MW01099020

SITTING LADY SUTRA

SITTING LADY SUTRA

Kay Stewart

TouchWood
Editions

TouchWood Editions
www.touchwoodeditions.com

Library and Archives Canada Cataloguing in Publication
Stewart, Kay L. (Kay Lanette), 1942–
Sitting lady sutra / Kay Stewart.

Print format: ISBN 978-1-926741-22-2 (bound).—ISBN 978-1-926741-23-9 (pbk.)
Electronic monograph in PDF format: ISBN 978-1-926741-40-6
Electronic monograph in HTML format: ISBN 978-1-926741-41-3

I. Title.

PS8637.T4946S58 2011   C813'.6   C2010-906346-5

Editor: Frances Thorsen
Proofreader: Lenore Hietkamp
Design: Pete Kohut
Cover image: Goddess: Miskani, istockphoto.com
Red streak: Tony Kwan, istockphoto.com
Author photo: Gary Ford

Permissions information: Four lines from page 240 to be used as an
epigraph {"If your heart is full . . . filled."} from *Think on These Things* by
J. Krishnamurti. Copyright © 1964 by the Krishnamurti Foundation of
America. Reprinted by permission of HarperCollins Publishers. Short excerpts
to appear on page 245 from the poem "Speaking in Tongues" by Anne Le Dressay
(1997) from *Sleep is a Country*, page 58. Reprinted by permission of McGill-
Queen's University Press. A short excerpt to appear on page 13 from "The Friend"
from *Circles on the Water* by Marge Piercy. Copyright © 1982 by Marge Piercy.
Used by permission of Alfred A. Knopf, a division of Random House, Inc.

We gratefully acknowledge the financial support for our publishing activities
from the Government of Canada through the Canada Book Fund, Canada
Council for the Arts, and the province of British Columbia through the
British Columbia Arts Council and the Book Publishing Tax Credit.

The interior pages of this book have been printed on 100% post-consumer
recycled paper, processed chlorine free, and printed with vegetable-based inks.

1 2 3 4 5 14 13 12 11

PRINTED IN CANADA

This book is dedicated to the men at William Head who are active in *William Head On Stage*, *Out of Bounds* magazine, the Restorative Justice program, and First Nations spirituality. You inspired me to create Ritchie and his friends. I hope I have done justice to your experience.

sutra:

a brief expression of a principle,
general truth, or rule of conduct,
or a collection of such teachings.
Literally, thread. Hence, a thread-
ing together of basic lessons . . .

PART 1

Man's character is his fate.
—Heraclitus

The universe is transformation; our life is
what our thoughts make it.
—Marcus Aurelius Antoninus

Prologue

She was alone on a beach, her uniform hot under a blazing sun. Her boots squelched through the wet sand as she waded out, gun drawn. A towering wave suddenly raced towards shore, sweeping her off her feet. She grabbed for a log floating past. Not a log but a body, the fish-nibbled face turning to stare at her. She tried to push the thing away but it stuck to her fingers, pulling her down . . .

RCMP Constable Danutia Dranchuk, Serious Crimes, Vancouver Island Division, awoke with a pounding heart and a tight grip on her buzzing alarm clock. It was 6:00 AM on Labor Day Monday. She silenced the alarm and lay still, trying to breathe through the panic as her therapist had recommended. In . . . and out . . . In . . . and out . . . until her pulse slowed, her stomach unknotted, and the face faded.

Stupid buzzer. It was all her own fault. Exhausted by a frustrating case in which she'd finally made an arrest in the wee hours, she'd completed her paperwork and fallen into bed without turning off the alarm. Now she was too wired to fall asleep again. She turned on the bedside lamp and wrote down as much of the dream as she could remember, her stomach clenching again as she described the drowned face. Cheeks and nose nibbled away, but lips and eyes beckoning her into the depths. Bits of seaweed clinging to tangled gray hair. The face by turns that of the suspect she'd shot the year before, her Winnipeg ex-lover, her father. What would her therapist make of that, she wondered.

Enough of that. She stuffed her notebook into the nightstand drawer. Her first day off in three weeks stretched invitingly before her. A long cycle ride with a gang from work on the Galloping Goose Trail to stretch her muscles, then dinner with Arthur to stretch her mind. What more could she want?

On a quiet street not far from Danutia's apartment in downtown Victoria, Corporal Surinder Sharma, head of Island Division Forensics, roused himself from *savasana*, stowed his yoga mat, and joined his mother at the kitchen shrine. Setting the photo of his dead sister Sita back in its place, Ajji took a few grains of brown rice in her fingertips and looked up at him, waiting for his signal. The fire already burned in the copper pan. At precisely 6:32, just as the sun popped over the horizon, bathing lower Vancouver Island in golden light, he nodded and together they chanted "Soorya'ya Sva'ha'," Ajji flicking the rice grains into the fire, "Soorya'ya Idam Na Mama, Prajapataye Sva'ha'," another offering of rice, "Prajapataye Idam Na Mama," their voices becoming one with the flames, one with the healing ash. As he stood watching the flames die down, Sharma brought each of his troubles from the recesses of his heart— the old sorrow about his sister Sita, his worries about his sons, his uneasiness about the truce he'd engineered between his mother and his niece—and mentally cast them into the fire, silently repeating "This belongs to the Sun, not to me."

The morning coolness burned off. Across the water, at the tip of a peninsula southwest of the city, the afternoon sun beat down on William Head Institution, reflecting off the guard tower and blanking out the windshield of a car turning into the prison grounds.

Hearing the engine's low hum, Ritchie Taylor dropped his arm-load of firewood onto the stack and moved closer to the chain-link fence. This was not a tourist destination. The driver, seeing the sign, would probably turn around and leave, as the last one had. Today was a holiday, however, and for once there were enough guards on duty to allow afternoon visitors. Excited voices rose behind him from the playing field near the water, and the breeze carried the smell of roasting wieners.

Ritchie watched as an old Volvo the color of faded denim nosed through the trees and pulled into the parking lot. As he waited to see who would get out, his eyes ached with the effort not to blink. He'd told her not to come here, to meet him in town tomorrow, when he would be a free man. Still he waited, as he'd waited for Santa Claus when a kid, afraid to close his eyes lest the coveted skates, bike, BB gun would materialize and then, because he wasn't paying attention, vanish again. Sleep had always claimed him, and so he awoke to find only the usual flannel shirt and a few of his favorite comics under the Christmas tree. Now he waited, his eyes burning, for the most precious gift of all, his daughter. She was a grown woman now, or almost. He wondered what she looked like. Dark and thin, like him, or blond and busty like her mother? He'd asked her to send photos, but she hadn't. Let it be a surprise, she'd said.

At last the car door opened and a stoop-shouldered old fart emerged, straw hat in hand. He settled the hat on his head and made his slow way towards the entrance. Shit. Ritchie turned away. Old Santa had let him down again.

What was he thinking anyway, she wouldn't be driving; she wouldn't be old enough even—or would she? He hadn't seen her since he went in, that botched convenience store job. How old was she then? Two? "Nineteen months," he heard Kelly's querulous voice say. "Your own daughter, you'd think you'd remember."

Truth was, he didn't remember much from those days. Kelly's voice, her long nose, her fingernails digging into his back when they made love. She'd come to see him at first, when he was in Ontario prisons, though she wouldn't bring the baby, said no child of hers was going to grow up knowing her dad was behind bars. From time to time he'd sent her a little money, saved up from his measly daily wage, to buy Crystal something special from her dad. He never knew whether she did or not. After the riots he got transferred to BC, where the overcrowding wasn't so bad, first Mountain, then William Head. That's when they'd lost touch. It was easier, when you were doing time.

His time was almost up. Tomorrow he would be out of here, a free man. Or at least as free as you can be living in a halfway house, on parole. His mouth went dry. What if he couldn't handle being out? Lots of guys couldn't, people expecting stuff from you and you don't know how to act, except the ways that got you into trouble in the first place. What did she expect from him, anyway? What did he know about being a parent? He should have told her to wait a month, till he got his shit together. Maybe he shouldn't have answered her letter at all. But he had, and now who knew what would happen?

A seaplane droned overhead, beginning its descent into Victoria's Inner Harbor. Usually he liked watching their lazy flight, like bumble-bees heavy with nectar, but today he couldn't tear his eyes away from the road. He wiped the sweat from his forehead. He'd better make a move or the guard would wonder why he was standing around gawking.

An angry metallic buzz split the air. Christ! Time for afternoon count. He couldn't be late, not now. One little thing and they could cancel his parole. Ritchie sprinted towards his unit through the dry grass, dust devils rising up behind him.

A couple of miles down the road, where the forested Department of National Defence lands gave way to a sprinkling of cottages and fields of sheep, a young man dozed behind the steering wheel of his Honda, music playing softly. Then the haunting voice of Nusrat Fateh Ali Khan faded away into the heat of the afternoon and Sunil Sharma yawned and stretched. His leg muscles cramped and he wanted a beer. He flicked off the ignition and climbed out.

"Aren't you finished yet?" he called to his new-found cousin, who sat cross-legged in the shade of an ancient apple tree, intent upon the sketchpad in her lap. Hard to believe they were kin, with her gray-green eyes and spiked hair the color of golden syrup. Only the rich tones of her skin hinted at a mixed lineage.

"Two minutes," Leanne responded, looking not at him but at the twin rows of Lombardy poplars marching up the narrow lane across the road. She'd been drawing them for the past hour. Strange to see her so still; she was a typical big-city type, always in a hurry.

Sunil lounged against the hood, waiting. He could feel the heat through his thin shorts, but he didn't care. He liked the heat. Hot sun, cold beer—the thought made him impatient. He glanced at his watch.

"Thirty seconds," he called. She ignored him, her face tight with concentration. Selfish bitch. Nothing mattered except what she wanted.

Take that call to his dad from Toronto a couple of weeks ago. 6:00 AM in BC and she's phoning an uncle she's never met. Someone had dropped out of the Emily Carr School of Art at the last minute and she'd been offered a place. Could Uncle help her find somewhere to live in Vancouver? As though she didn't know or care that the two cities were three hours and a ferry ride apart. And his dad, without even consulting him, says why yes, my son Sunil lives in Vancouver, he goes to university, you know, the University of British Columbia, and he was telling me a few days ago that one of his housemates is moving to Calgary, he will be happy to have you. That is, if your mother doesn't mind. There are two or three other girls in the house as well, all very respectable. No problem, what else are families for?

For getting away from, Sunil had wanted to retort when his father phoned him with the news. Why else was he at UBC? But of course he hadn't. He liked his family, most of the time, anyway. He wanted to live his own life, that's all, and now he was saddled with this pushy female. He'd drawn the line at playing tour guide to Vancouver on the last weekend before classes. On Friday he'd driven her straight from the Vancouver airport to the Tsawwassen ferry terminal, where they'd had a two-sailing wait because of the holiday. She'd stewed about that, but he didn't care. If Dad's so keen, he'd said to himself, let him entertain her.

Though of course it hadn't worked out that way; his dad was working overtime, as usual. His mother, who was busy cleaning and cooking holiday treats for Ganesh Chaturthi, had asked a few polite questions and then appointed him Leanne's chauffeur. He'd appealed to his sister-in-law Nandi, but she'd said "I must help your mother" with such a note of regret he couldn't be angry at her. Leanne was another matter.

"Time's up. Let's go. I want a beer," he said, pushing himself away from the car and opening the door.

Leanne sprang to her feet. "I'll be right back," she said. "I want to take down what that historical plaque says about these poplars. They're almost a century old."

Beside the plaque, blackberry bushes flung themselves invitingly across scattered boulders, and so for a moment Sunil was tempted to follow her. He liked to squish the dark berries between his fingers, feel them slide down his throat. But he was too old for that. He slid behind the wheel and rummaged through his CD case.

He was about to pop in Sheila Chandra's *A Zen Kiss* when a city bus drew up near the plaque. When it pulled out, a small figure in jeans and pink halter top stood looking around like she'd been abandoned on a strange planet. Plopping down on a boulder, she crossed her legs, stuck out her thumb, and stared across at the Honda. She wouldn't come over and ask for a ride, Sunil could tell from the way she'd thrown her head back. She was playing it tough. He could have laughed, she seemed so young, a kid really, long dark hair hanging limp under a pink polka-dot bandana.

He was halfway out of the car when Leanne yanked open the passenger door and climbed in.

"Okay, let's go," she said.

Sunil gestured towards the girl. "Let's give the kid a ride."

"This light won't last forever," Leanne objected. "I want to do some sketching at those falls we passed, Sitting Lady. Carr must have some paintings from there."

Sunil slammed his door shut. "So who cares about Emily Carr?"

"*I* care. And so does everyone who knows anything about art. She's just the most original painter Canada has ever had, that's all. She spent almost all her life in Victoria, as you'd know if you weren't such a geek."

"Look, I've spent the whole weekend driving you around to gawk at Carr's house, Carr's paintings in the galleries, places where she might have sketched this or gotten the idea for that. I need a break. Let's give her a ride and then have a Piper's or two at that café down the road."

Leanne did that eye-rolling thing that drove him crazy. "You're the one who insisted on coming to the island. I told you I needed to get started on my Carr project this weekend, and you said, then Victoria's the place to be. But I spent the whole of Saturday morning making clay figures of some silly elephant-headed god. Every night I've had to sit through some boring ceremony and listen to your grandmother drone on and on in a language I don't understand. She can't even remember my name, keeps calling me Sita. So don't make me waste any more of my time."

"She's your grandmother too," Sunil said. "And the culture is part of your heritage. Or did your mother forget to mention that?"

"Don't worry, my mom told me lots. Like the fact that *your* grandmother refused to have anything to do with us because my dad's Anglo. If that's your culture, you can have it. I'm Canadian. Like Emily Carr."

Sunil drummed on the steering wheel. Arguing was getting him nowhere. "Come on," he coaxed, "let's call it a day. We can stay over another night, come back tomorrow."

"That's fine for you," she said. "Your classes don't start till Thursday. I have life drawing tomorrow afternoon, and I'm not about to miss it so you can pick up a hitchhiker."

"You don't have to say it like I'm a pervert or something."

"She wouldn't even get in the car with you. You're—"

Sunil waited for the putdown—*you're fat, you're ugly, you're Indian*—but Leanne must have caught something in his expression.

"—a total stranger," she ended lamely.

Sunil grinned. "I'll tell her my dad's RCMP."

Leanne laughed. "I bet she hasn't heard *that* line before. It may not help anyway. At my school, cops' kids were the worst."

The laugh was a good sign, so he ignored the jibe. Maybe if he suggested a compromise.

A white Chrysler slowed. Crystal scrambled up from her boulder and stuck out her thumb, now stained with blackberry juice. The driver was an old bat with tight white curls and a tight white face, and

Crystal knew she'd never stop. When the car turned down the long row of poplars beside her, Crystal shot a finger.

Bitch.

She should have asked that guy in the Honda, and she would have if he'd been alone. The girl he was with was a cow, she'd never have agreed. If she didn't get a ride soon, the whole trip would have been a waste. No wonder Ritchie—Dad, she corrected herself, the word sweet as peaches on her tongue—no wonder Dad had said don't come to the prison, wait till I'm at the halfway house.

She'd been lucky though, caught a ride all the way from Lake Temagami to Thunder Bay with an old guy who'd been fishing at the lodge. He'd fallen for her story about her dying father, given her sixty bucks when he dropped her off late that night at the bus station, where she said a friend was meeting her. No way she wanted to end up in some cheap motel with him. Her boss had been a bastard, wouldn't pay her the wages she'd had coming, so she'd had to take most of what was in Brad's wallet. Luckily he always left it in the room when he went out in the boat. She'd pawned her mom's jewelry the next morning before she got on the bus. By the time she reached Victoria four days later, most of the money was gone.

Winnipeg, Regina, Calgary had passed in a blur. She'd done her best to sleep through the dreary miles of forest and prairie, sleeping to fend off nosy strangers and the wandering hands of drunks who got on and off the bus at night, like it was a traveling motel. After the Rockies she slept to blot out the thoughts that crawled into her brain like spiders. Now the spider thoughts came creeping back.

What if her mom was right? What if Ritchie didn't want her and never had?

Aiming a half-hearted kick at the boulder—she was wearing sandals, no point in breaking a toe—Crystal slumped down again. She should have paid more attention. The driver had told her that the #54 bus went down William Head Road, all right, but not all the way to the prison. A few blocks, she had thought, I can handle that. So she could hardly complain when he pulled up here in the middle of nowhere, said that's as far as he went. How much farther? she'd asked, not wanting to repeat, to the prison. Coupla miles, he'd said, as though that was nothing. She'd never walked that far in her life.

Not that there was any point in trying. She'd called from downtown to check the visiting hours—they would be over soon. So if the next person didn't give her a ride . . .

Sheep bleated from the field across the road. Crystal bleated back.

All this Labor Day 1996 the sun shone on the holidaymakers at Witty's Lagoon Regional Park, the sunbathers on the beaches, the hikers along the trails, the passing tourists who stopped for a quick look at the Sitting Lady. As the sun set, flushing the sky pink, they dragged themselves back to their cars and trucks and headed for home. Finally even the spiky-haired artist who had given her such close attention closed her sketchbook and set off up the Lagoon Trail.

The Sitting Lady Falls adjusted her watery skirts and settled to a soothing murmur for the night. She was dressed lightly in her summer finery, a fine mist swathing her head and shoulders, thin ribbons of water tumbling into the quiet pool below. Bats darted above the pool, and night creatures came to drink at its edges, until driven away by alien sounds and movements.

As the night deepened, the cooling air began to blow the spray about, to tug at leaves and twigs. Black clouds boiled out of the west, blotting out the moon and stars. The wind blew harder, churning the water and setting the treetops swaying. Large branches were torn from arbutus trees and flung to the ground. The earth rumbled as shallow roots gave way. In the gully, above the bridge, an ancient Douglas fir tree leaned into the wind, creaking like the mast it might have become. Another blast shook the tree. With a wrench the roots broke free and the fir thundered to the ground, concealing the body that lay in its path and smashing the footbridge beyond.

All night the wind blew. Towards morning, it subsided and the creatures that had cowered in their caves and bolt-holes came out to see how their world had changed.

PART 2

Thanksgiving/Dussehra
October 14-20, 1996

he said, cut off your hands.
they are always poking at things.
—Marge Piercy, "The Friend," from *Circles on the Water:
Selected Poems of Marge Piercy*

One

RCMP Constable Danutia Dranchuk pinned another crime scene photo to the board, this one showing Esther Mike's distorted face, her eyes and neck bulging from the red ribbon used to strangle her. Ordinarily, the pressure would have forced the tongue from her mouth. Not in this case. Rammed down her throat was her severed right hand.

Sick, sick, sick. Bastard. She steeled herself for the photo that she knew came next: the severed left hand protruding from the woman's vagina. After this batch, she would have to examine the photos of the second victim, with the same gruesome mutilations.

Danutia had been on the periphery during the initial investigations into the two Aboriginal women's deaths. After a few months the investigations had ground to a halt. With no suspects, no leads, the files would normally have become inactive. But these deaths were part of a larger pattern that drew media attention. Up and down the West Coast, women were disappearing from bars and rooming houses and run-down streets. Sometimes their bodies turned up months later, sometimes not. Most of them were sex trade workers. Many of them were Aboriginal. No one seemed to pay much attention until the media seized upon the words "serial killer" and denounced police inaction.

In response to public pressure, police authorities in the Greater Victoria area had dropped their jurisdictional squabbling and appointed a joint Special Investigator, in charge of these cases and any subsequent ones with the same hallmarks. Still there was no progress. On Friday Sergeant Lewis had called her in for a briefing. The Special Investigator had been transferred and Lewis was putting her in charge. "What we need is a new pair of eyes," he said, though he hadn't sounded too hopeful.

Neither was Danutia. So far she'd spent the long weekend poring over the files, unsure how to proceed.

On the desk behind her the phone rang, a hollow trill in the cavernous room. It was Thanksgiving Day in Canada, the second Monday in October, and her colleagues in Serious Crimes were either off duty or on call at home with their families. Danutia, having no one to celebrate with, had volunteered to cover. She picked up. "Constable Dranchuk speaking."

Her sister Alyne's voice came in a warm rush. "What are you doing at work? You're supposed to be off. Anyway, happy Thanksgiving. Jonathan's recovered, so we're going out to the farm. You should have come."

"It was too late," Danutia said. "The flights were all booked. You were supposed to come here." That was the plan. Her sister's first trip to Victoria since Danutia had been posted here a year and a half ago. She'd booked the time off, made reservations for high tea at Victoria's famed Empress Hotel, checked out the Royal BC Museum, the IMAX showings, and the Undersea Gardens to entertain her nephew. Then on Thursday Alyne had phoned to say that Jonathan had the flu and she'd canceled their trip. "Tell Jonathan I'm glad he's feeling better. I missed our trip to IMAX."

On the other end of the line her sister rustled impatiently. "You haven't been home in almost two years. Have the flights always been booked?"

"Just don't start on that," Danutia said. "I've got a therapist, okay?" Alyne was not only her sister, she was a psychologist. She was the one who'd urged Danutia to find a therapist after an incident last year. Danutia had shot at a suspected killer and there had been the usual inquiry. She'd been exonerated, but the incident had continued to trouble her. Not because she'd used her weapon—in the circumstances she'd had little choice—but because, blinded by her attraction to an older man, she'd misjudged the case with almost fatal consequences. For months she'd slept badly, struggling with feelings of guilt her sister had understood but had not been able to alleviate. Finally Alyne had said, "I can't be your sister and your therapist too, and I can't stop being your sister. You need to find somebody else to talk to." And so, when her excuses ran out and her lack of sleep began to interfere with her work, Danutia had picked up a phonebook. After a couple of bad experiences she'd found Grace Tilman, who, not surprisingly, had proved to be an older version of her sister. Their talks had gradually moved beyond the shooting incident to Danutia's relationship with her father, bringing up a host of memories she didn't feel ready to face. Relations with her parents were strained at the best of times. She couldn't possibly visit them now and keep up the pretence that everything was fine.

Danutia changed the subject. "I've just been given two cold cases. That's why I'm at work."

"Tell me about it," Alyne said, settling into her older sister role as confidante.

Letting Danutia off the hook, as usual.

"Two Aboriginal women," Danutia said. "One killed at New Year's, the other at Easter. Both strangled." She didn't mention the mutilations—those details hadn't been made public. Nor did she mention the nickname that some smart-ass police guy had given the killer early on—Handy Dan. Danutia hated it, hated the similarity to her own name, the teasing it provoked, after her long resistance to being called Dan, Danny, Dannygirl, anything except her own name, which had seemed normal enough in the small farming community where she grew up, but marked her as an outsider when she left. When she applied to the RCMP Academy, she'd considered becoming Jane or Mary or even Emma, after her maternal grandmother; then she'd decided that Danutia was who she was, and people could call her that or nothing. Mostly they avoided calling her anything.

"A serial killer? In Victoria? There's been a lot of coverage lately about the Hillside Strangler and the Green River murders in the US, but I never thought I'd have to worry about you in Victoria."

"Not to worry," Danutia said. "Unless I get a break, I'll never get anywhere near him."

When Alyne rang off, Danutia found herself thinking about the timing of the murders. New Year's Eve. Easter. Was there a reason the killer chose holiday weekends? How many holidays had there been since Marie Wilson's death? Victoria Day, Canada Day, the August civic holiday, Labor Day, and now Thanksgiving. Had there been other victims?

Behind her the phone rang again. She picked up the receiver, bracing herself for what she might hear.

Was it time? Ritchie Taylor eyed the lumps of dough lined up on the blackened cookie sheet, then tapped one lightly, as though that would tell him whether the rolls had "risen till light." If he put them in too soon, they would be heavy. If he waited too long, who knew—

He'd never made rolls before. Pies either, for that matter, but there they were, two apple, two pumpkin, the crusts a little burned around the edges, but what the hell. Four pies should be enough for thirteen people. They had joked this morning about the unlucky number, Chuck suggesting they toss out Nancy, the relief staff. As though Leicester House could operate without a staff.

Thirteen for dinner then: seven parolees, five guests, and Nancy. The rest of the guys, the ones with families, somewhere to go, were out on passes. Ritchie was too antsy to sit around smiling and making nice with the guests—Pat's girlfriend, Frenchy's wife and two kids, Chuck's dad. Early that morning he had shut himself up in the cramped basement kitchen. Idle hands are the devil's workshop, his gran used to say. If he kept his hands busy, he wouldn't have time to think about who wasn't there.

The kitchen door inched open, letting out the warm air that would make the rolls rise. "I told you fuckers to stay out of here."

A freckled hand thrust a gallon pail past the doorframe, and then Chuck's gap-toothed grin appeared. "Frenchy's old lady brought some blackberries. Make a great cobbler, eh?"

Ritchie picked up the cookie sheet, "Tomorrow. Soon as these rolls are done, we're eating."

Chuck edged inside and set the pail on the counter, but didn't leave. He was a few years younger than Ritchie, late thirties maybe, a little flabby but not bad looking except for the missing teeth. He popped a couple of blackberries in his mouth. "Those kids sure will be disappointed. They picked them, you know, a Thanksgiving treat for their dad—Pearl didn't even ask them to."

Ritchie thought about Frenchy, the young native guy. He'd only been at Leicester House a couple of weeks and so was still on mid-day sign in. They'd been in a couple of crafts programs together at the Head, Ritchie making boxes and picture frames, Frenchy carving whales and hummingbirds and flat-faced beavers. In January he would start First Nations Studies at Camosun College, where Ritchie had applied for cook's training. If you wanted parole, you had to have a Plan. No use saying you wanted to lie on the beach and listen to the sea, or hang out with your buds, or spend all day making out with your old lady, if you had an old lady. Work or school or both, those were your choices. When the Leicester House director asked about his plans, Ritchie had said chef's training. What the hell. He'd slung burgers when he was a kid. People always gotta eat.

Ritchie stared at the pail, an old ice cream bucket with the words "Island Farms" barely legible. He'd used one just like it for years at the Head, where all the sunny spots were overrun with wild blackberry bushes. A month ago you could have filled a pail with sweet, juicy berries in no time. Now the vines would be frost-bitten, the season almost over. The kids would have had to hunt, brambles scratching their hands and arms.

Sliding the rolls into the oven, Ritchie hunted for his *Joy of Cooking*, the first thing he'd saved up to buy.

"Cobbler's easy," he said. "It can cook while we eat."

Chuck sidled out the door. "Too bad your daughter didn't make it, eh?"

"Just get the fuck out." Ritchie banged the pail into the sink and turned the water on full blast. That sleazeball. Why'd he ever mention Crystal to him, anyway? So she hadn't turned up. Big deal. He never really expected her to, did he?

Out in Metchosin, not far from William Head, Park Interpreter Joan Goodman wasn't expecting trouble. Yet after she drove through the gate across the service road of Witty's Lagoon Regional Park, she locked it behind her. You could never be too careful, especially on a holiday weekend. Keeping ATVs and motorcycles off the trails was getting harder and harder. Not that the young thugs intimidated her. Like her Jeep, she was built for toughness and durability. After twenty years with the park service she could deal with almost anything.

Except her parents. She'd done her duty by Thanksgiving and left them to their afternoon naps, full if not satisfied—when were they ever satisfied?—while, as she claimed, she took care of a little work. She needn't have come, of course, but she couldn't stand being in the house another minute, too much cooking and cleaning up, too much stale air, stale talk. Three years ago, Joan had let slip that her downstairs tenants were leaving. Her mom had immediately stepped up her complaints about the Prairie winters. In a fit of guilt, Joan had offered her parents the suite. Why hadn't she kept her mouth shut?

Making yet another resolve to endure what couldn't be changed, Joan parked beside the new toilets and headed towards Sitting Lady Falls. She could have parked in the lot by the Nature Centre, but she didn't want anyone following her past the barricade that had blocked off the old Lagoon Trail ever since the Labor Day windstorm took out the bridge. Joan had argued against merely rebuilding the footbridge, pointing out that erosion along the cliff would continue to make that stretch of the trail vulnerable to blow downs and washouts. For once she had prevailed, and the trail was rerouted across a corner of the neighboring school grounds. Now the work was finished, the workers were gone, the danger was past. Tomorrow she would officially open the new trail, with the school and parents as special guests.

Pale October light sifted through the towering trees, and fallen maple leaves rustled underfoot, sending up a dry, musty smell. As she walked, Joan rehearsed the story of Witty's Lagoon that she would tell the children tomorrow. She would begin with the story of the meeting in 1852 between the Ka-Kyaakan band of Northern Straits Salish, the area's original inhabitants, and James Douglas, the first governor appointed by the Hudson's Bay Company. She would bring a stack of the company's famous striped blankets to show what Douglas had paid for a huge parcel of land stretching from Albert Head to Pedder Bay, on the other side of the peninsula. The next year, Douglas sold three hundred and eighty-five acres around Witty's Lagoon to Captain James Cooper, another Hudson's Bay employee. Cooper named it Bilston Creek Farm. Why do you think he chose that name? she would ask, and talk with them a bit about how we name things before telling them he'd named the creek and farm after his home town in England. She would show them where the Ka-Kyaakan continued to live on the beach, transporting the settlers to Victoria by canoe.

Nearing the falls, Joan could hear a steady splash like a bathtub filling as Bilston Creek dropped a hundred feet to the deep pool below. To the right, a barricade like the one near the Nature Centre blocked access to the new trail from this end. Straight ahead two cedar platforms joined by stairs—part of the new design—provided safer, better views than the old footbridge had. Every year, several people who ignored the Steep Cliffs warnings would sprain their ankles or bloody their knees trying to get a better view. Joan leaned against the railing of the upper platform, its fresh cedar smell filling her with satisfaction, and contemplated Sitting Lady Falls.

She'd never discovered who had named the falls, though she had no trouble seeing the figure created by Bilston Creek as it divided and spilled over outcroppings of volcanic rock. In the winter rains, the Lady's bounteous waters thundered and roared, and a fine spray misted the ferns and stonecrop that clung to the cliff. Now she looked rather anorexic, her ample thighs and sturdy legs shrunk to a thin trickle. The long, hot summer had continued into the fall, with no rain to speak of since the Labor Day storm. Had the creek dwindled so at summer's end when the Ka-Kyaakan had their camp along the lagoon, she wondered, or only after white settlers cleared the surrounding forest?

Joan sighed. Her parents would be wanting their afternoon tea soon. She said goodbye to the Lady and made her way to the right of the platform, where a huge log blocked access to the old trail. All very well, she thought, climbing over, but she wouldn't be the only one who ignored the warning. She'd better make sure the trail was blocked off at the bottom as well.

The path was steep and rocky here, chewed up by the ground crew and not restored. Clutching at bushes when her hiking boots threatened to slip, Joan worked her way close to where the bridge had been. The ground crew had been out the morning after the Labor Day storm, clearing paths. They'd taken off the top twenty feet or so of the fallen Douglas fir, enough to assess the damage. Once the decision to reroute the trail had been made, the splintered bridge had been removed. Only the footings remained on either side of what in the spring was a marshy area rank with skunk cabbage. Now, though the ground was dry underfoot, there was still a strong odor, perhaps of rotting vegetation stirred up by the workers.

The trunk of the fir had been left as a nurse log for new growth. Gazing up the gully towards the exposed rootball, Joan caught a glimpse of something pink. A surveyor's ribbon, she surmised, left behind by the workers. It was almost hidden in the undergrowth, but still it nagged at her. She scrambled up to remove it.

Not plastic but faded cloth, she realized when she was closer, a strap of some kind. The smell she'd thought was rotting vegetation was much stronger here, a carrion smell. A cougar must have left his kill nearby. Bending down, she grabbed hold and yanked at the strap. It tore, she heard it, but it didn't come free. She reached through the ferns and salal and felt around. Her fingers encountered a sticky, pulpy mass and then something bony and her stomach heaved.

It's only an animal, crushed when the tree fell, she told herself. Yet she couldn't quite square that comforting thought with the pink strap that lay torn and soiled among the fallen branches.

Two

An hour after the phone call, Danutia put away her reports, changed into cords and a sweater kept ready in her locker, and set off on her bike. The call had not been from Handy Dan but from her colleague Surinder Sharma, inviting her to Thanksgiving dinner with his family.

"You must understand, you would be doing us an enormous favor. Here is the reason," he said, his voice deep and warm, with the lilting rhythms of British India. "It is our practice to celebrate Hindu festivals alongside Canadian holidays, so that our children feel at home in both worlds. Today we are celebrating Thanksgiving, but we are also celebrating the Hindu festival of Dussehra." He paused, as though searching for words. "Now here is our problem. We have a visitor this weekend, my niece Leanne from Toronto, who is studying art in Vancouver. I fear she finds our ways strange. My sister married an Anglo, you see, and Leanne has had no exposure to our culture. You will come and talk to Leanne, help her eat the Thanksgiving turkey, yes?" Before Danutia could reply, he added, "My granddaughter Kumala will be here also."

Danutia had readily accepted. She liked children, wanted a couple of her own. Or would, when she had a stable marriage and a less dangerous job. It didn't seem fair to risk leaving her children motherless. In the meantime, she would make friends with Sharma's lively granddaughter, whose photos adorned his otherwise Spartan work space. Now that she had committed herself, however, doubts assailed her. She had never met Sharma's family. Like the niece, she too was likely to feel awkward and out of place.

Still, how could she have refused? In charge of her first case, more than a year ago now, she had been faced with the choice of either rubber-stamping her superior's judgment of suicide or accepting the attending doctor's claim of homicide. Or so she thought. Sharma had helped her see how to keep her options open until she could form her own opinion. That had been a valuable lesson, and a boost to her self-confidence. She owed him a favor. If she could act as a buffer between his family and the troublesome niece, she would.

As she cycled through the light holiday traffic, Danutia found her muscles relaxing and her mind clearing. When she'd discovered how easy it was to get around Victoria, she'd happily sold her old jalopy and invested in rain gear and a good bike. In her job, it was hard to find the time and incentive to exercise. This way she could build exercise into her daily routine. When she needed a car for work, she signed one out of the vehicle pool.

After stopping at a supermarket for a box of chocolates and a Polly Pocket set for Kumala, she turned off Quadra onto a street of modest houses. Early afternoon sunlight slanted through the trees and cast a golden glow on gardens past their summer glory. At last she spotted the house number Sharma had given her. The small bungalow shone bright as a sunflower amidst a garden full of tinkling wind chimes, reflective balls, and old boots planted with late-blooming African daisies. Statues of gods and goddesses, some blue, some many-armed, rose above the flowers. A pot-bellied figure with an elephant head stood guard beside the front door. Danutia wondered who the gardener was. Surely not Sharma. He was too somber.

As she wheeled her bike up the curving path, the door flew open and a small girl in a bright pink sari and gold earrings dashed out, shrieking, "She's here! She's here!"

A sari-clad older woman appeared behind her in the open doorway, speaking rapidly. Danutia didn't recognize the language, but the angry tone and gestures were unmistakable. The girl halted, hanging her head and gazing up at Danutia through long dark eyelashes. Then she slowly backed up until her black patent shoes clicked against the bottom step.

"Hello, you must be Kumala," Danutia whispered, taking a plastic bag from her backpack. "I have something for you."

As Kumala took the outstretched bag, the woman grabbed the girl by the wrist and hurried her back inside.

Clearly the niece wasn't the only source of tension in the household. Was that Sharma's wife? The woman seemed older, but there were no telltale signs of age. Her hair was black and her back was ramrod straight. Feeling even more uneasy about the dinner to come, Danutia looked around for somewhere to put her bike.

"Here, let me take that," Sharma said, materializing beside her in his customary dark suit and tie. He was tall and well-muscled on a large frame; only the deep lines in his face hinted that he was nearing retirement age. Motioning Danutia to follow him to the carport, he said, "You must forgive my mother. She has no patience with Kumala."

Relieved to hear that the woman was not Sharma's wife, Danutia said the first thing that popped into her head, "But what wonderful posture! My mother already has a widow's hump, and she must be years younger."

"Mother is faithful to her yoga practice, more faithful than I am. It is a good discipline for the body and for the mind."

"I should try it," Danutia said, straightening her shoulders. "Kumala's a dear," she added, knowing that would please the proud grandfather.

In the entry they paused to take off their shoes. A long corridor papered in red ran straight ahead, with closed doors probably giving onto bedrooms and a bathroom. Shouts and groans and the muted sounds of a television penetrated the glass doors to her left. Danutia took out the box of truffles. Peace through chocolate, she thought as Sharma ushered her into the living room.

"Constable Dranchuk, my sons," Sharma said, "Rajit and Sunil." With lingering glances at the soccer game, the two young men, both dressed in black pants and white shirts, rose and bowed politely.

"Forget the constable business, call me Danutia," she said, making a face. "I'm not much older than you." Though she felt older, because of the terrible things she witnessed day to day. This must be the way combat soldiers feel, she thought, coming home to civvies who can't possibly understand what it's like. She remembered her distress after her first autopsy, when she'd walked with Sharma to a recycling center where Rajit worked. There Sharma had spoken soothing words about the unending cycles of death and rebirth.

"I saw you on the crane once," she said to Rajit. Seagulls had wheeled overhead as the crane moved metal mouthfuls of discarded paper goods onto a waiting barge.

Rajit shrugged and spread his hands. He was tall like his father but thin, with an ascetic's delicate cheekbones and soulful eyes. "It's a job. At night I study accounting."

"Drudge the dredger, we call him," Sunil said, punching his brother lightly on the shoulder. Sunil was shorter and heavier, with Sharma's bumpy nose and heavy brows. Danutia, a younger sibling herself, wondered how he had compensated for his brother's good looks.

"And you?" she asked. "Are you also working?"

"Not him," Rajit put in. "He's too busy chasing girls."

"Ah, but I don't let them catch me," Sunil replied with a smile and a knowing wink at Danutia. Charm was his weapon, it seemed. Something about his manner disturbed her, but she dismissed the feeling. She'd always distrusted charming men.

"I'm in third-year microbiology at UBC," he said. "I'm going into medical research—AIDS, malaria, that sort of thing. Like you, I want to stop the bad guys from hurting people; only my bad guys are viruses and bacteria."

"And like the killers we read about daily, they will continue to multiply, no matter what you do," Rajit said.

"Enough of your bickering," Sharma said. "I must introduce our guest to the rest of the family. Don't pay them any attention," he continued as he steered Danutia through the dining room, its long table as gaily decorated as the garden outside. "They have their differences, but they're both good boys."

From the kitchen beyond came the murmur of women's voices and, mingling with the pungent curry, the smell of roasting turkey. Danutia felt a sharp pang of homesickness. Maybe she should have tried to get a flight home, however difficult it would have been to see her parents just now. She pictured the women in her family making candied yams and brown gravy in the big farm kitchen, the men outside looking over her dad's latest piece of equipment, the kids kicking around a soccer ball. The easy camaraderie of a large family—until the vodka flowed and the quarrels began. She was so caught up in remembered smells, remembered faces that she barely caught the name of Sharma's wife and daughter-in-law. She forced her mind back into the present, to the strange food and the three women in brightly-colored saris preparing it, Kumala flitting back and forth like a brilliant butterfly.

Yasmin half-turned from the stove, her blue and silver sari shimmering like the night sky. "Forgive me for not coming out to greet you," she said. "This channa dahl must be fried at the last moment or it tastes like soggy Play-Doh."

Danutia felt herself relax. No question now about who had created the fanciful garden. "We've met, haven't we?" she asked. "A couple of weeks ago, at your spice shop. I was picking up some things for my friend Arthur."

"Yes, and if I hadn't stopped you, you would have bought that vinegary-beginnery chutney," Yasmin said, puckering her lips and wrinkling her nose as she had when she'd rushed up and snatched away the jar in Danutia's hand. Danutia, who knew nothing about Indian food, had shown her the list of things Arthur had asked her to buy for the dinner he was making. Yasmin, being shrewd and an RCMP spouse, had asked if she worked for the police. It must have been that chance encounter that led to her dinner invitation. She handed over the chocolates.

"Truffles, my favorite," Yasmin said. "And your friend Arthur, did he like the ginger chutney?"

"He said it was bloody marvelous," Danutia replied, mimicking Arthur's accent as best she could. Arthur Fairweather reviewed local drama productions for the Victoria *Post-Dispatch*. Danutia had run into him—almost literally—on Salt Spring Island over a year ago. She was investigating a case, Arthur was reviewing the Arts Festival, and together they had caught a killer. Since then they had had an occasional drink or meal together, during which he regaled her with stories about the latest young thing he was pursuing. Danutia, off men for good, countered by declaring romance a waste of time and energy. With a pang she realized she missed him, though he'd been gone little more than a week.

"I have been missing his pieces in the paper this week," Yasmin said. "I said to Sharma, 'He's too clever, and so they've fired him.' Is this true?"

"No, his mother had a stroke and he's flown back to England to see her."

"When he returns, you must both come to dinner. How hard I had to beg Sharma to invite you today," Yasmin went on, despite her husband's frown. "'Work is for work, and family for family,' he always says. But after that day in the store I always ask him about you, and when he mentioned your sister wasn't coming, I said we can't let you be all alone on a holiday, and finally he agreed, and here you are."

Sharma had set a trap for her, and she'd taken the bait. She caught his eye. "And your niece?"

He shuffled uncomfortably. "All in good time," he said. "First, my mother."

The elder Mrs. Sharma stood at the kitchen table, dishing up a great pot of curried vegetables. She bowed her head in greeting. "Namaste. Ajji."

"Namaste Ajji," Danutia repeated, assuming she was saying hello.

"You should be honored," Sharma said. "Only a few are invited to call my mother 'grandmother.'"

"I beg your pardon—"

"We are the ones who are honored." The young woman slicing melon grinned shyly. "My father-in-law has told us how much he respects your dedication to your job. I would like to have a job like that."

"So, Nandi, you too wish to be working-working, do you," Yasmin said. "And who would feed this hungry bird?" She blew on a piece of channah dahl and popped it into Kumala's gaping mouth.

"Women have to do more with their lives than have babies," declared a nasal voice from a far corner of the kitchen. A golden-skinned young woman with spiked blond hair and a gold nose ring sidled out from behind a half-open door, a sketchbook in one hand and a pencil in the other. Instead of a sari she wore tight black pants and a cropped top. This must be the niece.

"Leanne, the daughter of my sister," Sharma said, speaking over an angry murmur from his mother. "She is studying art at Emily Carr."

"Hi," Leanne said, and turned back to her drawing.

Danutia caught the scent of burning incense and the soft flicker of candles. Curious, she moved closer. Leanne, she could see now, was standing in front of a pantry that had been converted into a shrine covered with dozens of small statues, tiny dishes filled with rice, fruits and nuts, a red rose floating in water. Idol-worship, her Baptist mother would have pronounced it, just like your dad's crucifixes and icons. Some part of her couldn't help but agree. Still, she wondered what it would be like to give your gods your care and attention, instead of endlessly asking for favors.

"What are you drawing?" Danutia asked.

The young woman leaned over and tapped a small gold-plated statue of a potbellied elephant god, a miniature of the one beside the front door. "This is Ganesha, remover of obstacles and god of successful ventures." She regarded Danutia with doubtful eyes. "Do you know anything about Emily Carr?"

Danutia tried to recall the calendar her nephew Jonathan had sent her for Christmas last year, no doubt at Alyne's prompting. "I've seen a few pictures."

"When Carr was sketching around Victoria, she camped out in an old caravan she called the Elephant," Leanne said, passing Danutia a loose sheet of paper.

Danutia stared down at a grainy copy of an old black and white photograph, apparently much enlarged. It showed a small wooden hut propped up on girders. In the open doorway sat a stout woman in a close-fitting cap, surrounded by dogs and a monkey. With a few sinuous strokes of her pencil, Leanne had topped the caravan with Ganesha's head, its trunk poised to snatch the cap.

Danutia laughed. "I see Ganesha has a sense of humor."

From behind them Danutia heard Ajji's angry tones grow louder, then Sharma's soothing voice. Joining them, he said to his niece, "Ajji says you must not make fun of the god. Not to worry, I told her, she is your own flesh and blood, she wouldn't do such a thing."

"Oh, Leanne's a bit of a rebel," Yasmin said, gently removing the pencil and sketchpad as though they were Kumala's toys. "Or so you think, don't you, young lady, with your spiky-spiky hair and nose ring. The truth is, everything you young ones do is old, old, old in Asia and Africa. Just look at *National Geographic*."

Leanne glanced at Danutia and rolled her eyes. Danutia felt a momentary sympathy for the young artist. Her own small community had firmly squelched any signs of nonconformity. Still, there was no excuse for bad manners, either Leanne's or hers. She turned to Ajji and put her hands together as she had seen Sharma do. "I'm sorry if I offended you. I didn't mean any disrespect," she said, hoping the elder Mrs. Sharma would in turn understand her tone and gestures, if not her words.

Ajji nodded and carried on slicing cucumbers. Behind her, Yasmin opened the oven and took out the roasting pan. Danutia felt her mouth water as the rich turkey smell filled the room.

Sharma gestured towards an ornate silver frame atop the altar. "When you arrived, I was telling Leanne about today's festival. Dussehra marks Lord Rama's defeat of the ten-headed demon Ravana, who had abducted Lord Rama's faithful wife Sita. That is the royal couple."

To Danutia, the pair seemed strangely androgynous. They were dressed in the same sumptuous Indian attire, their lips red and rounded, their eyes large and soft and unfocused. Uncomfortable under their benevolent gaze, Danutia shifted her attention to a fading photograph of a dark-skinned girl in a red sari. "And who is that?" she asked.

She felt Sharma withdraw a little. He glanced over his shoulder. "My second sister," he said softly. "She died young."

"How did she die?" Danutia asked, and then regretted her question when Sharma's mother broke into an agitated murmur. She hurried past, bangles jingling. Grabbing the photo from the shrine, she thrust it into Danutia's hands.

"Sita," Ajji said. "She is dying." Then she pointed towards Leanne. "She is living again."

Danutia must have looked as puzzled as she felt, for Ajji said, "Wait. I am showing. Come. Come," she insisted, grabbing Leanne's arm. The girl again rolled her eyes, but allowed herself to be led off.

Yasmin bustled over in a rustle of silk and tapped the photograph with a lacquered fingernail. "This photo was sent to families of prospective husbands when Sita was sixteen. She died soon after. Ajji thinks Sita has been reborn as Leanne. She should know better. The soul of a dying person enters into a new body quick-quick, it doesn't hanky-panky around, waiting for the next girl child in the family."

"How can you say that?" Sharma asked, as though picking up a familiar debate.

"Never mind, time to carve the turkey," Yasmin said.

"The scholars tell us . . ." Sharma began as he picked up the carving knife, but Danutia's mind drifted away from the general case and back to the particular. What if Sita's soul had entered the body of someone who then died just as Leanne was born? She resisted the temptation to ask. Logic was one thing, belief another. Her mother's church taught the resurrection of the body, a belief her work had forced her to surrender. She had seen too many bodies hideously mangled and mutilated. Like those of Esther Mike and Marie Wilson. Perhaps their spirits persisted in some form, somehow. Let their bodies rest in peace.

Tinkling bangles approached and Ajji glided into the room. With a gesture like an impresario presenting a new act, she stepped aside.

Leanne, who had been following close behind, stopped abruptly, a gawky apparition in a red sari. One hand gripped the cloth draped around her head; the other clutched the folds at her waist. Heavy dark rings outlined her eyes and a red dot marked her forehead like a bull's-eye. She shifted nervously from foot to foot, a smile playing about her lips as though she half-enjoyed the spectacle she was making of herself. Her bravado had disappeared with her Western trappings, making her seem younger and more vulnerable. She dropped her eyes, folded her hands together.

Danutia's gaze dropped to the girl in the photograph: high forehead and broad soft cheeks, the bones merely hinted at. Nose wide but well-formed above thin, faintly smiling lips. Except for the darker eyes and skin, the girl could have been Leanne's twin. A sharp intake of breath beside her told Danutia she wasn't the only one startled by the transformation.

"Portrait of the Artist as Her Dead Auntie," Leanne said, giggling nervously. "Where's my sketchbook?"

Uttering a sharp cry, Ajji slapped her and Leanne's hands flew to her face. Ajji grabbed an elbow and shook it, letting fly a barrage of angry words. The girl yanked free and bolted from the room, Yasmin hurrying after. Sharma took his mother by the shoulders. At first she tried to fight him off, but soon she subsided and let him guide her to a kitchen chair. She sat slumped over, her hands covering her face, rocking to and fro and murmuring *Sita, Sita, Sita*.

So much for Danutia's illusion about happy families.

Nandi began putting dishes of food onto trays and, after an initial protest, allowed Danutia to help.

Yasmin, returning to the kitchen, nodded approval at her daughter-in-law. "Fine, fine, let's get these onto the table." When everything was in place, she took Ajji gently by the hand. "Come, Ajji, the food is getting cold. Sharma, show our guest where to sit and call the boys, will you?"

The sons arrived at the table still bickering. A few minutes later, Leanne, who had changed back into her black pants and cropped top, dropped into the empty chair beside Danutia. Dishes were passed in uneasy silence. Danutia complimented her hostess on the subtle flavors. "Much better than the Indian meal Arthur made for me," she said.

"Million thanks," Yasmin said, but even she seemed subdued by the tension.

Finally Sunil spoke up. "I have the perfect joke for today," he said. "A cop pulls a man over for speeding. As the man hands him his license, the cop says, 'Sir, I can't help but notice your eyes are blood-shot. Have you been drinking?' The man looked at him indignantly. 'Officer, I can't help but notice your eyes are glazed. Have you been eating doughnuts?'"

Everyone laughed, except Leanne and Ajji, and the tension dissipated.

Maybe she'd misjudged Sunil, Danutia decided. Charm has its place. She was no good at jokes, but she could fulfill her role as guest. She turned her attention to the sullen young woman beside her, picking at the turkey and refusing everything else. Danutia had asked Leanne a third question about art school when Sharma's pager sounded.

Her host pushed back his chair. "You must excuse me for a moment," he said, and their eyes met. Though the family had no doubt experienced such disruptions before, only the two RCMP officers could know the full reality of what such a call might mean.

Conversation flagged while they waited. Kumala, sitting across the table, played with her Polly Pocket until Ajji put a stop to it. Soon the murmur from the kitchen died away.

Sharma stood behind Yasmin's chair and laid his hands lightly on her shoulders. "Unfortunately, I must leave," he said, "and more unfortunate still, I must take our guest with me."

Danutia quickly took her leave and joined him at the hall door.

"A body at Sitting Lady Falls in Metchosin," he reported.

Danutia slipped into her flats. "That's West Shore's jurisdiction, isn't it? I don't want to butt in."

The wrinkles in Sharma's craggy face seemed to settle deeper. "You're the Special Investigator. You have all the authorization you need. It's a woman."

Three

"Where to?" Sunil asked as Leanne settled herself in the passenger seat of the Honda.

"Remember that spit of land we drove across on Labor Day? Eski—"

"EsQWYmalt," Sunil corrected. "Esquimalt Lagoon."

"That's it," Leanne said. "Let's try that. Carr camped there in the Elephant in 1934. Thanks for getting me out of there," she added. "I was dying of boredom."

"No problem," Sunil said. "I've seen the *Ramayana* dozens of times. You looked like you could use a break from the family, and so could I." He popped in a Sheila Chandra CD and turned up the volume. He could feel Leanne give him a dirty look, but he didn't care. The weather was perfect, sunny and crisp. He wanted to relax and enjoy the cool breeze against his face, the autumn colors splashed across city gardens and hillsides. Skirting downtown, he took the Bay Street Bridge across the Gorge and then Skinner and Craigflower. When he reached the Old Island Highway he relented and turned down the music.

"What was the thing about the sari, anyway?" he asked. "You pranced through the living room like you were enjoying yourself, and then two minutes later Ajji was hollering and you were in tears."

Leanne shoved the book she'd been reading into her black satchel.

"No wonder Mom kept me away from her family," she said. "Your grandma's a lunatic. First she drags me into her bedroom and dresses me like a belly dancer, then I say something she doesn't like and she slaps me."

They were stopped at a traffic light. Sunil contemplated his passenger. She'd thrown a black leather jacket over her cropped top. The kohl around her eyes was smudged, her spiked hair poked out in all directions, and the red dot on her forehead had spread into an angry blotch. "You don't look like a belly dancer now," he said. "More like a punk with a hangover."

"You're all crazy," Leanne said, frowning at her reflection in the visor mirror. She yanked a tissue from her bag and rubbed at the blotch. "I don't care if she *is* an old lady; she'd better not hit me again."

"Look, if you don't want people to get angry, you have to treat them with respect. Especially old people. What did you say that upset her?"

"I don't even know now. Something about the photo of that girl. She was pointing at it and pointing at me."

"That is her dead daughter. Sita. My aunt. Your aunt. And you were mocking her?"

"I didn't even know Mom had a sister. What happened to this Sita, anyway?"

"Died in an accident, I think. That picture's been on the shrine as long as I can remember, but nobody talks about her."

Leanne turned to him, tissue in hand. "If it were as simple as that, it wouldn't be a secret."

"You could be right," Sunil admitted, dredging up a half-remembered conversation. "When I was thirteen or so, Mom and Ajji had a big fight. Rajit was going out with Nandi. Ajji didn't approve of her. One day Ajji came to my mom with a photograph of a friend's granddaughter. Mom got really angry. She said no one in *her* family would be bought or sold. Maybe our grandparents tried to force Sita to marry someone she didn't like, and she committed suicide."

"Why would she kill herself when she could run away, like my mom? I bet the family disowned her too, and she's not dead at all."

"But then why would Ajji keep her photo on the altar?"

They fell silent, leaving only Sheila Chandra's fading voice and the mournful beat of a tabla until it too died away. Sunil thought about the August telephone call when he'd learned about the existence of Leanne and her mother. At the time, wrapped up in the practicalities of adding a strange female to the rented house he shared in Kitsilano, he'd accepted without question (or much interest) his father's explanation of the family rift and his decision to make peace. Now he wondered how Sharma, who hated all forms of lying, could have deceived them for so many years.

Leanne broke the silence. "I felt weird in that sari, you know. Like I'd stepped into another body. No, that's not it. Like I'd stepped into an unfamiliar part of my own body. My mother's always going on about how I look just like my dad. That's not true. I have his hair and skin, that's all. She wants me to be Anglo, but that's only half of me. The more she pushes, the more like an outsider I feel."

"Join the club," said Sunil. What did she know about being an outsider? He bet no one called her Paki, asked what she'd done with her turban, turned down her overtures of friendship.

Whether she was responding to his sarcastic tone or merely following her own train of thought, Leanne changed the subject. "I was reading Carr's journal earlier. Did you know she went to hear an Indian who was speaking about Gandhi in Victoria? She even invited him to dinner."

"Bloody white of her, what?" Sunil said, imitating the British colonials he'd seen in the movies.

"Sorry," she said. "I didn't mean it like that. Guess I think like an Anglo even if I'm not aware of it."

Sunil relented. "Why are you so keen on Carr, anyway?"

"Blame my dad," she said. "He grew up in a family of loggers in Prince Rupert. He liked to draw, but his dad got him a job in the woods. So he saved up his money until he had enough to go to Toronto to study graphic design at Ryerson. That's how he met my mom. She was working as a secretary there. We never had the money to come to the West Coast. But he loved the trees, and he loved the way Carr captured their souls. And he taught me."

Sunil grinned. "So you're your father's daughter after all."

They'd finished the slow crawl through View Royal and entered Colwood. Sunil turned left onto Ocean Boulevard, which wound down through a blaze of golden maples to the narrow spit separating Esquimalt Lagoon from Juan de Fuca Strait. He squeezed his Honda between two RVs and they got out.

Sketchbook in hand, Leanne wandered up the beach, crossed the road, and wandered back down the rocky path on the lagoon side, pausing here and there before shaking her head and moving on. Sunil followed in her wake, drinking in the salt tang, the play of light on land and water. He tossed sticks for a friendly black Lab, helped a kid get his kite up, tried not to disturb the birders stalking migrating waterfowl.

As they neared the car again, Leanne complained, "It's too crowded here. There's no place I can get a fix on what Carr would have seen."

"But what about the world *you* see?" Sunil objected.

"That's not the point," Leanne snapped. "I'm supposed to immerse myself in Carr's landscape until I can reinterpret her vision in my own terms." She flung her arms outward in a gesture Sunil found melodramatic. "To do that, I need to be alone with her trees, her sky, and her water."

"What about me?" he asked on principle, not at all minding the prospect of time on his own.

She glared at him. "You can play with yourself, for all I care. After I find the right spot."

"How about going back to Sitting Lady Falls? It's only ten minutes from here. And another two minutes away from the best fries in the Western Communities."

"After all you just ate?"

Sunil patted his stomach. "I'll work it off tonight."

"If you mean dancing, there's no way I'm going back to that place we went Saturday night. The DJ was awful."

"No dancing. Sword fights. Tonight's Dussehra. I get to dress up like Hanuman, the monkey god, and help Lord Rama rescue his beloved Sita from the evil demon Ravana."

"You know what they say about fairy tale princesses," Leanne shot back. "Every rescued princess ends up dead."

"So do the princes who rescue them," Sunil said. "So do we all."

When she reached Witty's Lagoon Regional Park, Danutia discovered that it was too late to rescue the body. The West Shore constable at the service road examined her credentials, radioed the officer in charge, and then unlocked the gate. At the bottom of the gravel path the Ident van stood in deepening shadows beside two West Shore cruisers. Sharma had made good time. He'd carried her and her bike to Headquarters in his SUV and then come ahead with the tech while she locked up her bike and checked out a car. She parked and asked a uniform for Corporal Farrell.

"I'm Farrell." A woman in a blue-gray pantsuit rose from a log she had turned into a makeshift table and strode over, a clipboard at her side. She was shorter and thinner than Danutia, with a small, tight mouth, snub nose sprinkled with freckles, and auburn hair sleeked back into a bun. She looked Danutia up and down and apparently didn't like what she saw. Was it the cords and cycling jacket? Or the untidy mop of curls?

"Sharma said the Special Investigator was coming. Why isn't Kevin with you?" Farrell asked, her voice quick, slightly nasal.

Danutia struggled to control her anger. She'd never met a redhead she liked, and it seemed that Farrell would be no exception. "I'm the new Special Investigator. You must have seen the notice. Any indication this is the same killer?"

"There's no way to tell until we get the tree off the body, and there's no way to do that tonight. I've shut everything down."

"I'll just have a quick look—"

"This isn't a peepshow," Farrell said, her gaze shifting to the broad path where the tech trudged towards them with a set of portable lights, Sharma a faint shadow beyond. She turned back to Danutia. "Look, I've secured the scene, set a guard, and sent the coroner home. We're meeting here at eight tomorrow morning. Bring me the paperwork and you can have all the access you like. Till then, the site's closed."

Sharma approached and set down his cases. "That's the last of the equipment. It will take me a few minutes to pack up. After that," he said to Danutia, "I would very much like a coffee. If you want to wait, there's a café a few kilometers south, the Crossroads. Dennis can drop me off there."

Aware that he would tell her what he could, Danutia nodded. To

Farrell she said, "I'll be back in the morning."

Long before she reached the crossroads that gave the café its name, she could see the bright lights that outlined the building. The parking lot was full, the entrance jammed with people waiting for tables. She wasn't the only one who preferred to have Thanksgiving dinner cooked by someone else, Danutia thought as she worked her way to the one empty seat at the bar.

The bartender appeared and Danutia ordered a coffee. The woman beside her, an aging Cher with unnaturally black hair, plunging neckline, and too much flashy jewelry, loudly demanded another Harvey Wallbanger. "If Harvey don't bang her, who will?" she cackled. The bartender, smiling tiredly at a familiar joke, cleared the woman's empty glass.

No place for a quiet chat, Danutia decided, and ordered Sharma's coffee to go.

A pimply busboy slammed through the kitchen door with a tray of wine glasses and began sliding them into the wooden rack above her, breathing heavily. His white dress shirt gaped between the buttons and she could see the soft fat of his belly and the deep circles of sweat under his arms. He would have to be nineteen to work here, Danutia assumed, but he looked younger.

The woman leaned over and clutched Danutia's arm. "That's my Trav," she said, her breath heavy with alcohol and stale tobacco, her words a little slurred. "How you doin', sweetie? Be careful with them glasses now. Sometimes you don't know your own strength." Her voice dropped to a stage whisper. "Know why I named him Trav? He was born with this black curly hair like mine, see, and the cutest dimple in his chin, the spittin' image of John Travolta. I just knew he'd grow up to be tall, dark, and handsome." She ran appraising eyes over the boy's pudgy face and soft belly. "Guess I should've named him Mitch, you know, for the Michelin Man!"

The boy flinched as though he'd been hit and his face and neck turned bright red. He grabbed a handful of dirty glasses and shoved them in the tray. "Fuck off."

Danutia pried the woman's fingers off her arm.

"You hear how he talks to me?" she demanded of no one in particular. "Kids these days ain't got no respect. He's movin' out, he says, and me with cancer."

Over the woman's shoulder Danutia glimpsed Sharma making his way towards her. She laid a five-dollar bill on the bar and rose from her stool. "Do you need a ride?" she asked. "I'm a police officer and I think you've reached your limit."

A loud crash and the tinkle of breaking glass. Danutia looked around. The busboy was wedged halfway through the kitchen door, trying to regain control of the tray, now almost empty.

"Give me the tray and get the broom," the bartender said. The boy did as he was told.

"Hopeless, that kid," said his mother. "And the police too, if you ask me. Sittin' here drinkin' coffee and harassin' a sick woman." She grabbed Danutia's arm again. "Where were you when my rings got stolen, eh? A month I've been trying to get the cops around here to do something, and all they say is it's not their business. Your ring disappeared from the Royal Jubilee Hospital, you got to talk to the Victoria police, they say. And me a sick woman who can barely get out of her house."

Danutia signaled the barman to cut off her supply and handed Sharma his takeout coffee. "Let's go."

"What was that all about?" Sharma asked as they crossed the road to where she'd parked her car.

As they headed back towards the city in the gathering darkness, she told him about Trav and his mom. "Did you see him drop his tray when I said the word police? I figure he must have snitched her ring, and who can blame him," she concluded. "Poor kid. No dad in the picture, far as I can tell. Too bad Child Protection didn't apprehend him at birth. Maybe he would have had decent parents."

"Or perhaps he would have grown up with foster parents who abused him. Or perhaps they would have loved him and treated him well, but he would have hated them anyway, because they weren't his 'real parents.' We never know what will happen when we interfere in people's lives."

"You and your Indian fatalism." Her headlights flashed over the sign for Witty's Lagoon Regional Park. "Your turn," she said.

"Hard to say much until I can get a better look. The body's been there a while, I'd say. Maybe six weeks or so."

Six weeks. The bloating would have lessened, the flesh turned blue, green, purple, brown. The maggots would have come and gone, having feasted upon the soft flesh around the body's openings, natural or unnatural. The bones would have been gnawed by animals, possibly scattered. Or severed by the killer.

"Did you get a look at the hands?"

"Too many branches in the way. All I could see with the light was a bit of flesh and bone here and there."

"It's a wonder anyone found the body."

Sharma repeated the story Joan Goodman had told Farrell. "Goodman says the tree came down in the Labor Day storm. She thinks it must have fallen on an early-morning jogger," he concluded.

"And you?" Yawning black holes stretched away on both sides of the road, with trucks and cranes scattered here and there like abandoned toys in a giant sandbox.

"According to Corporal Farrell, there have been no recent Missing Person reports in this area. As for me . . ." He folded his hands in his lap. "There was an American television show I watched growing up. *Dragnet*, it was called. In every show, Joe Friday would say, 'All I want is the facts, Ma'am.' I am like Joe Friday, ugly but persistent. I want the facts. But the facts are not always as they appear. I will wait until the facts yield up their truth. As Krishnamurti says, truth is not permanent. It must be discovered from moment to moment."

One moment the demon Ravana seemed about to defeat Lord Rama; the next moment he lay writhing on the ground. As Lord Rama declared his victory, Sunil quickly crawled beyond the circle of candles in paper bags that lit the back garden. In the darkness he yanked off his demon mask, reversed his cloak, and put on the headdress of the fire god Agni. Then he crouched behind the picnic table, soon to become Sita's funeral pyre, and waited for his next cue.

With his father away tonight and Rajit playing Lord Rama, as usual, Sunil had stepped into the role of the demon, which he found both strange and exhilarating. He'd enjoyed the cut and thrust of their plastic swords as he and Rajit dueled; even more, he'd liked taunting Lord Rama about how he had defiled the virtuous Sita, Lord Rama's wife, while she was in his power.

Now Lord Rama was renouncing Sita, saying that her honor had been compromised. Astonished gasps went up from the assembled throng. Sita, played by Nandi with an energy that surprised Sunil, demanded the right to prove her innocence in a trial by fire.

That was his cue. He danced around the picnic table, lighting more candles and fanning the dry-ice "smoke" of the funeral pyre.

"If the fire god knows me to be innocent," Nandi proclaimed, "let him protect me from these flames."

Yasmin, waving Indra's thunderbolt in one hand and Brahma's lotus in the other, rushed towards the pyre to protect Sita. Ajji and Kumala, costumed as other gods, followed after. Leanne straggled along behind, thumping on a small drum. Suddenly she cried, "Look, it's Uncle."

Furious at Leanne for interrupting the ritual, Sunil peered through the billowing smoke. His father stood in the shadows near the side gate, making a calming motion with his hands. How long had he been there, Sunil wondered, knowing Sharma would never have interrupted the *Ramayana*.

"What's going on out at Witty's Lagoon?" Leanne shouted. "I was going to do some sketching out there, but the police wouldn't let me past the barricade."

Sunil knew his father wouldn't answer. Sharma never discussed his work at home, though he'd reluctantly visited Sunil's Grade Five class on Career Day to talk about fingerprinting. The other kids had stared spellbound while his father used sprays, powders, and solutions to make prints appear and disappear. Terrified by his father's unsuspected powers, Sunil had shrunk deep into his desk. Never again had he sneaked coins from his mother's purse.

"It will be on the news soon enough," Sharma said. "More important is the reunion between Lord Rama and his beautiful wife Sita. Carry on."

Sunil wasn't sure he believed the old stories any more. Still, each time the fire god laid Sita in Lord Rama's arms and asked him to treat her kindly, something magical happened inside. So he tried to bring his mind back to that place, to become Agni again, the fire god protecting the innocent Sita. But this time as he carried Nandi towards her waiting husband, he thought only of the next part of the story—Rama's second and final renunciation of Sita. Leanne was right: Rescued princesses always die.

Four

Early the next morning, Danutia set off on the trail from the Witty's Lagoon service road to Sitting Lady Falls, armed with the notice appointing her Special Investigator. So far she had made no progress in investigating the deaths of the two Aboriginal women and had no suspects. She didn't want this to be another of Handy Dan's victims—how could she want anything so gruesome to happen to anyone?—but if he was responsible, she would at least have a chance of finding new evidence, new leads to follow up.

Soon she could hear a steady splash like a bathtub filling. Through the morning fog she caught a glimpse of Corporal Farrell, talking with a couple of uniformed constables beside a Parks Department barricade. Farrell's blue-gray pantsuit looked as fresh as yesterday, her auburn hair as tightly coiled. Stuffing the SI notice in her pocket, Danutia ran her fingers through her own mop of short blond curls. Then, tucking her shirt more firmly into her khaki trousers, she strode forward.

"Here's the paperwork," she said.

Farrell took a quick look and slipped the notice under the other papers on her clipboard. "See where that tree's come down?" she asked, pointing. Beyond the barricade, a steep trail descended to a gully and rose again on the other side. At the bottom, the sawn upper end of a massive tree trunk stopped just short of the trail. "The body's under there, about thirty feet uphill. Soon as Sharma and the Parks foreman figure out how to get the tree off, we'll take a look. Assuming the coroner's here."

"What can I do?" Danutia asked.

"Everything's under control." Farrell tucked an unruly wisp of hair into place and turned back to the constables. "Don't start the house-to-house till I've examined the body. In the meantime, don't allow any unauthorized access from either end of this trail."

Danutia retreated to the viewing platform and paced to and fro, trying to warm her body and cool her temper. Who did Farrell think she was, anyway? Danutia had worked with a couple of West Shore officers but had never heard her mentioned. Maybe she was new to the posting and determined to prove herself, just as Danutia had been not so long ago. Or maybe, a small voice whispered, you're envious of her rank and good looks.

The air, heavy with the scent of cedar, was cold and clammy, the Sitting Lady partially hidden by patches of fog that swirled off the lagoon and drifted through the trees. A buzz of excitement seemed to surround the men as the Parks ground crew and the forensics tech— Carl, that was his name—dumped gear beside the barricade and went back for more, while Sharma and the Parks foreman headed up from the gully.

She was the only one without a role. She didn't want this to be another victim of Handy Dan—who would want that?—but if it was, she would coordinate evidence from the three murders. If the killings were unrelated, she could forget about this case and get on with her own investigation. She glanced at her watch. Two minutes to eight. Where the hell was the coroner?

In the province of British Columbia, she'd discovered, anyone could be a coroner. Well, not exactly anyone, but you didn't have to be a medical doctor, though some were, especially the full-time city ones. The part-time Community Coroners, common in rural areas and the Gulf Islands, were mostly lawyers and science teachers and social workers who'd been trained in the proper procedures at the Justice Institute. Today they were waiting for Paul McCasland. He was a former lawyer and a widower, Sharma had said last night. The two men had worked a couple of cases together.

Danutia's thoughts drifted to the message on her machine when she arrived home last night, Alyne's cheery voice saying, "Hi Sis, where are you? Sorry I missed you, hope you had a good Thanksgiving, I'll try again soon." She hadn't called back, though it wouldn't have been too late. She'd been in no mood to hear the latest family gossip or to endure Alyne's gentle prying. For the next few weeks, at least, she would be too busy with these investigations to think about her relationship with her father or other men in her past. She'd left a message on her therapist's answering machine this morning, canceling her Thursday appointment.

A noisy rattling sound drew Danutia's attention to a bird skimming across the lagoon.

"Kingfisher," said a man's voice behind her. She felt the platform shake and looked around. There he was, Paul McCasland, bounding towards her like a friendly puppy. He was a comfortable-looking man with short curly hair and a short curly beard encircling a round face, gold-rimmed granny glasses perched on a button nose. His leather briefcase was scuffed and battered around the edges.

She checked her watch. Eight o'clock. Exactly on time.

McCasland must have noticed. "Sorry if I'm late," he said as Farrell and Sharma joined them. "What's the plan?"

Sharma explained the procedure he had worked out with the foreman. "We must try to coordinate the winches so that the trunk rises straight up," he concluded. "That is our best hope for avoiding further damage to the body."

"It's risky, but it can't be helped. Do your best." He looked around the circle. "We'll wait here."

Farrell opened her mouth but seemed to think better of objecting. Until the body was removed, the coroner was in charge of the scene.

Sharma and the tech pulled on their disposable whites and set off down the trail with their equipment, the ground crew following with chainsaws and cables and a couple of winches.

McCasland opened his briefcase. "I always carry binoculars in case there's a chance to do a spot of birding. We should be able to follow most of what they're doing. Any takers?"

Danutia reached out her hand. Farrell intercepted. "This is my case," she said, taking the glasses and raising them to her eyes.

McCasland winked and handed Danutia a second pair, keeping a telescope for himself.

"Thanks," she said, but not too warmly. She didn't want him getting any ideas. Her therapist had suggested that she avoid any entanglements for at least six months, and Danutia had agreed. Besides, McCasland wasn't her type. Too soft and cuddly.

Through the lenses she watched the men below disappear into the foggy hollow, then reappear. The ground crew, ghostly apparitions dragging their chains, first secured two cables around the upper trunk of the tree, then ran them out to either side of the gully, wrapped them high up on sturdy firs, and hooked them to the winches. The foreman checked the cables and then positioned himself down slope.

"That guy could be in trouble if something goes wrong," Danutia said.

"There's no help for it," McCasland said. "He has to be in line with the trunk to make sure it's rising straight up. The undergrowth's too thick higher up for him to have a clear view. Besides, they won't lift the whole trunk; they'll use the root ball as a pivot."

Danutia shifted her attention. Sharma and the tech were making their way up the gully, Sharma videotaping the path ahead of him, the tech carrying a chainsaw. They stopped near the spot Farrell had pointed out, the spot where the body must lie. Sharma videotaped some more, and then switched to the still camera. A few minutes later he passed the camera to the tech, faced towards the parks foreman on the slope below, and circled his arm as though throwing a rope.

"Ready," called a faint voice. Sharma dropped out of sight.

"He's on his hands and knees, clearing some brush," McCasland said. "Now he's signaling Dennis to start the winches."

McCasland's telescope must be more powerful than the binoculars. Danutia could see only the trembling undergrowth and then the tech making large circles in the air. One . . . Two . . . As he completed the third circle, the winches creaked and clanked. Branches slowly rose through the fog, snapping and tearing. A sharp "cut" gesture and the winches creaked to a halt. A chainsaw buzzed eerily from the undergrowth.

"A branch must have caught on something," McCasland said.

"Damn binoculars," Farrell muttered. Danutia, vainly trying to focus her own pair, silently agreed.

The buzzing died away and the winches started up again. Slowly, and with stoppages when it edged off course, the trunk was hoisted.

At a double "cut" signal the winches fell silent. Sharma stood upright and gave an "all clear" signal. The ground crew slowly swung the tree trunk towards the far side of the gully, the tech began stringing up crime-scene tape around where the body lay, and Sharma walked around with his cameras. Finally, motioning the party on the platform to join him, he headed back towards the trail.

Danutia was stiff from the cold and glad to be moving. Handing McCasland his binoculars, she fell in behind Farrell. The trail was steep and she concentrated on her footing. At the bottom, the ground was torn up and chunks of fir strewn about.

McCasland pointed up the slope to where the root ball of the fir made a dark circle like writhing bullsnakes. "Just imagine the force of that tree. The old bridge must have splintered like it was made of matchsticks."

Danutia studied the terrain, thinking not of the tree but of the body that had lain in its path. Sharma had given her the bare facts on their way back from Metchosin last night; now she could fit them into what lay before her. The fog had lifted, revealing a narrow deer track, almost overgrown by ferns. The track led up the gully from the bridge site to the crime scene. That must be the path Sharma and the tech had used, and before them Joan Goodman, the parks interpreter. And the victim?

"Why would anyone go so far off the main trail?" she asked.

Sharma didn't reply. He was gazing at the ground, his expression troubled and his hands palm to palm in that gesture almost like praying. She waited for him to speak, to lay out the facts he'd gathered so far with the serene calm he'd shown in other cases. Still he said nothing.

Something about the body or the scene must have reminded him of his sister. She wondered again how the girl had died.

McCasland broke the silence. "She could have been killed here and carried up there, out of sight, don't you think?" When Sharma still didn't reply, he added, "Guess we'd better have a look."

At that Sharma dropped his hands and lifted his head. "Forgive me. Follow in my footsteps, please. We'll need to search along this track."

As they made their way upwards, the bittersweet smell of death grew stronger. McCasland stopped to light a fat cigar. Danutia coughed as the smoke drifted towards her. She hated the smell and the smoke irritated her lungs.

"Sorry," he said. "It's the only thing that keeps me from throwing up."

When they came to where the yellow crime-scene tape drooped from shrub to shrub, they stopped. The body lay in a small mossy clearing freshly littered with fir branches and sawdust. Even at this distance Danutia could tell the girl hadn't been smashed like a china doll. "That outcrop must have taken the weight of the tree," McCasland said, gesturing with his cigar. Farrell slid under the tape and McCasland followed. They would conduct the head-to-toe visual inspection of the body, and then Sharma and the tech would comb the area for evidence. Again Danutia felt unnecessary, out of place.

McCasland had left his briefcase beside her. She helped herself to his telescope and focused in on the body. The girl was lying on her right side, her legs slightly drawn up and her soiled jeans twisted around her knees; across her torso, a tattered halter top, once pink, with the trailing strap that had caught the park interpreter's attention. Half covering what was left of her face, a polka-dot bandana. A thin branch, its end freshly cut, protruded from just below the ribcage.

"Maybe the tree did her in after all," Farrell said.

McCasland blew around the branch stub and sawdust flew. "I'd say she was already dead when the tree fell. The wound's been messed up a bit from the chainsaw, but there's no sign of bleeding."

Was she one of Handy Dan's victims? That was the question uppermost in Danutia's mind. The answer would determine whether this became her case or remained in Farrell's hands. She focused the scope on the left arm, which stretched over the skull at an impossible angle and then ended abruptly at the elbow. She took a deep breath. "Left elbow. Cut or chewed?"

McCasland bent to examine the jagged bones. "One or both, it's hard to tell. There's not much flesh left after six weeks in the bush. The arm could have been dragged off by some animal any time. We'll have to wait for the autopsy."

Danutia wasn't in any mood to wait. She focused on the bandana knotted loosely under the ear hole. Her assailant would only have had to grab and twist, twist again. "She's been strangled, like the other two."

"Perhaps," Sharma said, adding so softly Danutia barely heard him, "and yet he tried to cover her face."

She studied the head and neck area more closely. It was true that a flap of polka-dot material lay slanted across the lips and left jaw. But to assume, after all this time, that it had been placed there by the killer? She was the one who leaped to conclusions, not Sharma. She thought of the cloth draped around Sita's head in the photo she'd seen. Had she too been strangled, her face partially covered? If so, that would explain Sharma's reaction. But if the cases were similar, would he be able to remain objective, to see the facts as they were, undistorted by memory? If he lost his objectivity, he could jeopardize the case. She'd have to talk to him privately, and soon.

As it happened, she didn't have the chance. After the head-to-toe, Farrell left to set the investigation into full swing. McCasland, who couldn't leave the area until Body Transport arrived, invited Danutia to a little bird watching. "Best time of year for migrating waterfowl," he said.

"No thanks," Danutia said. "I'll stay and watch the finger search. You never know what might turn up." Nothing much did, though: bits of vegetation that might or might not yield body fluids or trace evidence, and a smashed beer bottle that might or might not yield fingerprints.

When Sharma and Carl finished searching the cordoned off crime scene, Sharma paged McCasland, who called for Body Transport on his cell phone. While they waited, the coroner chatted about a rare spectacle he'd seen: red-necked phalaropes spinning in circles to stir up food from the lagoon's marshy bottom. "Couldn't tell if they were males or females," he said. "They were probably juveniles, this late, and the plumage is the same in both sexes. It's a different story with the adults. One's larger, with brighter plumage, and I bet you think it's the male, but it's not. The phalaropes are one of the few bird species where the females put on the sexual display."

McCasland's chance remark about "sexual display" sent Danutia scurrying back to review her files on the two Aboriginal women. Soon she found what she was looking for. According to the second victim's housemates, Marie Wilson liked to go dancing on theme nights at the Castaway Club. On the Easter Saturday she disappeared, the theme was Hawaiian Luau. Marie had been strangled with the lei of artificial flowers she'd worn as part of her costume. A server named Sybil Swanson had identified Marie from a photo, though Swanson couldn't say when the woman had left, or with whom, nor could any of the other staff.

The first victim, Esther Mike, had been strangled with the red choker she was wearing and her body dumped on a reserve in Central Saanich, some twenty minutes northeast of Victoria. Her movements on the days before she was killed had not been so easy to establish. A thirty-three-year-old status Indian from the New Songhees Reserve in Esquimalt, she'd been charged with various offences by both the Victoria police and West Shore RCMP. Her mug shots showed a woman losing her good looks as addiction and a hard life took their toll. In the last one, taken the previous October, a half-moon scar disfigured her left cheek. By that time, according to family members, she'd lost her three children to Social Services and was drifting from man to man. During the Christmas holidays she had been sleeping on a friend's couch, on the nights she came home. The last time she'd been seen, as far as anyone had been willing to say, was the Friday before New Year's. When her body was found, she was wearing a flounced red skirt with black fishnet stockings and a garter belt. The investigating officer assumed she'd been hooking.

McCasland's comments had reminded Danutia that street corners are not the only places women indulge in sexual display. On a hunch, she called the Castaway Club and asked what the theme had been for their New Year's Eve party. The manager put her on hold while he checked his calendar. "Moulin Rouge," he said. "You know, can-can dancers."

Images of can-can dancers flashed into Danutia's mind. Flounced skirts. Fishnet stockings. Choker ribbons around their necks. "I'll be right out," she said.

Twenty minutes later she pulled into the club's parking lot off Esquimalt Road. The Castaway was a long, low building, the entrance up a flight of stairs covered by a blue arched canopy, like the gambling clubs in old gangster movies. Roger Waldrip, the manager, a tall, thin Fred Astaire type without the smile, showed her into his office. While he studied Esther's last mug shot, he fingered his thinning hair. Finally, he said, "It's hard to tell people apart when they're in costume, and I don't remember the scar. Short woman, a bit heavyset?"

"That's right," Danutia said. "When did you see her here?"

"I can't say for sure. I'm not bad with faces, it's part of the job, but dates now, that's different. A year ago, it must have been, maybe longer. If it's the same woman, she was drunk and pestering people, and I had to ban her from the club. You'd better ask Sybil. She's like an elephant, never forgets."

Danutia recognized the name from Marie Wilson's file. Sybil Swanson had served Marie several pina coladas during the Hawaiian Luau. She hadn't been interviewed during the investigation into Esther Mike's murder because no one had connected the dead woman to the club. Now there was a possible link.

"You say she was pestering people. Who, exactly?"

"I guess it was mostly one guy at a table. I didn't pay much attention to him, just moved in and walked her out the door, told her not to come back."

"What can you tell me about him?"

"He wasn't a regular, just some guy, average looking. It was a theme night, I remember that, so he might have been in costume, but I don't remember anything flashy."

For someone who claimed to be not bad on faces, Waldrip was singularly unhelpful. Fat? Thin? Hair color? Eye color? Facial hair? Glasses? He thought maybe glasses, but was vague about everything else. Danutia could only hope that Sybil had been more observant. While Waldrip wrote out the server's address and phone number, Danutia found herself thinking about the girl at Sitting Lady Falls. Her left foot was bare. On the right, as McCasland discovered when he shifted the body slightly, was a high-heeled pink sandal.

"By the way," she asked, "what were your theme nights for August and September?"

Waldrip paused in his writing. "I run a clean operation here. Why do you want to know?"

Danutia had checked out the Castaway Club before she came. Fights were common and drug deals went down in the parking lot. Though Waldrip had been cooperative so far, he might well clam up if he thought she was on a fishing expedition. "You'll hear it on tonight's news," she said. "Another body's been found. I'm trying to establish whether there's a connection."

Waldrip swivelled in his chair and flipped back the pages of the wall calendar behind his desk. "Theme nights are once or twice a month, usually around holidays. August 3, the long weekend, was Arabian Nights. Labor Day weekend, August 31, Guys and Dolls." He turned the page. "September 21, Harvest Moon."

Danutia thanked him and left. As she drove back to Headquarters, she considered what she'd just learned. The club's theme for the Labor Day weekend, the only one that fit the probable time of the girl's death, was Guys and Dolls. Did the girl's clothes fit that theme? Not if you were thinking of the movie, a favorite among the old musicals she watched to unwind. That was Fifties gangsters and their molls. What about more recent "dolls," such as Barbie dolls? She could imagine Barbie dressed as the girl had been, in jeans, pink halter top, pink polka-dot bandana, pink high-heeled sandals. The sandals were hardly what you'd choose for a hike in the woods. But then, how much choice had the girl had about what happened that night?

That night Ritchie Taylor was channel surfing from the beat-up couch in the living room of Leicester House when he caught the words "body discovered near Sitting Lady Falls in Metchosin." Fuck. He clicked to another channel.

"Hey man," Chuck protested from the doorway. "That's out by the Head. I wanna hear what's goin' on."

Ritchie tossed the remote onto the coffee table and stood up. "I need some smokes."

Chuck grabbed the remote and clicked back to the local news. "Hold on a minute and I'll go with you."

"Dammit, I want out of here," Ritchie said, but his feet wouldn't move.

"West Shore RCMP say it is too early in the investigation to release any details," the announcer went on in his oily voice. "Asked whether there's any connection with the unsolved murders of two Aboriginal women earlier this year, the RCMP officer refused to comment, saying only that the investigation into those deaths continues, but no arrests have been made." The announcer grinned into the camera, displaying perfect white teeth. "Stay tuned for sports right after these messages."

"Bastard," Ritchie muttered.

When they were outside at last, Chuck paused to fiddle with the zip on his old sweatshirt. "Whatcha wanna bet the Head's locked down?" he said.

"Will you hurry up?" Ritchie said. "Fairway will be closing soon."

"Why not Mini Mart, it's open till eleven. Oh, I get it." Chuck gave up on his zipper and fell into step beside Ritchie. "It's not just smokes you want, is it? What is it this time—more of that goat's cheese to stink us out with? Just kiddin'," he protested when Ritchie cuffed him on the shoulder.

Cutting through to Gorge, they strode silently past struggling motels offering cheap off-season rates. As they neared a bus stop, a beefy young guy in a hoodie stepped in front of them. "Spare some change for the bus?" he said, opening a grubby palm to reveal a couple of quarters and a dime. "My car broke down and I'm a little short."

Ritchie was about to slip him a coin or two just to get away when Chuck tugged on his arm.

"Try AA," he told the guy, dragging Ritchie across the street. "Man, what are you *doing*? That's the oldest scam goin'. Didn't you learn anything in all those programs? You can't go around enabling addictions. Look at me and my old man, the booze nearly killed us both. You see him at dinner yesterday? Hands a bit shaky and he can't wait to leave, but for a few hours, no drinking. That's the rule, and he knows it. Not just at Leicester House, either. If he wants to see me, that's how it's gonna be."

Ritchie felt the bitterness rising in him. "You're lucky he wants to," he said.

"Yeah, well, it's been a long time comin', for both of us."

The neon supermarket sign was only a block away. Ritchie slowed down, thinking about his interview tomorrow for the chef program at Camosun. He wanted to impress the guy by saying he knew how make a cheesecake, they were on all the dessert menus. But the ingredients were expensive and all he had was a tenner and some change, and half of that would go for a pack of smokes. What was the point, anyway? He was still an ex-con, wasn't he?

Chuck, who must have sensed his shifting mood, grabbed his arm. "Say man, let's have a look at the rapids. That's really something at night."

Soon the two men stood leaning over the railing of the Gorge Bridge, their backs to the streetlights and the traffic. A short drop below, the black waters of the tidal inlet, churned into foam where the waterway narrowed, spilled over jagged rocks and raced towards the sea.

"My old man used to bring me up here all the time," Chuck said. "The falls was bigger then, with a huge rock in the middle of the channel. Dad had an old canoe, and he'd fill it with food and fishing tackle and a case of beer, and we'd set off for the day. He always seemed to time it so we were headin' home when the tide was going out and the water was racing over the rocks. He'd grin and yell 'Ain't this fun?' while I paddled for dear life. Then some guy blasted out the big rock and we didn't come any more. Guess it wasn't any fun if there wasn't much chance of drowning."

You could still drown down there, Ritchie thought. He could feel the goose bumps rise along his arms. His T-shirt was thin and there was a cold breeze, but it wasn't that. The water was tugging at him, whispering sweet promises of peace if only he would yield himself. "Let's get out of here," he said.

Chuck didn't move. "Frenchy says clothes washed in this foam will protect you from drowning. If I'd known that then, I'da been down here every day, scrubbin' the bejesus out of my raggedy old jeans." He hawked and spat, the stringy gobbit stretching out like the tail of a meteor as it plummeted towards the black water.

Ritchie's eyes followed as it was swept away. "Just shut up. I'm going to the store. You coming or not?"

"What's got into you? It's just a story." A car screeched past, rap music blaring out the open window.

Ritchie shot a finger at the receding car. He let a bus pass and then jogged across Tillicum Road as the light changed.

Chuck panted up beside him. "I know what's makin' you jumpy. You're thinking about Crystal, and wondering why you never heard from her, right? She got cold feet, man, that's all. She's just a kid. Betcha she's home in Ontario, safe and sound, and don't know how to make things right. You gotta get in touch, let her know she can try another time. Then you can quit worryin' and get on with your life, you know what I mean? You got a phone number? I got some time left on my calling card."

"Who says I'm worrying? She said she was coming to Victoria. She told me when to meet her at the bus station. What would she be doing way out in Metchosin? Just forget it. I got no address for her, no phone number, nothing. All I know is, she said she was staying with a friend. Probably some no-good she's shacked up with."

"How about her mother? You could call her."

"Kelly? You must be joking. Even if I knew how to find her, she'd never talk to me."

"Think, man. There must be somebody."

Ritchie paused at the entrance to the store. Kelly's parents, if they were still alive, in Mississauga. Maybe they would pass on a message. There was a phone box at the service station on the corner. But then he remembered the grim satisfaction on her dad's face when the judge gave him life–15. He'd served every year of the fifteen, and now he'd be on parole for life. If he didn't end up back in prison.

"Nobody," he said. The glass doors closed behind him with a sigh.

Five

Danutia turned into the Witty's Lagoon service road. The Ident van, a minivan, and a couple of cruisers stood in front of the entrance gate. She parked and joined the group clustered around Farrell.

"Sorry I'm late," she muttered. After pursuing leads from the Castaway Club all day, she'd fallen into bed with a blinding headache and slept fitfully, waking every few hours to the image of the polka-dot bandana half-covering the girl's ravaged lips and jaw. She hadn't worked in Serious Crimes long, hadn't had a lifetime of observing mangled bodies. "It's the kids that get to you," older hands had told her, and maybe that's what she was troubled by, the senseless death of one who seemed little more than a child. Sharma was also troubled by this death, she sensed. She'd hoped to talk to him privately this morning, but she wouldn't have the chance now.

Farrell nodded brusquely and introduced the two dog handlers from Vancouver, Mike and Barb. The decision to bring in dog teams had been made late the previous day. The long dry summer, which had carried on through the Thanksgiving weekend, was due to end soon in heavy rains, further compromising any evidence that had not already been dispersed or destroyed. The area needed to be searched thoroughly and quickly. Given the difficult terrain, sniffer dogs were an obvious choice. None with the right training were available on the Island, and so the search had been postponed until the dog teams could arrive.

Spreading a map on the hood, Farrell directed their attention to the green band representing the regional park, which surrounded the blue of the lagoon like a misshapen horseshoe.

"These are the hiking trails and bridle paths leading into the park." Farrell tapped her index finger at half a dozen spots on the outer edges of the horseshoe. Her hand was small and freckled, Danutia noted, the finger dainty, the nail well shaped and covered with a clear polish. Danutia, who had inherited her own large hands from her farmer father, felt a pang of envy.

"Too far for anyone to carry a body," Sharma said.

"Right. So she wasn't killed and dumped like Handy Dan's victims," Farrell said dismissively, fixing her gaze on Danutia for a moment. "On the other hand, the sandals suggest she didn't set out with hiking in mind. So most likely she was lured to the falls and then killed. This map shows the trails as they were before the Labor Day storm. The parking lot at the Information Centre is the closest public entrance to where the body was found," Farrell ran her finger down a dotted line. "It's less than a quarter of a mile from there to the crime scene by way of the old Lagoon Trail. This"—her finger moved to the right—"is the service road we've been using. It's about a third of a mile from here to the falls, and the gate is always kept locked. The Beach Road access"—Farrell pointed again—"leads to a favorite hangout for kids from the area. There's a small parking lot with steps down to the beach, and no gate. It wouldn't have taken much persuading to get the victim down to the beach, even in sandals. Then he could have lured her up Beach Trail and down the Lagoon Trail to see the falls," she said, tracing the route.

"That looks a long way," Danutia objected.

"Less than a mile," Farrell said, "and most of it's easy going. Even in sandals. I think we can assume they came by car, and the killer left by the same route. If not . . ." Her hand swept over the map.

If not, Danutia thought, he's almost certainly a local who knows more ways in and out than we have the time and resources to cover.

"The dogs will find what they find," Sharma said, as though reading her thoughts. "And we will decide what it means."

They soon agreed upon a plan.

Sharma, who proclaimed himself too old to go chasing after dogs, would take Dennis with him to the crime scene. There they would pick up where they'd left off the day before, Sharma focusing on the area around the bridge site, Carl combing through the undergrowth along the deer path.

The dog teams would split up. Mike's dog Ruby was a cadaver dog, trained to sniff out human remains even if buried or underwater.

That pair would start from the crime scene and work outward in search of the missing forearm. Barb's dog, trained to alert only on the scent of a specific person, would search for any of the victim's possessions that might have been scattered along the most likely access routes, working their way down the service road and then up the old trail to the Information Centre and on to the Beach Road parking lot.

"Do you want us to radio if we find something, or are you sending a walk-along?" Mike asked. He was a good-looking guy in his early forties maybe, wavy brown hair, blue eyes, a body he obviously took good care of, so Danutia wasn't surprised when Farrell said, "I'll come with you."

"Fine with me," Danutia said, mindful of her therapist's advice to avoid entanglements. She smiled at Barb and said, "Guess that means we're partners."

When the others had left, Barb opened the side door of the minivan and released a muscular black and tan terrier about the size and build of a Jack Russell. "Her name's Penny," Barb said, scratching between the cropped ears. "What else would you call a mini pinscher?"

Danutia liked Barb's straightforward gaze, open smile, well-worn jeans, and boots. The dog she was less sure about. Good for squirming through deadfalls and down rabbit holes, she could see that. But finding objects?

"Anything the girl had on her has been out in the weather for six weeks or more," she said. "You think Penny can pick up a scent that old?"

Barb laughed. "Give her a good sniff and she'll find the handkerchief you lost a year ago."

Barb snapped a leash on Penny and they moved around the locked gate, stopping just inside while Danutia drew on gloves and removed the girl's pink sandal from an evidence bag. A thin ankle strap, a wider toe strap, a narrow band joining them. Cheap plastic, except for the cork heel. "I wouldn't wear these for walking in the woods, would you?" she said, passing the shoe to Barb.

"I wouldn't wear them anywhere," Barb said, grinning, "but it's perfect for tracking. See how grimy the insole is? It should have a good strong scent." She held the sandal near Penny's nose.

The dog sniffed, her eyes dark and alert.

"Go find," Barb said, and they were off.

The sun had burned off the early morning mist, though the air was still cool. The woods were fairly open at first, and so Barb was able to take Penny in long loops on both sides of the service road. As they neared the water, the undergrowth thickened and Barb had to let the dog off the leash. Still nothing.

When they reached the viewing platform, they stopped for water and a doggie treat for Penny, who couldn't seem to settle despite Barb's pats and ear-scratching. Another sniff of the sandal and she was off.

"She's caught a scent," Barb said as Penny darted down the trail towards the old bridge site. Pockets of mist still clung to the lagoon and curled up the banks like steam from a kettle, obscuring the dog's movements. When Danutia and Barb caught up, they discovered Sharma on his hands and knees doing a finger search through the trampled vegetation and Penny casting back and forth over the churned up ground where the park crew had removed the smashed bridge.

"Have you found something?" Barb asked. "Is that what she's picking up?"

Sharma gestured to his open evidence case a few feet away. "Some odds and ends. But your dog doesn't seem to be keying in on them."

"It's this gully," Barb said. "Breezes get stifled or bounced around, so it's hard to pin down a scent." Calling the dog, she led her to the case and one by one held the evidence bags to her nose. No response.

"We agree then," Sharma said solemnly to the dog. Penny took no notice. Her ears pricked up and she bounded up the slope towards the crime scene, leaving behind a wake of swaying ferns. Barb and Danutia hurried after her. They found her barking and quivering at the base of a hollow cedar tree ten feet west of where the body had lain.

"Good dog! Good Penny!" the handler said, taking a treat out of a plastic bag. "You're the best sniffer dog ever, you are!"

Pulling on a fresh glove to prevent cross-contamination—and spider bites, she thought ruefully—Danutia felt around inside the dark hollow. Decaying leaves, twigs, fir cones stashed for a rainy day. Then her fingers touched something hard and unyielding. Carefully she brushed away the leaf litter.

"It's the other sandal," she said. She took out the camera Sharma had sent with her and snapped a dozen shots, hoping the flash was strong enough to reveal the sandal nestled in the hollow tree. Then she slipped a twig under the toe strap, shook off the debris, and raised the sandal to the light. "How would it get here? I can't see the killer hiding it. A murder weapon, maybe, but this is a long way from any trail."

"Raccoon, probably," Barb said. "Maybe rats, though this is a little far from the water. The teeth marks will tell." She scratched between Penny's ears and the dog shivered with pleasure. "Anyway, you found it, didn't you?" she said in a high-pitched sing-song voice, as though she were talking to a baby. "Maybe now Constable Danutia will show you a little more respect."

And she looks so sensible, Danutia thought as she followed the stocky woman in jeans and boots back to the bridge site. She liked dogs, always had, but didn't consider them baby substitutes. Barb evidently did. Maybe it's her biological clock ticking. Maybe in a few years Danutia would find herself cooing over a shih tzu, or a black and white cat named Bootsie.

As Sharma added the sandal to his evidence case, Danutia noticed again the melancholy that had clung to him since he'd first viewed the body. The lines in his craggy face seemed deeper, his shoulders braced against a heavy burden. She doubted that he confided in anyone, except perhaps his wife, but she could at least try to find out what was troubling him. "Lunch at the Crossroads when we finish up here?" she asked.

Before he could reply, Penny, who had been sniffing the ground not far from where he was standing, sank to her belly, whining softly.

"Good dog," Barb said, and then turned to Sharma and Danutia.

"She isn't as certain as when she found the sandal, but she thinks there's something here."

"And I missed it," Sharma said. "I must tell Sergeant Lewis he made a wise decision."

Danutia bent over to inspect the ground. Small rocks and twigs poked up, and here and there she could see the faint imprint of boots. "There's nothing on the surface," she said. "Something must have gotten buried."

"Then we'll have to dig it up," Sharma said. "I'll set up a grid."

Leaving him to his sticks and string, Danutia and her partner headed up the old Lagoon Trail towards the Nature Information Centre, Penny bounding ahead. As they worked their way up the steep hillside, the shouts and squeals of young children at play punctuated the roar of the falls. A Montessori school, Danutia recalled, lay between the Information Centre and the service road. According to the park interpreter's statement, the new trail ran across Montessori property near where the body had been discovered. Would the school continue to allow public access, Danutia wondered, or would the parents try to seal off their world from the evil outside? As though that would forever keep their children safe.

The trail grew steeper. Barb played out leash as the sure-footed pinscher edged her way back and forth along the rocky cliff. They were nearing the top when they heard her bark, the sound barely audible above the splash of the falls. Barb secured the leash around a tree trunk and they peered over the side. No Penny. Then Danutia spotted the swaying ferns that signaled her whereabouts, about halfway down the cliff, wet and slippery with spray.

She swung a foot over the edge and hesitated.

"I'll go," Barb said, as though reading Danutia's mind. "If you're worried about me contaminating the evidence, I can at least see what's there and mark the site, then the tech can collect it later."

"Just give me a minute to figure this out," Danutia said, knowing that if she let her fear of heights win out, she'd have to quit her job. She scouted back down the trail to see whether she could work her way to Penny from the side. Possible, but there was nothing big enough to rope herself to in case she fell. She'd have to go over the top.

Luckily Sharma's cases held what she needed. "I'm a good Boy Scout, always prepared," he said, digging out a hundred-foot climbing rope and a pair of leather gloves.

When Danutia was roped up and ready to drop over the edge, Barb shoved a couple of doggie treats at her. "Here, don't forget to give Penny these."

Slowly Danutia descended through ferns and ocean spray, facing into the cliff as though she were going down a ladder. Where she was unsure of her footing, she used the plants for handholds. She didn't dare look down; she stared straight into the cliff face or darted quick glances upwards for Barb's signals to move right or left. Penny's barking grew louder and the footing became more treacherous. She slipped on a rock wet from the spume of the falls and felt herself lurch sickeningly outwards.

She was up and over, gripping the pole too long, turn loose, turn loose, her foot knocking against the bar, voices shouting, her father, Coach, his hands pumping over his head, hands settling on her arm her breast . . .

Then the rope swung her back into the cliff and safety. She clung to the wet rock till her breathing slowed, and then continued her descent.

When at last she reached Penny, the pinscher shook herself excitedly, spraying Danutia with water. "Good dog," she heard herself saying, her voice high-pitched with relief. "Good Penny."

While Penny gobbled down her treat, Danutia examined the surrounding vegetation. She was beginning to think her ordeal had been for nothing when she caught a glimpse of pink. Her heart beating fast, she parted a clump of sword ferns. There, tangled among the wet, heavy fronds where it might never have been found but for Penny's good nose, lay a pink plastic handbag.

The heavyset young guy with the zits handed Ritchie a five. "Keep the change," he said.

"You sure?" Ritchie asked as he set down a coffee and double chocolate cookie. The kid nodded. Only one other customer was left, a regular who sat hunched over a book with his veggie sandwich and cappuccino. Part of the granola crowd the Grind catered to, with its organic bread and fair trade coffee, but who was Ritchie to complain. He made the stuff, but he didn't have to eat or drink it. Elaine had given him the job despite his record, and that was what mattered.

"Man oh man," the young guy said. "You see this?" He'd picked up the *Post-Dispatch* and was pointing to the photo on the front page. "They've found a body at Sitting Lady Falls. That's out near where I live."

Ritchie had taken care not to look at the paper all day and he wasn't about to start now. He picked up a stack of dirty dishes and headed for the kitchen.

The bell over the door jangled.

"Hey Ritchie," called a familiar voice.

Shit. He was dead tired and didn't want Chuck holding him up. Pretending not to hear, he carried the dishes to the back. When he reemerged with a tray of assorted squares, Chuck was perched near the cash register, a bike helmet on the stool beside him.

"You know how geekie you look in that thing?" Ritchie asked, shoveling Whole Wheat Fruit and Nut Bars into their appointed slot.

"It's the law, and I'm a law-abiding citizen," Chuck said. "Else I'm back in the slammer. Anyways, an old bike's a hell of a lot cheaper than a monthly bus pass, and I gotta save my money. Soon's I get more hours, like the boss promised, I can rent my own place and leave you little rays of sunshine behind."

Chuck had been saying the same thing ever since Ritchie moved into Leicester House, but he let it pass. Maybe someday the big boss at Pharmacity would come up to Chuck and say, "I've been noticing how well you stock bum wipes and Gas-No-More, so I'm giving you a full-time job with decent benefits and a wage you can live on." But somehow Ritchie doubted it.

Chuck nodded towards the young guy in the corner. "What's he doin' in here?" he asked in a stage whisper.

Ritchie shifted to the apricot-almond squares. "Getting his caffeine fix, like everybody else."

The kid must have heard them talking, because he stood up suddenly, jiggling his cup and spilling coffee across the table.

"Here, I'll get that," Ritchie called, but it was too late, the kid was already out the door.

"Don't you know who that was?" Chuck asked. "That's the asshole who was panhandling last night."

"Him? Can't be." This guy was always clean, white shirt and black pants, the uniform of the restaurant trade. He'd asked Elaine about a job a few weeks back, said he was going to school and needed the extra bucks. Sometimes she could barely pay Ritchie, so she turned him down, but every few days he dropped in for a coffee and a chat.

"I tell you, I got a good look at him—dimpled chin like a fat baby, bad case of zits. It's the same guy."

"So? What's the big deal?" Ritchie poured a regular coffee and set it in front of Chuck. He was about to empty the pot anyway.

"If he knew you, why didn't he act like it, say he'd pay you back? Why rush out just now? Bet he stiffed you, didn't he?"

"Just leave it, okay?" Chuck could be a real pain. When he got his teeth into something he wouldn't let go. Unless you offered him a different stick. "Speaking of assholes, you shoulda heard that guy at Camosun this morning."

Chuck sipped his coffee, tipped in another spoonful of sugar. "Yeah, how'd the interview go?"

"He came on like Clint Eastwood," Ritchie said, tucking the last of the apple-walnut squares into the display case, "allowin' as how he'd let me into the chef's program if I keep my nose clean till January." Ritchie had almost told the asshole to stuff it but he'd been down that road before, so he'd kept his mouth shut and counted to ten, mentally shrinking the man until he looked like a baby throwing his toys around. It was a trick they'd been taught in anger management. It had worked, too, he couldn't help smiling, and then the fathead had smiled back.

"Way to go, man," Chuck said, digging in his pocket for some change. "I better run. I'm pickin' up my old man for the AA meeting. You got any of them day-old cookies? The old man don't eat so good."

Ritchie shook his head. He wasn't about to start feeding that old soak. He laid the coins in front of the cash register. Never open the till when you're on your own. That way you can't be blamed if it comes up short. "Say hi to your old man, okay?"

"Will do." Chuck shoved his bike helmet onto his head. "Say, you called Crystal's mom yet?"

Ritchie picked up the empty tray. "I told you, I don't even know where she's living."

"Don't give me that crap," Chuck said, tightening his chin strap. "You're just too chickenshit."

Right on, buddy, Ritchie thought as Chuck stalked out the door. And if you had any sense, you'd be scared shitless too. You with your big dreams about getting ahead, turning that old rubbie into a dad who loves you more than he loves his bottle. It's all bullshit. Dreams like that get you into trouble. They make you careless. You think you have rights like everybody else, start complaining, wanting to fix things. So they punch you in the gut and throw you back in prison. Better to keep your head down. Stick it in the sand if you have to. Down deep, where there are no dead girls, no missing daughters, no daughters at all. Otherwise you're just dead meat.

"No meat for me today," Danutia said, closing her menu. The thought of chomping on a burger after the morning's hunt for human remains made her queasy. "Leanne and I were the only ones eating the Thanksgiving turkey, I noticed. Maybe you vegetarians have the right idea."

Sharma nodded at her over his menu and Danutia smiled. By the time she and Barb had completed their sweep, Mike was waiting at the bridge site and Farrell had left for the West Shore. The handlers had bundled the dogs into their cages, said hasty goodbyes, and raced off to catch the next ferry back to Vancouver. Sharma had reluctantly agreed to take a quick lunch break while Carl began excavating. Now, perhaps, she would learn what was troubling him.

The Crossroads wasn't busy today: a young mother with a fractious toddler, three older women in biking gear, a couple of Hydro guys. Nothing like Monday's Thanksgiving crush. Fewer servers, though, and so the service was no faster. No sign of the surly busboy or his obnoxious mom.

After they ordered, Sharma spread a map of Witty's Lagoon on the table. As Danutia read from her notes, he mapped Penny's finds: P1, the left sandal in the hollow tree; P2, the unknown object or objects buried at the bridge site; and P3, the purse on the cliff face.

"The killer must have hoped the purse would go into the lagoon," Danutia said. "Lucky for us it didn't."

"We can't be absolutely sure that the purse belonged to the victim," Sharma said. "I don't have fingerprints yet to match. Still, I will go over it as soon as I get back to the lab. It may tell us something." He tapped a spot north of the service road labeled R1. "This is where Ruby found the remains of the forearm, six feet off a bridle path. I would guess it was dragged there by a dog, or various dogs. The bone has been chewed; the microscope will tell us whether there are knife marks as well. The hand is still attached, though the fingernails have fallen off, which is unfortunate. The assailant's skin or blood might have been caught under the fingernails."

Their orders arrived. Sharma folded the map and put it away. Hungry from the morning's exertions, if not for meat, Danutia attacked her grilled cheese and fries. When she'd dampened her hunger pangs, she voiced the thoughts that had been running through her mind. "No severed hands, then. So it seems either Handy Dan has changed his MO or he was interrupted. Maybe the storm scared him off."

"Possible," Sharma said. "It is also possible that this is not his work. There are many differences. All we know for certain is that a young woman has died. We will have to wait for the autopsy to see how she died, and whether there are similarities to the other murders."

He was right, Danutia had to admit. One killer was undoubtedly responsible for the deaths of Esther Mike and Marie Wilson: they had been strangled and mutilated in the same fashion; their bodies were found on First Nations lands within twenty-four hours of death, Esther's in Central Saanich northeast of Victoria, Marie's in the opposite direction, on Beecher Bay land, southwest of Witty's Lagoon. In both cases, the bodies had been discovered as a result of an anonymous call to Crime Stoppers. The calls, placed from different pay phones, had ended with the same ritualistic chant: "If they want this to stop, they'd better keep their hands off our land." Analysis of the heavily disguised voice suggested that the speaker was probably male, probably middle-aged, probably Canadian-born, probably with a grudge against First Nations. Nothing any half-intelligent officer couldn't guess and nothing that would help to identify the killer. And yet Danutia was reluctant to concede that they might be hunting two killers.

"Serial killers don't always follow the same pattern. If things didn't go as he intended, Handy Dan might not want to claim responsibility. Like control freaks who won't admit when they screw up."

Moving his empty plate aside, Sharma put his fingertips together in a gesture Danutia recognized as the prelude to one of his sayings, most of them on the theme of keeping an open mind. So she was surprised when he said, "You want it to be Handy Dan, don't you? Is that because the evidence points in that direction, or because you don't want the case to be yours, not Corporal Farrell's?"

Danutia could feel her face grow warm. "It's true that I don't like Farrell much," she said. "But it's more than that. I keep seeing that girl's mangled body. I can't seem to let go."

"And since you didn't see the bodies of those Aboriginal women, they are not quite so real to you? That's where your first duty lies. If you neglect it," he said, his voice dropping, "those are the faces that will haunt you."

Danutia studied his homely dark face. The lines that furrowed his cheeks and brow had deepened and his gaze seemed distant, unfocused. She sensed that if he was ever going to confide in her, this was the moment. Gently, she asked, "Whose face is it that you see? Your sister's?"

His fingertips parted and he reached for his water glass. He drank deeply, set the glass back in the centre of its paper coaster, and brought his napkin to his lips. She'd gone too far. He wasn't going to answer.

"Yes, my sister's," he said. "Sita's."

She breathed again, and waited.

"It's the bandana," he said at last. "Sita was wearing one when she died. A blue paisley one. I didn't know she wore them. As I discovered, there were many things I didn't know about her. After my sister Pramilla, Leanne's mother, eloped with an Anglo, my parents tightened the rules. Sita was forbidden to have Anglo friends or to wear Western clothing. She fought with my parents constantly. One Friday lunchtime she left school and never returned."

Danutia sipped her coffee, cold now. "Did you ever learn what happened to her?"

"Eventually I pieced together part of the story. It happened during my first posting, in Halifax. My father called me on a Friday night in May to say that Sita was missing. He refused to go to the local police. You see, my parents had reported my sister Pramilla missing when she eloped with her Anglo boyfriend, and the police had treated them badly. So I agreed to do what I could over the weekend. On Monday, if there was still no word of Sita, we would go to the police. I took emergency leave and flew back to Toronto. My parents still lived in Richmond Hill, a suburb to the north. That's where my parents settled when we came to Canada. I went to school there and my sisters were born there. When I searched Sita's room, I discovered only one clue. Underneath the ring tray in her jewelry box there was a scrap of paper with a Toronto telephone number. Pramilla's number. I sneaked out of my parents' house to call her. Pramilla—Pam, as she now calls herself—admitted that they often talked on Sunday evenings when my parents were out visiting friends. Pramilla sent her clothes and money through a classmate, a Swedish girl new to the school. When I later opened Sita's locker, I discovered beneath her school books a pair of well-washed jeans with four assorted tops and matching bandanas. Every day, it seems, Mother would walk Sita to school in her sari or *lehenga choli*; every day before she went to class Sita would change into pants and tops and then change back again to go home. Pramilla insisted that she hadn't seen or heard from Sita since she went missing, and promised to let me know if she did.

"Over the next two days I talked to my parents' friends in Richmond Hill's small Indian community and to their children who went to school with Sita. On Sunday I was allowed to see the Swedish girl, who was at home with the flu, or so she said. Her story was that she and Sita had eaten their lunches together outside the school, then she had gone home because she wasn't feeling well. She hadn't heard from Sita, had no idea where she might have gone. I thought she was not telling the truth, but I had no authority. She did say that Sita was worried about the report card she'd received just before the lunch break. She thought Sita had failed chemistry, and was afraid of what my father would say.

"I would have kept this news from my father if I could. He had served as a medic in the British Army in India, and after we immigrated to Canada, he became a medical technician and went to work for the Ontario Public Health Authority. Sita had always been brilliant in math and science. How could she fail in this subject he cared about so passionately? He blamed himself, and did not long outlive her.

"Sunday evening came and went. My mother cleaned closets, my father and I played endless games of chess. I slipped out to call Pramilla. Still no word of Sita. I had done all I could. On Monday morning we went to the police. My mother described the clothes Sita had been wearing the day she disappeared. The red sari you have seen in the photo. That night I went back to my job, my wife, and my small son. Three weeks later, my parents had a call. The body of an Indian girl had been found deep in a forest of red pines to the north of us. This girl was wearing flared jeans, a turquoise tank top, and a blue paisley bandana. Nevertheless, it was Sita."

"I'm so sorry," Danutia said.

Sharma spread his hands in a gesture of letting go, and as he did so, the lines in his knobbly face seemed to soften. "It was a long time ago," he said.

Now there was another girl dead in a forest, with a bandana over her face. Danutia wondered whether Sita too had been murdered but didn't want to ask. Some memories are too painful to share.

As though he had read her mind, Sharma said, "The autopsy revealed that she had been thrown against a tree with great force. There were signs that a motorcycle had skidded."

Motorcycle. Danutia felt her stomach knot up. Her only brother had died in a motorcycle accident, twelve years ago now. He had plowed into a concrete bridge abutment. No obvious cause. New bike. Straight dry road. No drugs or alcohol. She knew now that Andrew would have been badly smashed up. Her parents hadn't talked about that part, not in front of her. She'd been almost delirious with fever at the funeral, couldn't remember whether the casket was open or closed, not that it would have mattered, he would have been so prettied up she wouldn't have known him anyway. The fever had hung on for weeks, a bad case of flu, the doctor said, but she knew better, knew she was in anguish that such things could happen with no cause, no one to blame. That's when she decided to go into police work. Now it was her job to find out who was to blame and to see that the guilty were punished.

Sharma's voice brought her back from that pit of grief, into the present where he was saying ". . . never identified."

She struggled to put together the words she had only half heard. "The biker just left her there? And he was never found?" she said.

Sharma shook his head. "At the time I blamed the Ontario Provincial Police who investigated. If I had gathered the evidence, I told myself, the culprit would not have escaped. So I switched to forensics. Eventually I learned humility. We must do our best to determine the facts of what happened, that much is true. But when we have the facts, what do we do with them? That is a much harder question. A young man—for so we must presume—has an accident on a motorcycle and a young girl dies. Is he any more responsible for her death than the parents who tried to control her every move? Or the older sister who secretly sent her Western clothes and spending money? Or the brother, older yet, who counseled patience when she cried on the phone instead of interceding for her? Is the young man more responsible than the girl herself, whose deepest wish was to make her own choices?"

"How can you say that?" Danutia demanded. "That's like saying she asked for it."

"No, I'm sure she did not wish to die. Nevertheless, that was a consequence of a choice she made. We are responsible for our choices, even if we cannot foresee the consequences."

"The biker made choices too. So he should pay the consequences."

Sharma folded his napkin into a triangle and laid it across his plate. "Oh, I expect he has," he said. "Just as my parents have, and my sister Pramilla, and I. There are worse punishments than going to prison. The pangs of remorse bite deep. A killer who is filled with remorse may arrange the body in a respectful pose or cover the face, so I've read."

"The bandana across the girl's face yesterday. Is that what you meant? That we're looking for a remorseful killer? Then we can forget about Handy Dan. Nothing he's done suggests that he feels any remorse."

"We will see what we find," Sharma said. "Then we will know."

"Speaking of knowing," Danutia said as they gathered their things. "Give me a call when you've examined that purse. Maybe the killer's left his prints."

Sunil dropped his backpack on the hall floor while he checked messages on the communal phone. He'd have to hurry—it was his turn to make dinner tonight and he'd forgotten to stop at the store. He listened impatiently to half a dozen messages for his housemates before he heard a familiar voice.

"Sunil, it's your father. Call me as soon as you can." Without waiting to hear more, Sunil hit the delete button. His dad's calls were never as important as they sounded, and he had an exam tomorrow. He could always say he hadn't got the message.

Six

The low reception building of William Head Institution, its edges softened by the mist hanging in the air, looked more like a well-protected small factory than a medium-security prison, Danutia thought as she pulled into the parking lot the next morning. No massive concrete walls, no armed guards patrolling a catwalk, no hint of grim cell blocks with clanging doors and barred windows. Just a high chain-link fence topped with razor wire, halogen lights on tall poles, and, overlooking Juan de Fuca Strait, a guard tower that might equally have been a fire lookout. No wonder the place was called Club Fed. Escaping from a place like this would be easy. Sitting Lady Falls wasn't more than a couple of miles away . . .

Stop it, Danutia told herself. Checking out the prison population is West Shore's job. You are here to interview Henry Mike, remember? Henry Mike, Esther's estranged husband, was already incarcerated here when Esther was murdered, and so hadn't been considered a possible suspect. In the statement he'd given at the time, he'd denied any knowledge of other men in her life, anyone who would want her dead. That was before Marie Wilson was killed, before Danutia found out about the Castaway Club. Now she had some new questions.

At the entry gate, a friendly guard checked her ID, made sure she'd locked her gear in her glove compartment, paged the intelligence officer through whom she'd arranged her visit, and offered her coffee, which she declined.

"No sniffer dog?" she asked. On her only previous visit to William Head, she'd come at night with her friend Arthur Fairweather to see performances of two depressing plays, *No Exit* and *End Game*, by the prison theater company. They'd had to deposit their valuables in a locker, pass through a metal detector, and then stand at a white line, hands at their sides, while a German shepherd checked them out. Arthur had laughed off the incident, but Danutia hadn't liked the sense of being on the wrong side of the line.

"That's only for people who might be smuggling drugs," the guard replied, and they both laughed, knowing how easily drugs flow into prisons, whatever the security measures.

Danutia pushed open the glass door leading to the grounds and stepped outside to get her bearings. High winds and rain were forecast for later in the day, but for the moment the air was still and cold. Trees, shrubs, even buildings seemed to bleed at the edges as though painted with watercolors. Here and there a diffuse yellow glow from windows promised warmth and human activity. Beyond, gray sky melted into the gray waters of the Strait. The damp air beaded her face and hands, seeped into her clothes. If she didn't get moving, Danutia thought, she too would dissolve, lose her edges.

A gravel road to her left ran past what she guessed to be the Administration building, from the flag barely visible in the soft mist. A uniformed figure passed through its glass double doors and hurried towards her. As they met, the man thrust out a beefy hand. "Bonkowski, SIO." He was built like a rain barrel, round and solid, with a fringe of grizzled hair. Friar Tuck in a different uniform. "Henry'll be in the woodcarving shed," he said. "We can pick him up from there."

Danutia checked her watch. "We arranged the time. I thought he'd be at your office. Can't you page him?"

"Believe me, it will be faster this way," Bonkowski said. "You page somebody, they don't turn up for maybe an hour. You been here before?"

"Only at night, for a performance," Danutia said.

"Good. I'll give you a tour as we go." He set off down the gravel road with such a jaunty step that Danutia suspected he'd used her visit as an excuse for a break in his routine.

With the perimeter fence and guard tower behind her, the place looked even less like a prison. More like a modest resort, with low buildings scattered over a grassy lawn and magnificent views of the ocean and the Olympic Peninsula. Club Fed indeed.

"You must get a lot of escapes out here," she said. "Though it's hard to see why anyone would want to leave."

"It hasn't always been like this," Bonkowski said. "The new duplexes you see, that's where the inmates live. They're part of an experiment. The idea is that a lot of prison riots are caused by over-crowding. You give inmates more space, you get less trouble. And here we've got lots of space. But the Head was never one of your concrete block prisons. Some of the buildings are left from the time it was a quarantine station." He stopped abruptly, pointing to where a rocky beach curved around to create a safe harbor. "You see that bay on your left? That's Quarantine Bay, where ships' passengers and crew were inspected for smallpox and other infectious diseases before land-ing in Victoria or Vancouver. The prison is here for the same reason. Isolation. So yeah, guys go AWOL occasionally. But it doesn't take long to get them back."

"So no one could slip out, commit a crime, and slip back in?" Danutia asked, thinking again of the girl murdered only a few miles away.

"No way. There's count four times a day, and the guys are locked in their residence after the last count. But we did have a guy one time . . ."

So much for that theory, Danutia thought, tuning out Bonkowski's story of an attempted escape by sea. Interrupting him, she asked, "How much farther?"

If he was annoyed by the interruption, he didn't show it. "See those carved house posts on the left up ahead? That's the woodwork shop," he said. "Built by the native guys. They wouldn't raise a stink about being quarantined for two weeks, I tell you, not like those hoity-toity English passengers that made life hell for one poor sod of a medical officer until he hanged himself. Two weeks ain't nothin' to these guys. Some of them been here ten, twelve years. Lifers, most of them, no danger to anybody. You tell them they're out in two weeks and they'd kiss your feet."

"I don't let just anybody kiss my feet," Danutia said.

"Ah, they're not bad sorts, most of them," Bonkowski said. "It's the addictions that get them into trouble. Drugs. Booze. Take Henry, now. You've read the charge sheet: auto theft, assault, unlawful confinement, kidnapping. It's all true, but it's not the whole story. Henry gets drunk and when he gets drunk, he steals a car. He's been in and out of jail who knows how many times, mostly because of parole violations. Last October he got drunk and tried to steal a car so he could get to a cousin's wedding in Bella Coola. Only this time the owner caught him, so he knocked her out, threw her into the back seat, and drove onto a ferry. The police picked him up at the Tsawwassen terminal, and here he is again. In here he's sober, and he's a good guy. You find a way to keep him sober outside and he won't be back."

Thick posts carved like totem poles loomed up out of the mist, with a carved house front behind them. The three men sitting out front, smoking, returned Bonkowski's greeting as he passed into the shed. Conscious of their stares, Danutia followed. The building smelled of varnish and damp cedar. The front part was taken up with saws and lathes and chunks of wood. Under a small window at the back, a man with a thick braid of black hair was bent over, paintbrush in hand. Although it seemed colder to Danutia inside than out, his arms were bare. Their shadows fell across his work and he looked up.

"You are like this Raven, stealing my sun," he said, holding up the carving.

A raven with its feet tucked up, a red disk of sun in its open beak. A black hump of body and wing; black eyes. On the table, a dozen or so ravens, orcas, and totem poles in red and black were spread out to dry.

"Beautiful," Danutia said.

"Hey Henry, how you doin'," Bonkowski said. "This is Constable Dranchuk, Serious Crimes. She wants to talk to you about Esther."

"Eh? What was that?" Henry Mike said, dipping his brush into the pot of red and touching it to the raven's beak. "I don't hear so good."

Bonkowski laid a beefy hand on the painter's shoulder. "Come on, Henry," he said mildly. "The lady doesn't have all day."

Henry Mike jerked around, freeing himself from the unwanted touch and splattering Bonkowski's uniform with red. His black eyes were hard and his jaw moved as he struggled to control his temper. Snake tattoos rippled down his bare arms. The two men were about of a size, but Henry Mike was at least ten years younger, she guessed, and in much better shape. She felt her muscles tense in readiness for the move she hoped she wouldn't have to make. So much for getting pal-sy with the cons, letting your guard down.

Bonkowski stepped back, Henry Mike shrugged, and the tension dissipated. He laid aside his brush and carving and pushed back his chair. He poked a finger at a red splotch on Bonkowski's jacket. "Too bad about that paint on your nice clean uniform," he said. "You give it to me, I'll take it back and wash it."

"Shit happens," Bonkowski said.

Soon Danutia and Henry Mike were alone in the Security Intelligence office with cups of strong coffee, Danutia at Bonkowski's desk, the inmate across from her in a straight-backed chair. Bonkowski had offered to sit in, but she'd declined. She didn't need him messing up things.

"I'm following up a lead about an argument Esther had with a customer at the Castaway Club a few months before she was killed," she said. "August of last year. That's before you came back to the Head in October, right? Can you tell me anything about that argument?"

Henry Mike gazed out the window where the mist was thickening into fog. Under the bright lights, moisture glistened on his bare arms and reflected back rainbows from his thick black hair. "Esther loved to dress up and go dancin'," he said. "Sometimes, when I was home, I went with her. That was before Social Services took the kids away. Jesus, that was hard. After that, I kinda lost the heart for it, eh? Not Esther. She'd go off to the thrift stores and buy bits of this 'n that. I remember it was a real hot day when she come back with these little baby doll pajamas, sayin' I should come, I wouldn't need no costume, I sleep nekkid as a jaybird anyways. But me, I was tryin' to stay off the booze, so I didn't go. Must have been one, two o'clock when she come bustin' in, cussin' and throwin' stuff around. Seems she tried to bum a smoke off some guy and he got her thrown out."

"Did she say anything about the guy? What he looked like?"

"Some white guy, that's all I know."

Danutia leaned forward across the desk. "There must be more to it than that. She must have asked for things before and been turned down. The manager said she was harassing the guy. Did something upset her, or was she drunk?"

"Jesus, she was drunk all right, but that wasn't all. Seems the guy kept goin' on about drunken Indians, always sticking their hands in your face, gimme this, gimme that." He stuck his hands out to demonstrate, and Danutia pulled away.

"Anything else?" she asked.

"Yeah, one thing, and I think it's what really made Esther mad. 'Better keep your hands off,' he says. 'This's our land now.'"

Hands in your face. Hands off. Danutia could feel the back of her neck prickle. "Those were the exact words he used?"

"How would I know? I wasn't there. But that's what Esther said, near as I remember. I figured it was because of the longhouse exhibit up at the museum that summer, showin' where our people camped and smoked fish around Victoria in the old days. There was a lot of talk about land claims, and some people said the exhibit showed the bands around here was tryin' to claim all this area. I figured he was just another fuckin' white guy—excuse my language—goin' on about natives stealing their land. That's a rich one, eh?"

He leaned forward, his hands gripping his knees. They were a mechanic's hands, shiny and supple as though well-oiled, covered with nicks and scratches and smudges of paint. He brought the left one up to show Danutia a gold ring with a raised carving, eagle or hawk, she couldn't tell which at that distance. "In all those years I never hit her. But that night she started throwin' punches and I put my hands up, you know, to protect myself. My ring caught her face," he said. "That was the last time I seen her."

Danutia remembered the scar on Esther's last mug shot. "That was the end of August. You were returned to the Head on October 15. You didn't see her in all that time?"

"Like I told them other officers, she left and she never come back. And I didn't go lookin'."

"Esther had been banned from the Castaway, but from what you say, she really liked going there. Do you think she would have tried to sneak in on New Year's Eve?"

"Sure she would. People all dressed up, who's to know? She was always hopin' for one of them big prizes, you know, a trip to Vegas and such." Henry Mike shook his head. "So you think some crackhead from the Castaway killed her, eh? That's what you get in there. Crackheads, twisted cops, horny navy guys."

Danutia left the prison mulling over what she'd heard from Henry Mike. The sky had darkened and the wind blew yellowing maple leaves across the road. She could feel the wind's urgency in her bones, or perhaps the urgency was her own. Henry's story seemed to confirm what the Crime Stopper calls suggested: Esther hadn't been killed by an angry husband or lover, but by someone with a sick mind, acting out of racial hatred. The same person had undoubtedly killed Marie Wilson. And a killer like that wouldn't stop with two murders. Maybe he had already taken a third life. She had to track down this faceless man who raged about hands. But how?

The facts, Ma'am. You need more facts. Back to the Castaway.

By the time she reached the club, the wind had strengthened and the rain was bucketing down. She made a dash for the building and pounded on the door until Waldrip let her in.

He'd spent the morning struggling with a new bookkeeping program and was only too willing to take a break, though he shook his head at Henry Mike's story.

"I didn't hear any of that stuff about land or hands," he said. "First thing I knew, Esther was waving a beer bottle around and shouting obscenities, so I hustled her out, told the bouncers not to let her back in."

She asked him the same question she'd asked Henry. "Could she have sneaked in on New Year's Eve?"

"Sure, if she was wearing a costume. Nobody would look too close unless she started making a nuisance of herself."

When Esther was murdered, investigators had assumed she was a random victim, easy prey. Perhaps they were wrong. Perhaps Esther's attempt to bum a smoke had triggered violent fantasies that the killer had spent months refining. Where to find his victims and how to kill them. Where and how to dispose of the bodies. How to disguise himself to escape detection. Theme night costumes would provide a perfect cover.

"How many people would come in costume?" she asked.

"Maybe a hundred to a hundred and fifty an evening, twice that many at Halloween and New Year's," Waldrip said. "We try to encourage them by charging a ten dollar cover for anyone who doesn't come in costume, and by giving lots of prizes for most authentic costume, funniest costume, things like that. Some people, especially the men, throw on something obvious, like a cowboy hat for Wild West night, but that won't win you a prize. Neither will dressing like the posters. You have to be more creative. Take a look at the bulletin board between the washrooms and you'll see what I mean. That's where I post photos of the winners."

Danutia felt a leap of hope. "Would you still have photos or negatives from the nights the women disappeared?"

"Afraid not," Waldrip said. "They're just Polaroids for people to carry off the next time they're in. If they're not claimed before the next theme night, I throw them away. I keep copies of the posters, if that's any help."

"Let me have the ones for the nights closest to the murders—New Year's Eve and Easter."

While she waited for Waldrip to fish the posters out of his filing cabinet, Danutia thought about his comments on costumes. The murders were premeditated. The killer would not want to draw too much attention to himself by competing for prizes, yet he would need to be well disguised. The posters might provide valuable clues. Waldrip was no help in identifying the images—an art student who'd since left for Toronto had put them together—so she took them to her favorite video store; the owner had an encyclopedic knowledge of popular culture.

Danutia wasn't disappointed. He took one look at the Moulin Rouge poster of a can-can dancer and said, "That's a steal from Toulouse-Lautrec, a late 19th century French painter who drank himself to death. The poster made the Moulin Rouge—which means Red Windmill—the most famous dancehall in Paris. The painter himself was a little shit, if you believe the film." The owner, a grumpy balding man with a limp, obviously did.

There was no male figure in the poster, so Danutia had no idea what kinds of costumes the men might have worn. "There's a film about him?" she asked. "Do you have it?"

"Should be on the shelf." He stumped over to the British Drama section and handed her a video. "John Huston, *Moulin Rouge*, 1952. Anything else?"

She handed him a Hawaiian Luau poster that showed grass-skirted dancers among a sea of male faces.

He frowned. "This one seems to be a collage of television shows set in Hawaii. See that guy with the Detroit Tigers cap, that's Tom Selleck from—*Magnum PI*. The one next to him is William Conrad, from *Jake and the Fat Man*, and then Jack Lord from *Hawaii Five-O*. I'm not so sure about the rest. Is it important?"

"Could be," Danutia said. "This is a murder investigation."

"Then leave me the poster and I'll see what I can do," he said, limping off to answer the phone before she could say thanks.

While she was inside, the storm had hit with full force. She was drenched by the time she reached the car. Rain poured down the windshield and she had to fight the wind to stay in her lane. Her hands were shaking when she turned the car in at the vehicle pool. Head lowered, she splashed to the office building. When she'd changed into dry clothes, she called the forensics lab. Sharma didn't answer. She left a message. Why hadn't he called her about the girl's purse? There was no ID in it, no surprise; still, it might yield fingerprints, either the girl's or her killer's. Surely he would have had time to test it by now. She was gathering up paperwork to take home when her phone rang. It wasn't Sharma.

"This is Jill at Crime Stoppers," said a shaky voice. "I just took a call you'd better listen to. I'll play it back."

There was a whirr and click on the other end of the line. Then came the voice she'd listened to so many times, the voice she'd resolved to silence.

"Can't you assholes tell the work of a professional from an amateur? You haven't heard from me for a while. But you will. Soon."

Seven

"We'll be back soon with more on the storm that's battering Victoria and southern Vancouver Island," the radio announcer chirped. "Now it's time for a little drive-home music to soothe the savage breasts of all you frustrated commuters out there."

Ritchie reached up with a wet hand to lower the volume. Rain pounded against the Grind's leaky roof. He went back to scrubbing cookie sheets. He didn't give a fuck about the storm.

For three days now, wherever he turned, everybody was talking about the murder out at Sitting Lady Falls. The radio, television, newspapers were full of it. There were rumors about a serial killer. Ritchie hadn't wanted to listen, had wanted to drown out those smug voices getting their rocks off on tragedies that could never happen to them, but something wouldn't let him. He had a daughter, and he didn't know where she was. At first he'd tried to cling to his belief that she'd never come to the island, that she was safe back home in Toronto. But as the days passed and no one came forward to claim the body, his fear grew. Now his mind couldn't, wouldn't let go. He might miss the one report that would tell him his worst fears weren't true, that it wasn't his daughter's body lying in the morgue.

"You still open?" said an uncertain voice behind him.

Startled, Ritchie looked around. He thought he'd locked the front door. The fat kid with the zits stood dripping water on his clean floor. No jacket, just a hoodie pulled up over his head. He shook himself like a big puppy and water drops flew everywhere.

Ritchie swiped at his hands with a towel and took a few steps towards the doorway. "I was just about to close up," he said. "What are you doin' out in weather like this?"

"That tire place across the road said they'd give my mom a good deal on some retreads, but they're already closed up. You're closin' too, eh?"

He looked so woebegone that Ritchie took pity on him. "I already threw out what was in the pots, but I can make you a cup," he said.

"Bring a stool from out front and you can watch while I finish these. And turn the deadbolt while you're there, would you."

The kid drew a plastic bag from under his hoodie and laid it on the counter, then did as he was told. Ritchie put the kettle on to boil and made a filter coffee. He put a couple of day-old muffins on a plate and set it down on the counter.

"You look like you could use these," he said.

"That's not what my mom would say," the kid said, picking up the banana chocolate chip. He looked like Humpty Dumpty, perched there on that slender stool. "She's always goin' on about how fat I am. I wish I could move out, live in town."

Ritchie ran more hot water into the sink and went back to scrubbing. "Why don't you?"

"I was goin' to this fall, put down a deposit on a basement suite near campus and everything. Then my mom had to have this cancer operation and now she says she can't do without me. Can't drive, can't lift anything, because her arm's too sore."

"Anybody else who can help out?"

"You kidding? She can always find some guy to buy her a drink, but that's as far as it goes. Maybe she'll drink herself to death, and then I can have a life."

"What about your dad?"

"What dad? My mom doesn't have any idea who my dad is. She likes to tell the story about the first time I asked about my daddy, when I was just starting to talk. She told me, 'You don't have a daddy, you have a sperm donor.' Every time she tells that story, she laughs. I could kill her."

Ritchie picked up the towel and began drying cookie sheets. "It ain't worth it, kid," he said.

The kid had polished off the second muffin, a lemon poppy seed, too sweet for Ritchie's taste. He inched off the stool and picked up his plastic bag. "I'd better get goin'. Elaine's gone home, I guess. I brought my resume just in case something opens up."

"School called, she had to go pick up her kid."

"Can you give it to her?" He reached into the bag and shoved a piece of paper Ritchie's way. His hand, like his chin, was dimpled with fat.

"No problem," Ritchie said, sucking in his gut. He'd put on a few pounds since he started work here. At the Head he'd spent a lot of time on the weights, all the guys did, what else was there to do? There was no weight room at Leicester House, and even if there had been, he probably wouldn't have worked out much. He was a free man; he had better things to do, except usually he ended up in front of the TV like everybody else. He walked to work and back, didn't he? And on his way home he munched away on the day-olds Elaine gave him for the guys, trying to satisfy some deep craving for life's good things. Some days, by the time he made it back to the house, there was nothing left.

Ritchie glanced at the resume and tossed it on the counter. Then he found a cloth and began cleaning the floor where the kid had splattered it.

"It's a freakin' hurricane out there. Need a lift?" the kid said, backing out the kitchen doorway. "You live at Leicester House, right? It's on my way."

Ritchie's guard went up. "It's none of your business where I live."

The kid waved his fat hands around. "I didn't mean nothing by it. Friend of mine lives on that street. I saw you come out one day. It don't matter to me if you've done time. I live out that way, you know. Metchosin. Near where that girl got herself killed—"

Ritchie jumped to his feet. "You know something about that?"

The kid clutched the plastic bag in front of him like a shield. "Course not. I live out there, that's all, and so I can't get it out of my mind. Look, you want a ride or not?"

"Not." Ritchie waited for the kid to fumble his way out the front door, and then stood watching him through the rain-streaked front window. That business about having a friend who lived on Leicester, that was just bullshit. You could tell by his eyes the kid was lying. That was the trouble with trying to be nice to people, they just

messed you around. The kid splashed across the street and climbed
into a small white car. Something about it looked familiar, Ritchie
thought; then he pushed the thought away. The world was full of
small white cars.

The car drove off and Ritchie went back to the kitchen. The radio
was still making noise about the storm. He punched a button and the
sound died away. His eyes fell on the kid's resume littering his clean
counter and he picked it up. The name on it wasn't Mitch—that's
what he'd said his name was, just a couple days ago, Mitch like the
Michelin Man. The name on the resume was Trav, Trav O'Donnell.
Ritchie wadded up the sheet of paper and tossed it into the garbage,
then retrieved it and smoothed it out, thinking.

What kind of game was Zitface playing, anyway?

Handy Dan was playing with them and Danutia didn't like it. The
call repeated itself over and over inside her head on her slow crawl
home by taxi, her bike in the trunk. The message was unequivocal.
He hadn't killed the girl at Sitting Lady Falls, but he would strike
again soon.

There was nothing she could do until the storm abated. Roads
were closed and power was out in many parts of town. By some twist
of fate, her own neighborhood still had electricity. She paid the driver
and climbed the stairs to her third-floor apartment. Ignoring the
plant pots and balcony furniture she'd hurriedly brought indoors this
morning, she ran a hot bath. She was shivering from sitting around in
wet clothes. And from the shock of the phone call, she had to admit.
Time for a little self-care.

While the bath ran, she stripped off her wet clothes and made
herself a hot toddy. Then she set two chunky candles aflame on the
dressing table, two more on the edge of the tub. She didn't burn candles often because the smell made her cough. Tonight the soft light
was soothing, and if the power went out, she wouldn't be plunged into
darkness. She poured lavender bath salts and slowly eased into the
water, her toes recoiling from the heat, then stretched out, trying to

release the tension in her neck and shoulders. The chill left her bones but her eyes remained open, staring into the flickering darkness.

When she emerged half an hour later, her fingers and toes were wrinkled, like a baby's or an old person's. She pulled on warm sweats and turned her attention to dinner. The fridge held containers of lamb saag and butter chicken, vegetable pakoras and basmati rice that she'd brought home from Yasmin's spice shop the day before. She spooned some of each onto a plate and popped it into the microwave. While the food heated, she tried Sharma's numbers. Still no answer at work or at home.

Danutia set up the video in what used to be the spare bedroom, now transformed into an exercise room with a futon couch. The can-can dancer on the Moulin Rouge poster had obviously inspired Esther's costume—flounced skirt, black fishnet stockings, long-sleeved white blouse, the broad ribbon around her neck that had been used to strangle her. She retrieved her microwaved curry and settled in to watch *Moulin Rouge* for clues about what Esther's killer might have worn on New Year's Eve.

Would he have disguised himself as the artist-hero, Toulouse-Lautrec? Although the bowler hat, glasses, neat beard, and mustache would be easy to copy, Danutia felt sure the killer would never identify himself with the painter's stunted legs and awkward gait, nor would he want to attract undue attention. The mutilated hands and the calls to Crime Stoppers suggested a plan carefully executed by someone with a sense of superiority. That meant the killer would more likely have chosen the top hat, tails, and white gloves worn by many men in the film. The top hat, in particular, suggested aristocracy and authority. Add a beard, a pair of glasses, even tinted contact lenses, all easily obtainable, and you would have a person of distinction whom his own mother might not recognize. Tomorrow she would check out New Year's rentals or purchases of such costumes at the local shops.

Drawn in by something twisted yet fascinating about the artist's relationship with women, Danutia put aside her notebook and watched the rest of the film. The early scenes in Paris had shown Toulouse-Lautrec as alternately worshipping and mistreating the streetwalker who became his model, his anger masking his dependence on her. With a later lover, he disguised his fear of rejection by acting indifferent. In a flashback, the young Toulouse-Lautrec declared his love to a woman of his own aristocratic class, who contemptuously rejected him because of his deformity. Danutia found the scene disturbing, and not just because of the young woman's atrocious behavior. The film seemed to suggest that this rejection had caused all the painter's subsequent problems: his treatment of women, his depression and alcoholism.

Her head throbbing, Danutia wandered into the living room. Fresh air, that's what she needed. She slid open the balcony door and slammed it shut again, shivering in the icy blast. Try caffeine then. Caffeine and work would calm her nerves. She made coffee and carried it back to her desk. After staring blankly at a form, unable to concentrate, she jumped up and began to pace the floor.

What was wrong with her?

Images from the film had lodged in her mind and she couldn't seem to shake them. She wondered about that young woman, the upper class girl who rejected the painter. What was she supposed to do? Would it have made any difference if she'd turned him down gently? In their last therapy session, Grace Tilman had talked about the cultural messages that many women grow up with: If a man wants you, you should feel grateful. If a man wants you, you have no choice but to say yes. Was the film endorsing those messages? Consider the corollary: If women don't feel grateful, don't say yes, men feel betrayed. And that sense of betrayal fuels men's anger at women.

Yet there is a crucial difference between men like Toulouse-Lautrec and psychopathic killers like Handy Dan. For all his harsh treatment of women, the painter had turned most of his hatred inward, against himself. He had not entirely lost the ability to empathize with others' pain. In the film, he had rescued his can-can dancer from a mocking crowd after she'd lost her job as a result of the Moulin Rouge's success.

Psychopaths like Handy Dan feel no such compunction. No one had rescued Esther. No one had rescued Marie. Would Danutia succeed in stopping him before he killed again?

A thousand tiny hammers were attacking her brain. She rummaged in her backpack for the ibuprofen she always carried. Instead she found another video, this one a set of yoga lessons Yasmin had recommended.

"From your work you must be all the time tense," Yasmin had said, pulling a video case from the shelf behind the till. "No wonder you get headaches. Like Sharma, you must learn to stretch the muscles and relax the mind." She must have sensed Danutia's resistance, because she wrinkled her face. "No 'I don't have the time' excuses. See?" she had said, turning the case over. "Three sets of lessons—ten minutes, seventeen minutes, and thirty-five minutes. Easy, easy. You take it, try it, bring it back if you don't like it."

Danutia thought now that she might as well try it. She could do no good for herself or anyone else in the shape she was in. She headed back to the spare bedroom, turned on the television and popped in the video. The instructor, an Indian woman based in California, was as slim and supple as a girl, though she looked to be in her forties. Her voice was soothing, her manner unhurried, her instructions precise. Danutia tried to clear her mind and focus on her body. As she worked her way through the first two sessions, she could feel her headache lessen. But with every break in concentration, thoughts about the film came flooding back. So she carried on.

The final poses, the instructor informed her, were designed to stretch the spine and open the chest. Danutia worked her way through cobra, locust, downward-facing dog to relax. Then the bow. Her muscles were strong from regular workouts, but she was less flexible than she expected. She did her best, lying on her stomach and pulling her legs up with her hands until only her abdomen rested on the floor. When she tried to lift her head up, leaving her throat exposed, her breathing quickened and fear fluttered in her belly. She felt like a girl again, young and vulnerable. She collapsed onto her stomach and lay there panting until the instructor's soothing voice invited her to make herself comfortable for *savasana*, the corpse pose.

She tried. She lay on her back, eyes closed, legs slightly apart, arms out from her sides. Relax your face, your shoulders, your abdomen, your thighs, your feet. Clear your mind, breathe slowly and deeply. In two three four out two three four five six seven eight. In two three four . . . A hand seemed to be stroking her belly, circling lower and lower, towards that place of shame. The butterflies beat their wings more fiercely.

Danutia held her breath until the panic subsided. When she couldn't hold it any longer she gasped for air, her chest racked with sobs and tears spilling down her face. Turning on her side, feet drawn up, she tried to soothe herself with her childhood prayer. "Now I lay me down to sleep . . ."

When she woke the power was out and the wind was still howling.

Eight

"The power should be on soon, Mum," Parks Interpreter Joan Goodman said into the phone. "If you can't wait for your tea, you can boil some water on the woodstove. I'll call in at lunch time. Right now I have work to do."

Joan rang off and sat staring out her office window at the fine rain barely visible against the Douglas firs, their tops swaying. The wind had diminished since yesterday's gale, but the forecast was for more wet, windy weather. Trees would be coming down for days as the ground became saturated and shallow roots gave way. Like the one that smashed the Lagoon bridge on Labor Day, and that poor girl—

The outer door of Park Headquarters opened with a bang, startling Joan from her reverie.

"Sorry I'm late," Marge said, closing her umbrella and giving it a shake before dropping it into the stand. "There was an accident, looked like someone going too fast around that curve where the 1A joins the Island Highway."

"Anyone hurt?"

"Don't know," Marge said, shrugging off her coat. "By the time the traffic was moving, the car was being loaded onto a tow truck. The side was bashed in. It must have hit a telephone pole."

"I called the schools to cancel today's programs, but they're closed anyway," she said. "I thought I'd post notices at the Nature Centers in case anyone is foolish enough to show up, and check out the trails while I'm at it. How about holding down the fort?"

"Glad to," Marge said. "It's warm in here. Thank goodness for the generator."

"Your power out too?" Joan zipped up her rain jacket and tightened the drawstrings on the hood. "There's no woodstove in my downstairs suite, so I had to move my folks in with me last night. I'll pop in and see about them on my way back."

"You should move them into one of those assisted living places," Marge said.

Joan shrugged, knowing she would continue to ignore Marge's advice about her demanding parents, as Marge ignored her advice about her wayward kids. They had worked together for years, gradually smoothing the rough edges until they'd become, if not friends, at least companionable colleagues.

"Hope you don't find any more dead bodies," Marge said.

Joan shoved the door open against the wind. "I won't look, that's for sure."

The roads were almost empty, a good thing since the traffic lights were out. Twigs and branches crunched under her tires. As she zigzagged over to Metchosin Road, she saw a Hydro crew working on a downed power line and a parked car crushed under a fallen cedar. Again her thoughts drifted towards the body under the tree, but she forced them back.

Descending the steep grade towards Witty's Lagoon was like plunging into limbo. Sky and water were heaving masses of gray. No machinery moved in the gravel pits, now full and spreading into lakes; no lights shone from houses; no cars toiled towards her. Joan parked in the empty lot outside the Nature Center and taped her cancellation notice to the window. She could have gone inside and donned the hard hat kept there, but she decided against it. If a tree fell on her, it fell on her. She had decided long ago that she wasn't going to live her life in fear, as her parents had. The line from an old song her mother used to sing popped unbidden into her head. *Que sera sera.* Remember that, Mum? *Que sera sera.*

She made her way to the Lagoon Trail, yellowing maple leaves as slippery underfoot as those plastic toboggans. Where the new trail broke off from the old one, tattered crime-scene tape fluttered from an overturned barricade. Down below, the tarps that had covered the old bridge site since Tuesday were gone. Had the dig turned up any clues? Joan wondered. She came to the place where the new trail crossed the grounds of the Montessori school. The school was dark, no doubt closed like the public schools in the area. When she'd gone over Tuesday morning to postpone the trail-opening ceremony, she'd encountered a couple of parents insisting that the teachers keep the children inside until the killer was caught. Joan had repeated the RCMP officer's reassurance: There was no need to cancel programs because people in groups were not likely to be in any danger.

"Just let us know if anyone hangs around and asks a lot of questions," Corporal Farrell had said. So far, the only overly inquisitive person, Joan thought, was herself.

Parents were not so easily convinced. A school had cancelled on Wednesday and now two more days had been lost to the weather. Joan felt sorry for the children trapped inside their classrooms, squirming at their desks. She'd squirm too if she couldn't get out of the office and into the fresh air, air that this morning was heavy with the smell of wet cedar.

Joan could hear the thunder of Sitting Lady Falls long before she stepped onto the viewing platform, sturdy and intact as she knew it would be. A fine cold spray played across her cheeks. The Lady was bursting at the seams this morning, roaring and rampaging like Mum in a fit of temper.

So far Joan had noticed only minor damage—broken maple and arbutus branches and a few small firs down, but nothing obstructing the trails. Now, turning away from the Lady, she saw that a section of the bank beside the old trail had caved in. She set off to investigate. When she reached the log she had climbed over on Monday, she hesitated. Here too there was a barricade, not visible from the platform, and yellow crime-scene tape was strung across the path. Taking a calculated physical risk was one thing; trespassing was another. Nothing short of an emergency would justify crossing the police line. As she turned back, a great sense of relief washed over her. Only then did she realize that she had steeled herself against another nasty surprise.

Leaving the tumultuous Lady behind, Joan followed the main trail towards the quieter waters of the lagoon. Though the rain had stopped, a brisk wind still blew, ruffling the water's surface. Soon she came to her favorite spot, a low bank where a huge twisted arbutus, its trunk almost horizontal, snaked out in search of sun.

Half a dozen crows landed in the arbutus, quarreling loudly. A moment later something sparkling splashed into the water, then was swept against a trailing branch maybe ten feet from the water's edge.

Curious to see what the crows had been fighting over, Joan shed her boots and rolled up her pant legs. The lagoon was shallow here, though the current could be strong. Holding onto the arbutus with one arm, she waded out. She was soon up to her knees in icy water and the thing she was after was still out of reach. Retreating a few steps, she broke off a thin dead branch and advanced again. Using her stick like a hook, she drew the leafy branch towards her, careful not to dislodge her prize. Woman the tool-user, she thought triumphantly. Then a sudden wave lifted the branch over her stick and the thing—some kind of chain, she could tell now—slid into the water. She grabbed for it and felt it settle into her hand.

Clambering out, Joan examined her prize. A tiny locket, a child's perhaps, on a thin gold chain, lost who knew where or when, or stolen from a campsite or beach towel by a thieving crow. The chain looked new, the locket worn. She was tempted to open it, see whether it contained a photo or lock of hair. Better not, she decided. She might let in moisture that would ruin whatever was inside. On her way back she would drop the locket into the lost and found box. More likely than not, it would lie there, among the unclaimed mittens, hats, sunglasses, socks, shoes, and sundry other items, until the next clean-up day, when it would be tossed or sent to a thrift store.

Que sera sera.

As soon as the shops were open Danutia walked the dozen blocks to downtown. Too much storm debris littered the streets to take her bike. A light rain was falling and the wind was brisk at her back. Except for Hydro crews and city trucks, the streets were almost deserted, the sidewalks given over to the homeless hunkered over their rucksacks and garbage bags.

She'd found listings for four costume shops. Two were in outlying areas where the power was still out; two were in downtown Victoria. All she had to go on was the slim chance that the killer had bought or rented a Victorian gentleman's costume for New Year's Eve. That and the call saying he would strike again soon. Halloween was approaching, a perfect opportunity for a costumed killer.

Outside Troy's Tricks and Trappings she paused to examine the window display. Nylon skeletons, witches' hats, broomsticks, glow-in-the-dark cats, pumpkins, gargantuan spiders suspended in equally gargantuan webs. Towards the back, two costumes that might appeal to a man with sadistic tendencies. The Grim Reaper. The Executioner.

Inside, Halloween paraphernalia jostled with tasteless party items. A young guy with wispy brown hair falling into his eyes sat on a stool behind the counter, reading a comic book. She asked for the owner.

The young man barely looked up. "The boat got smashed yesterday. He's down at the marina, talking to the insurance guy."

Danutia eyed the false beards, mustaches, and wigs on the shelves behind him. "Do you work here regularly?" Silence. She repeated her question.

"What's that? Oh, no, I'm just filling in. Dad needed somebody in the shop, and my school's closed."

Better reading comics than smoking dope, Danutia figured. She would have to come back.

A few blocks away, Island Masquerade seemed more promising. In its window, ghostly mannequins of Elvis Presley, Buddy Holly, and John Lennon were jamming among gravestones bearing their names. Just the sort of place that would appeal to an attention-seeker.

A middle-aged woman in a bright gypsy costume was stocking shelves behind the counter. When Danutia asked about rentals for last New Year's Eve, she shook her head.

"Sorry, I'm afraid I can't help you," she said, her gold hoops dancing. "We didn't open till February, just in time for Mardi Gras. And we don't rent costumes, we sell them." She pulled a plastic bag from under the counter. "They come already packaged, like this pirate costume—pants, shirt, eye patch, wig, large handkerchief to tie around your head or use as a sling."

Danutia nodded towards the window. "Does Elvis come in a bag like this?"

The woman laughed. "No, I put those costumes together from odds and sods. It's the masks that make them work. Here, I'll show you." She lifted two flesh-colored plastic masks from a rack behind her and laid them side by side on the counter.

"This one," she said, pointing to the mask with heavy brow ridges and a gaping mouth, "is your basic monster. You build it up with face paint and scars or what have you and attach it to your face with spirit glue. We carry a dozen standard masks of this sort. But if you want a custom job," she said, picking up the plain mask, "you bring in a photo and we scan it onto the mask. That's how I made the ones in the window. Then I painted them to make them look dead. With wigs, colored contact lenses, rubber dentures that slip over your teeth, makeup, you can look like anyone."

You can look like anyone. As the words sank in, Danutia realized that she had assumed the costumed killer was like an actor, changing his identity but within a basic set of physical features that she could discover. Now she had to consider the possibility that he was a shape-shifter, unrecognizable in his different roles. Images from the posters flowed through her mind like the changing patterns of a kaleidoscope. Tom Selleck. William Conrad. Jack Lord. Anyone who recognized the face would fill in the body type to match, whatever the reality might have been.

She was grasping at straws. She needed another angle. As she set out on foot for Headquarters, she thought about the Castaway's clientele: druggies, cops, navy guys, or so Henry Mike had said. When a drug deal went bad, the offender went down in a moment's anger or in a gangland execution. No one played dress-up or called Crime Stoppers to brag. That left cops and sailors. Both wore uniforms, which were costumes of a sort; both were trained to handle weapons and to kill if necessary. She would check the records for police and military personnel who had been in trouble with the law over the last two years. She might run into another dead end, but then, where else did she have to run?

She was just settling at her desk when the phone rang.

"I have found something," Sharma said, his voice as slow and deliberate as always. "Come over and I'll show you." He hung up.

At last, Danutia thought, the purse. Not bothering to grab her jacket, she dashed to the forensics unit, a squat two-story building adjacent to Headquarters. The windowless lower floor was given over to a firing range and a bay where vehicles, boats, and other large items were examined for trace evidence. As she climbed the enclosed stairs, she could hear the whine of a portable vacuum cleaner seeking out dust, hairs, fibers, anything that might link a suspect to a crime.

Sharma worked on the second floor, one large room divided into various work stations. As Danutia entered, he put his hands together and dipped his head in greeting. "Namaste," he said. The lines on his face were deeply etched and he seemed to sag a little inside his dark suit. The unit was short-staffed, as always, but it wasn't just his work that was weighing him down, Danutia felt sure, it was the similarities between the sister who'd died and the Sitting Lady, the unknown girl at the falls. Then she remembered the dark circles and puffy eyelids that had stared back from her own mirror this morning. When she'd woken on the floor of the spare bedroom in the middle of the night, stiff and cold, she'd stumbled off to bed, where she'd listened to the wind and tried to still her breathing. The yoga workout had troubled her, she remembered, but she no longer knew why. *Our ghosts rise up to haunt us.*

But this was not the time to lay ghosts. Just the facts, ma'am. "So what do you have?" she asked.

"Two things," he said, handing her a plastic evidence bag. "First, a key, and if I'm not mistaken, a key from a locker at the bus depot."

The key had a bright orange plastic head. Cut into the metal was the number 508. "Where was it?" Danutia asked.

Sharma reclaimed the evidence bag. "Right where Penny Pinscher told us. Carl hadn't found anything at the bridge site yesterday when the rain began. I decided to have one last look before the gully flooded, so I went back with a metal detector. The archeologists would not have approved my methods, I'm afraid. Still, I found the key, a handful of rusty nails, and five shiny beer bottle caps."

"Any prints?"

Sharma picked up an index card from his desk. "The beer caps were too smudged. Here's what I found on the key."

The index card contained two prints, a partial right thumb and a right index finger. "Notice the ridge pattern on the index finger, how it rises into a sharp wave," he said, pointing. "That's called a tented arch. Plain and tented arches together make up only five percent of ridge patterns."

"It's the girl's, isn't it?" Danutia said, imagining the girl's slender finger, the hand turning the key. "That's why no one has reported her missing. She's from out of town and everyone thinks she's somewhere else. But after six weeks, you'd think someone would be worried."

"There are so many reasons for the things we do and don't do," Sharma said. "In the end, the reasons don't matter." He took back the card and studied it for a moment. "I don't have the girl's prints yet, so I don't know whether these match or not. The autopsy was rescheduled for this afternoon. The Medical Examiner won't find it easy to get prints after so long. If he succeeds, Corporal Farrell will bring me the results. Then we will have our answer."

"In the meantime, I'll drop by the bus depot and see what I can find out," Danutia said, reaching for the key.

Sharma laid his hand over the evidence bag. "I suggest you talk to Corporal Farrell first."

"Why wait?" Danutia asked impatiently. "I want to nail this guy before he kills again."

Sharma stroked the air in a soothing motion. "All things unfold in the fullness of time. This key was buried in the ground for six weeks or more. What is a few minutes, or even a few hours? If you are patient, you will have Corporal Farrell's cooperation. If you are not, these skirmishes over territory will become pitched battles, and to what end? She will remind Sergeant Lewis that the killer of the Aboriginal women has denied responsibility for the girl's murder and ask him to take you off the case. Is this what you want?"

"You're right. Like it or not, I have to work with her. Even if she's a redhead."

"What is this about redheads?" Sharma asked. "That's like saying you have to work with me even though I'm brown."

Danutia grinned sheepishly. "You weren't the most popular girl in my Grade Seven class who teased me mercilessly about my braces."

"Neither was Corporal Farrell," said Sharma. He locked the key and prints in a desk drawer and sat down at his computer. "Time for us both to get back to work."

Danutia stopped halfway out the door. "Say, what about the pink purse? I thought that's what you were phoning about. I left you a message last night."

"Ah yes, the purse," Sharma said, eyes on his monitor. "It has been out in the weather a long time. I don't have the equipment to deal properly with objects in its condition. I have sent it to the lab in Vancouver."

Something in his manner made Danutia uneasy. She'd never known Sharma to be anything but straightforward, but now he seemed to be avoiding her gaze. "How long before you get a report?"

"I asked for a prelim as soon as possible, but so does everyone else. A week, I would guess."

"Maybe by then we'll know who she is. Call me when Farrell arrives."

Sharma didn't respond with his customary goodbye.

"Namaste," she called softly.

Back at her desk, Danutia phoned the Military Police at CFB Esquimalt to ask for incident reports involving military personnel over the last two years. The Military Police officer said he'd have to get back to her; the computers were down. "I'll need clearance before I can release any information, of course," he said.

More delays. She'd have to start with the police files. She'd known a few cops who'd roughed up suspects or lifted product at a drug bust, knew about others who'd sexually assaulted women or killed their wives. Racist comments about Aboriginals weren't unheard of. So she had to admit that Handy Dan could be a cop, though she hoped it wouldn't prove to be the case. Every time a police officer stepped across the line, there were calls for an inquiry, for tighter regulations that often hampered their work. Imagine the outcry if there was a serial killer in their midst.

By the time her phone rang, she'd found three cases in which off-duty officers were mentioned in connection with altercations. None of them had been charged.

The voice on the phone was Farrell's, sounding tired and irritable. "Krahn worked for an hour trying to get some usable prints," she said. "First saline, and then—"

"Did he get any? Did they match?" Danutia broke in.

"Enough for Sharma. A tented arch on the right index."

"I knew it," Danutia said. "Let's hit the bus depot. I've got a car booked."

"Tomorrow," Farrell said. "Right now I'm heading home for a hot bath and a stiff whiskey."

"The office shuts for the weekend at five o'clock. It'll be less of a hassle if we go now. I'll drive if you like."

Grumbling, Farrell agreed to meet at the car pool. As soon as they were in the car, she leaned the passenger seat back as far as it would go, shut her eyes, and began a soft tuneless humming. Danutia drove in silence. She had seen the grim lines around Farrell's mouth and eyes and thought she understood. Autopsies are never easy.

As they neared downtown, Farrell straightened her seat back and inspected her hair in the vanity mirror. She plucked out the pins holding her bun and stuck them in her mouth.

"Caucasian female, around five feet, slight build, maybe a hundred pounds," she said around the hairpins, "Hair medium brown at the roots, dyed black. No eyes, so no eye color. Age sixteen to eighteen, judging from the incomplete eruption of the wisdom teeth and the sharpness of the sternal areas. Teeth crowded, nicotine stained. Three fillings and some unfilled cavities, so any dental records could be old. Bruises and abrasions from the tree branches, as well as the puncture wound, all apparently made after death. Unhealed fracture of the right scaphoid bone." She paused. "You know what that is?" she asked.

Danutia glanced over. "No," she said.

Farrell twisted her auburn hair into a knot. "I didn't either," she said, trying to capture a stray tendril. "It's a small kidney-shaped wrist bone below the thumb. What you break when you fall down rollerblading. The break's old. Probably her mom thought it was just a sprained wrist and slapped an ice pack on it. The fracture can't be diagnosed until the swelling's gone down, maybe a couple of weeks later. By then no one's paying attention."

Danutia pictured a slight, dark-haired girl eagerly lacing up birthday rollerblades; another part of her mind waited to hear how the girl died. Meanwhile her hands steered, her foot braked for a light, a horn beeped behind her, a senseless stream of traffic stopped and started under a blank gray sky.

"Any identifying marks?" Danutia asked.

Farrell shook her head. "Not that I want to make public. There's a tattoo on her chest that looks so recent it could have been done by the killer. You saw her face, or what was left of it. It will have to be reconstructed. The artist says it will be a week before he can get us a sketch." She poked in the hairpins, inspected the results, and then leaned back.

"He wasn't facing her head on," she said. Her voice had lost its clipped assurance. "He was angled to her left and considerably above her. She might have been kneeling. He twisted her left arm, wrenching it out of its socket. There were ligature marks on what was left of her throat. Most likely he grabbed the bandana and twisted it. She would have died from asphyxiation within a few minutes. No obvious signs of rape, though we'll have to wait for the tests to know for sure. No signs of mutilation. Looks like Handy Dan was telling the truth."

Danutia could feel Farrell's attention focused on her now, waiting for a response. "Guess that means this case is all yours," she said, her jaw tense. "So why am I driving you to the bus depot?"

"Beats me," Farrell said. From the corner of her eye Danutia could see her tight lips relax into a smile.

Because I insisted, Danutia thought. *Because Sharma told her the same thing he told me, about working together. Because we want to catch this guy, and two heads are better than one. Even if one of them is a redhead.*

A block ahead was the bus depot, an eyesore in the middle of Victoria's tourist zone. On the left, next to the provincial museum, stood a Coast Salish longhouse similar to the woodcarving shed at William Head, with totem poles and a carved bear grinning at her with huge white teeth. That's the place Henry Mike mentioned, she thought. The exhibit that fanned talk about Aboriginal land claims.

Danutia pulled into the bus station and parked in a vacant taxi spot. Gray metal lockers lined the building's north side. They found Number 508 in front of the loading bay for Pacific Coach, the line connecting Victoria and Vancouver via the Tsawwassen ferry. The locker was empty, another key with a bright orange head in the slot.

"The agent didn't mention this part," Danutia said, pointing to a small notice. "'After twenty-four hours contents may be removed and held for thirty days and then sold for charges.' It's been more than six weeks. We may be too late."

Inside, passengers lined up in front of the ticket window or lounged on the metal benches. Danutia rapped on the frosted glass door marked Staff Only and they walked in.

The tracing agent, a harassed-looking young man with a mustache, was shoving papers in a drawer. "The office is closed—"

"RCMP," Farrell said, presenting her ID.

The man pushed at the overstuffed drawer and gave up. "Two

minutes and I'm gone. I've got to pick up my kid at daycare. Costs me a dollar a minute if I'm late."

"I spoke to you this afternoon," Danutia said. "We're looking for items left in locker 508 around Labor Day and never claimed."

"I meant to check but I've been swamped," the man said. "Everybody who couldn't travel yesterday because of the storm is trying to get out." He extracted his keys from his pocket and unlocked a door behind him. "We cleaned out the storage room last week and sent a lot of stuff to the Salvation Army. You may be out of luck." Scuffling sounds as he moved things around, then he was back.

"Bingo," he said, handing a large black plastic bag to Danutia. He shoved a form towards Farrell. "Sign this and let's get out of here."

Soon the black garbage bag was sitting on a bare stainless steel examining table in Sharma's lab. Pulling on gloves, he cut the bag open, exposing a faded red carry-on, the nylon covering scratched and abraded.

Danutia said it first. "No tags." No claim tag to tell them whether she was coming or going. No tag with a name and address. Any name. Any address.

Farrell reached for the case. "Maybe there's some identification inside."

"Patience," Sharma said. "First I must check for prints. We are assuming that the suitcase is the girl's, but we do not yet know that for certain. Nor do we know, if it is hers, who else may have handled it. The bus depot staff, you say, and no doubt that will prove to be the case. There may also be others. Perhaps her mother helped pack her bag. Or a kindly gentleman lifted it onto the bus rack for her. Or it belonged to the boyfriend she was running away from, who followed her and killed her. At this point we don't know. And so we must proceed slowly and carefully."

The two women exchanged looks that said, *We should have opened it in the back seat of the cruiser.*

"How long?" Danutia asked Sharma.

"The whole process will take until about noon tomorrow—"

"I'm out of here," Farrell said, heading towards the door.

Sharma held up a hand. "Wait, let me finish. It should take no more than half an hour to test enough surfaces to allow opening the suitcase. I will do the rest after."

Farrell looked at Danutia. "If I'm going to wait, I have to have coffee."

"Done," said Danutia.

A few minutes later they were sitting in the Daily Grind, a nearby bakery-cum-coffee bar Danutia had recently discovered. Over blackberry scones and double espressos Farrell filled Danutia in on West Shore's search for the girl's killer.

"No visitors of the girl's description at the prison, and no one in the population admitted to knowing anything about her," Farrell said. "If they did, they probably wouldn't admit it. They'd be afraid of getting into trouble either with the authorities or with their mates. Snitches don't live long inside. The door-to-door's also been a total waste. Metchosin isn't like the city, where houses are set close to the road and there's always somebody around. Out there, the houses are up long driveways or hidden behind trees. Residents near the beach access said they wouldn't have taken any note of cars if they had seen them; in the summer, cars are parked there till all hours. The ones who might have been walking their dogs that night were kept indoors by the Labor Day storm.

"That leaves Metchosin Road," Farrell went on. "On one side of Witty's Lagoon there's the Montessori school, on the other a church. Both are a long way from the Nature Centre parking lot. There was a pre-term staff meeting at the school on Thursday, then everyone scattered for the holiday. There was a wedding at the church on Saturday night. The minister said the girl didn't sound like anyone from his congregation, though she could have been a guest who'd wandered off."

Danutia called up her mental map of the area. "What about the golf course across the road? Sunny holiday weekend, it must have been busy."

"Nothing so far. The clubhouse was open till 11:00 PM all weekend except for Labor Day, when the power went off about nine thirty. The staff closed up by candlelight. According to the manager, everybody was out by about ten fifteen. He passed Witty's Lagoon on his way home, says he didn't notice any vehicles in the parking lot, but then he probably wouldn't have been able to see one unless it was parked close to the road. As soon as I have the artist's sketch, I'll send constables to interview everyone at the wedding and on the club's sign-in sheets for the weekend. If the girl was around, someone may remember seeing her."

"What about the north end of the park, where Ruby found the forearm?"

"We're working on it," Farrell said, draining her cup.

"What I don't understand is why she hasn't been reported missing," Danutia said. "Surely she must have a mother, somebody who'd be worried about not hearing from her."

"You know how it is," Farrell said, standing up. "Mom has a new boyfriend, he doesn't like the kid, or likes her too much, and Mom doesn't get too excited when the kid leaves. Not to mention the sex trade workers who drift from place to place. They may be gone six months, a year before anybody notices. Speaking of which, any leads yet on Handy Dan?"

Danutia slid a five under her cup. Though she could feel herself losing some of her hostility towards Farrell, she was still wary. For the moment she would keep her theory about a costumed killer to herself.

"I'm working on it," she said.

Nine

First thing Saturday morning, Danutia bought spring bulbs and winter pansies from her local nursery. Then she filled her big patio containers two-thirds full with fresh potting soil. In went the tulip bulbs and another couple of inches of potting soil. Then Siberian iris and more soil. Crocus bulbs just below the surface. She topped off the pots with the perky cream and rose pansies, bright splotches of color against the approaching winter. Before the pansies were finished the bulbs would begin to bloom, first the multi-colored crocuses, then the iris with their touches of gold on dark blue, last the pink and purple tulips.

Her spirits lifted by contact with rich black earth, Danutia biked to Headquarters and checked out a vehicle. Power had been restored to the two outlying costume shops. At Tillicum Mall, a bored assistant told her to come back Tuesday, when the manager would be in. At Fantasy World in Esquimalt, the softly permed owner wasn't sure what she'd done with her receipts from the previous year. Perhaps her tax accountant still had them, she'd have to check. Danutia left her card and asked the woman to call. That's all she could do.

As she drove back, a Bible verse she'd memorized as a child floated into her mind: "Whatsoever thy hand findeth to do, do it with thy might." Time to tackle the files again.

By the time she'd cycled home, she was chilled to the bone by the cold, damp wind.

She stepped into the shower and let the warm steam envelope her. When she finally turned off the water, she heard the phone ringing, then the click of the answering machine and her sister's voice. She grabbed a towel and ran to answer.

"I'm glad I caught you in," Alyne said. "I've left a ton of messages this week. Why haven't you called back?"

"I've been—"

"Yeah, I know, you've been busy. Anyway, I've just emailed you an article on how to tell when someone's lying. Maybe you can find time to read it, since it's relevant to your work. Too bad you couldn't make it for Thanksgiving, everyone was there." She plunged into an account of the latest births, marriages, and divorces in their dad's large Ukrainian family.

Danutia propped the cordless phone under her ear while she toweled herself dry, then wandered into the bathroom in search of her sweats. The bottoms were no problem, but when she tried to pull the top over her head, the phone fell.

"Sorry about that," she said.

"I was just saying that everyone sends their love," Alyne said. "We all missed you. Especially Mom and Dad." When Danutia didn't respond, she added, "They don't understand why you haven't been home in over two years. They say it's been months since you even called. Is that true?"

Danutia loved her sister. Alyne had cuddled her, shown her how to blow bubbles, let her lick her ice cream cones. Like most older sisters, she was also bossy. She had never let Danutia hold the cone. And here she was, still trying to control Danutia's life. "Like I say, I've been busy," she muttered.

"Too busy even to call and leave a message when you know they'll be in church?"

"Has it been that obvious?"

"They're not dumb. If I figured it out, they have too."

"But you're a psychologist," Danutia said. "That's your job."

"And they're your parents. What have they done that's so horrible you can't call them once in a while?"

"Nothing," Danutia said. She swiped at the bathroom mirror with her sleeve and peered at her reflection, a little blurred by the steam. Who was this person? Her mouth seemed to be trembling, her eyes wide with fear. Danutia felt her stomach clench and turned away. "Look, I just got out of the shower and I'm freezing to death. I've got to go."

"That's what you always say. What are you running from? They're my parents too, remember. They're not addicts, they didn't beat us, and they're no more neurotic than anyone else. So what's the problem?"

Danutia sat on the closed toilet seat and drew her legs together against the ache inside. Her breathing was fast and shallow and she couldn't speak. Breathe, she told herself. Breathe. At last her throat opened. "Physical abuse isn't the only kind," she said.

She could feel Alyne go still, there in her split-level house in Calgary with its view, the Rockies like a wall between them. Her fingers hurt like she'd punched a hole in that wall, but it was just her grip on the phone. She switched hands while she waited for her sister's angry denial.

"What are you saying?" Alyne asked.

Encouraged by her sister's cautious response, Danutia said, "I've been working with this therapist, you know, about liking older men. It's starting to come back to me. My senior year. Going out for track. The meet where I broke my ankle. Then Andrew died and I was sick and I blanked it all out. Only I couldn't climb a ladder because I couldn't make my hands stop shaking and I couldn't bear for anyone to touch me."

"I remember," Alyne said, her voice lower. In the background Danutia could hear the hockey game on television, excited yelps from Jonathan, "Way to go, Flames," from his dad. "When I came back for Andrew's funeral, you wouldn't let me hug you. You said you didn't want me to catch whatever you had. That was so hard. You were the only sibling I had left, and you wouldn't let me be close."

"I was angry at God, the universe, Mom and Dad, you. I know now that I blamed you all for Andrew's death. If you hadn't failed him somehow, Andrew would be alive. So I cut myself off from everybody. My two years at university, my year at the Police Academy, I didn't make friends, I didn't date. And then when my anger began to fade, I found I was attracted to older men. I'm beginning to understand why."

"Father substitutes," Alyne said. "You were always Dad's favorite."

"That's what I used to think too," Danutia said. "Then Dennis came along, and I realized that wasn't the whole story."

"Dennis was that doctor in Winnipeg, wasn't he? The one that dressed you up like a little girl?"

"That's right. I broke off with him, and then Mom gave him my home number here. I was angry about that too."

"I can see why," Alyne said. "Still, that's no reason to stop calling."

"That isn't all," Danutia said. "The therapy's been bringing up all this stuff. I don't feel I can talk to Mom and Dad about it, but it seems phony not to say anything, so I don't call. Lately I've been having these flashbacks about being touched—"

"Are you saying you were sexually abused? You don't mean Dad—"

"Yes. No. Not by Dad. Anyway, it's not as simple as that." Danutia took a deep breath. She'd cancelled her therapy appointment this week, trying to avoid the memories by burying herself in work. Then they'd come back despite her—the hand on her breast, the hand moving down her belly—and she'd called Grace to rebook. Grace had squeezed her in early this morning, and Danutia had told her about Coach.

"My name it sounds like gobbledygook in your mouths," he'd said on the first day of track season. "You are to call me Coach." A wiry, graying refugee from somewhere in Eastern Europe, he never let his students forget he had coached Olympic contenders. "You want to win, you listen to Coach," he said as he adjusted a foot position, pushed shoulders back and down. "Vacuum the stomach," he said, pressing Danutia's belly as she did leg raises. Keeping his hand there a second too long. That's how it started. That's as much as she'd had time to tell Grace this morning. Maybe she shouldn't say any more to Alyne—

"Yes?" said her sister and a lifetime's habit took over. They'd shared too many confidences for Danutia to hold back now.

"Do you remember the track coach I had my senior year? The refugee from Eastern Europe? Maybe you never met him. Anyway, he had this terrible accent and when we didn't understand what he said, he yelled at us. He was kind of funny looking, with a buzz cut and a little gray mustache, but for some reason I found him attractive.

He had this amazing body, strong and supple and totally under his control, not like the boys my age, who were all elbows and knees. He must have known I had a crush on him, because it wasn't long before he couldn't keep his hands off me."

"You, I can understand," Alyne said. "Hormones. That's what adolescence is all about. But this coach—he was in a position of trust, and he betrayed it. Did you tell anybody?"

"I told Dad I didn't want to do track any more, but he wouldn't hear of me quitting. You were off at university—"

"Oh Sis, you know you could have called me. Why didn't you?"

"You were busy," Danutia said, feeling a moment's grim satisfaction at turning the tables.

"And I've been busy ever since, haven't I, juggling university and marriage and work and motherhood," Alyne said. "No wonder you say you don't have time to talk to me. And in fact I'd better get dinner on the table by the time the first period is over or I'll never get my men folks away from the TV. But listen, those tickets I had to cancel at Thanksgiving are good for a year. I'll come out soon, by myself. Then we can talk. Like old times."

"Like old times," Danutia echoed as Alyne rang off. And like old times, Danutia hadn't had time to unburden herself completely before her sister had turned her attention elsewhere. Hadn't had time to tell either Grace or Alyne the whole truth. Coach had put his hand on her breast, stroked her hair, kissed her lips, explored the deepest recesses of her young body. And she had liked it.

Ten

When her phone rang on Sunday morning, Danutia ignored it at first. Then she glanced up at the clock. Almost ten. She could use a stretch. She'd finally been given access to the military files and she'd been poring over them for hours.

"Paul McCasland here," said a cheery voice. Classical music in the background, heavy on the strings. "Sharma gave me your number, I hope you don't mind. I'm working on my report for the Coroners Service on the unidentified body out at Sitting Lady Falls. I have a copy of the autopsy report and the photos, but I don't have a complete description of the purse. Can you help me out?"

"No problem," she said. "Give me a minute to find my notes. They're much more reliable than my memory." She rummaged for her notebook and flipped through the pages while Paul hummed along with the music.

"Here it is," she said. "Bright pink plastic shoulder bag with zipping foldover flap, no outside pockets." She gave him the bag's dimensions, folded and unfolded, and the length of the strap. "Big enough for a wallet, keys, and a bit of makeup. None of which has been found," she added, "except for the key to the bus station locker."

"The killer probably dropped the key when he cleaned out her purse," McCasland said.

"Maybe. Or she dropped it herself, earlier. Hers were the only fingerprints."

"On the key or the purse?"

"The key. We don't know about the purse yet. Sharma had to send it to Vancouver. Let's hope it has the killer's prints on it."

"A girl that age, you'd think she'd have a watch, some jewelry," McCasland said, his thoughts obviously elsewhere. "It helps when I can put something like that on the poster. You'd be surprised how many people remember a tattoo or a pair of earrings when they can't recall a face."

"Can't help you there," Danutia said. "Guess I'd better get back to my own paperwork."

"I'll be through here in an hour or so," McCasland said. "Sharma mentioned you're a cyclist. How about a ride out to the Potholes?"

Danutia hesitated. A stretch would do her cramped muscles good. She'd been on the Galloping Goose Trail, but never as far as the Sooke Potholes. However, she'd promised Grace she'd stay clear of entanglements. Not that McCasland was her type. She liked cool cats, not friendly puppies.

"I'm not dating right now," she said. "Thanks anyway."

McCasland's chuckle surprised her. "Thanks for being so honest," he said. "I'm not dating either. I just like company on my bike rides. Given the weather, today's the best chance for a while."

Danutia glanced out the balcony window. The system that had brought Thursday's storm had stalled. Low gray sky but no rain, though the forecast, as usual, called for scattered showers. She'd worked halfway through her stack of incident reports without spotting any obvious links to the Handy Dan cases. She would have liked to talk the case over with Sharma, but he seemed impossible to reach. She'd even been tempted to ring up Jennifer Farrell, but Jennifer would suggest the obvious: re-interviewing everyone who had been mentioned in the two investigations. She needed someone who would jiggle the kaleidoscope, help her see a new pattern. Someone like McCasland, whose comments on sexual display in the bird world had led her to the Castaway Club.

"Are you still there?" he asked.

Danutia could feel her resolve fading. She made one last half-hearted objection. "Isn't it too late?"

"We could skip the city part, start from Roche Cove," he said. "The Potholes are about an hour from there."

"I'll be ready at eleven thirty," she said.

By the time they reached the regional park, a few rain spatters had hit the windshield.

"What's a little rain?" Danutia said, hoisting her bike out of the box of McCasland's truck. She could feel her body relax and her breathing deepen as they skirted the Sooke Basin, warming up for the rise into the hills. The Galloping Goose Trail, named for the train that once carried mail and passengers between Sooke and Victoria along this rail bed, was still littered with twigs and branches whipped off by the wind, and twice they had to lift their bikes over downed alders. Here the trail hugged the east side of the narrow valley cut out by the Sooke River. The air was moist and cool but the rain held off. In the distance, green cedars and hemlocks and golden-brown maples rose out of the haze like the picture on a jigsaw puzzle she remembered from one snowy Christmas.

Rounding a bend, Danutia heard the splash of water and saw a long wooden trestle bridge curving away before her. She slowed down, her heart thumping and muscles tightening as the bike bumped over the first slats. The bridge was wide, with a chest-high guardrail. It was also high, a hundred feet or more above a tumbling creek. I'll be all right if I keep to the middle, she told herself, eyes glued on the far end.

McCasland, slightly ahead of her, stopped beside the railing. "Come have a look at the waterfall."

Reluctantly Danutia pulled up beside him. He must have seen something in her face, for he said, "Heights bother you?"

She could have denied it, claimed she was stifling a sneeze, whatever. But he'd been straight with her, and deserved the truth. "Ever since I broke my ankle in a high school pole-vaulting competition," she admitted.

"That must be tough," McCasland said, his brow wrinkling, his eyes bright with curiosity. "How did you make it through RCMP training?"

She probed his question for the criticism she expected, and found none. No criticism, no air of superiority, no quick fixes for her "problem." She'd never known a man capable of being such a good listener. "When we were doing obstacle courses and stuff, I made sure I knew what to expect," she said. "If I can prepare myself, I'm usually okay. The bridge took me by surprise."

Swallowing the lump in her throat, she peered down. Far below, the creek frothed over rocks and gathered in a quiet pool for its next leap into nothingness.

"These falls aren't like the Sitting Lady," McCasland said. "Here there's not much of a view from the bottom, because the road's too far away. But if you don't like heights, we can come back that way." He pedaled off. Danutia followed. She was beginning to understand the connection between her feelings about her Coach and her aversion to heights, but she wasn't ready to discuss her fears with a stranger. Still, she was grateful that he accepted her explanation so matter-of-factly.

Cycling down the forest path with only the whoosh of tires and an occasional bird call to disturb the silence, she thought about the life she'd shared with her sister. Giggling under the covers in their tiny bedroom wallpapered with climbing roses. Whispering in church until the noisier one, usually Danutia, was forced to squeeze in between her parents. Passing notes in the corridor at school. Until Alyne, four years older, crossed the magic threshold into high school and disappeared into a different world, like the children in the Narnia books. It was then that Danutia had developed some sympathy for their brother Andrew, between the sisters in age but shut out of their shared life. And then he was out of their lives forever.

McCasland, who had pulled ahead, dropped back to ride alongside her. "See those ruins?" he said, pointing through the trees to a tall rock chimney and the skeleton of a massive wooden structure. "Developer had big ideas about building a world class resort here. Then he ran out of money."

He crossed the road that now ran parallel to the Galloping Goose Trail and chained his bike to a tree.

"I'm hungry," Danutia said, following suit. "Let's eat first, explore later." She carried her backpack to a low outcrop of gray rock tipped with pink where the river spread out into a shallow basin. Seagulls squawked as they circled and landed, flapping, to tear at the carcasses of dead and dying salmon.

"Looks like a good run of chums," McCasland said. "If we hadn't had that storm to raise the water levels, they wouldn't have made it this far."

"Can we find somewhere to eat away from the smell of rotting fish?" Danutia asked. "I went out to Goldstream last December, my first experience of spawning season. I couldn't believe it. You read about it in school, how salmon come back to the rivers and creeks where they were born to lay eggs and die, but when you live on the Prairies, you can't really imagine what it's like. Salmon lying quiet in the shallow water or struggling to swim a few feet upstream, salmon packed so thick that you could practically walk across the river on their backs. Seagulls like here, not even waiting for the salmon to die, and dozens of eagles in the trees. It was incredible, but the smell— well, you know how it is. Shut up your apartment for a day with fish scraps in the garbage, and multiply by ten. It's not a smell I want to be reminded of in my free time."

"We could go back to those picnic tables we passed, they're farther away from the river," McCasland said.

Danutia took a few cautious breaths. "Actually, it's not so bad," she said. "As long as the wind doesn't get up." She set her backpack down on the rock and began taking out apples and oranges, a Thermos of lentil soup and one of coffee.

McCasland tapped his jacket pocket. "I can always light up a cigar," he said. "Though from the face you made on Tuesday, I don't think you like them any better."

"Hey, it worked," she said, pouring soup into the Thermos cups and handing him one, with a spoon.

"Trade you," McCasland said, handing her a wrapped sandwich and a granola bar. A jay lit nearby, beady eyes fixed on dinner. She shooed it away and settled into a hollow. McCasland dangled his feet over the edge of the rock, his eyes intent on the silvery forms moving below the water's surface. She wondered what he saw there: food for the body, like the seagulls; or food for thought, about the mysteries of life and death. She said, "Do you mind if I ask a personal question?"

"Go ahead," he said, swinging around to face her.

"In the other provinces where I've been posted, coroners have to be medical doctors. British Columbia is different. Sharma says you used to be a real estate lawyer." Unsure of how to proceed, she unwrapped a sandwich and took a bite. Ham and cheese on rye, with Dijon mustard and dill pickle. She approved.

"So what am I doing in this profession?" McCasland set down his cup and spoon. The curly beard covering his cheeks and chin made his expression hard to read, though his eyes met hers squarely. "I guess you could say I had a conversion experience a few years back."

Danutia wasn't sure what kind of answer she'd expected; maybe some flip comment about preferring clients who didn't talk back. Certainly nothing so honest. "Like Saul on the road to Damascus?"

He looked puzzled. "What's that?"

"You know, the Bible story: Saul persecuted Christians until he had a vision on the road to Damascus, and then he became an apostle called Paul, and a great preacher to the Gentiles."

"Exactly," he said. "Except my conversion had nothing to do with religion. The real estate market in Vancouver was booming—still is, all those Hong Kong millionaires trying to get out before Beijing takes over in '97. Anyway, I was raking in the dough, doing contracts for big projects, so I talked my wife into buying in North Van, fancy new estate up the hillside with fabulous views. Antoinette didn't really want to leave our funky house in Kits, or her friends, or her job managing one of those little boutiques along Broadway."

"I can see her point," Danutia said.

"So can I, now that it's too late. At the time, I insisted. I had to have a place where we could entertain my wealthy clients, or so I thought. I'm talking people with fifty to a hundred million dollars who don't trust the stock market, they want to buy something solid, like a shopping centre or an office building," he said, unwrapping the other sandwich.

"Finally Antoinette relented and we moved in the spring. All that summer it was dry, perfect for the parties we gave, everyone sitting around the deck admiring the view." He fell silent and his eyes narrowed. Danutia was about to say he needn't go on if the memories were painful when he cocked his head and held up his hand. "Hear that?" he said.

A high-pitched twittering, from somewhere in the towering evergreens. After a few misses Danutia spotted them, dozens of tiny birds clinging to the underside of boughs high in the canopy.

McCasland laid down his sandwich and pulled his binoculars from his backpack. "Know what those are?"

All small brown birds looked the same to her. "Chickadees?" she hazarded.

"Close. Yellow-crowned kinglets. You can tell by the call. Here, take a look."

Danutia shooed off the jay as it darted in for McCasland's abandoned sandwich. "I'll take your word for it," she said. "I'm more interested in your conversion experience."

"Are you sure?" McCasland said, reluctantly putting the binoculars away. "It's a long story."

"Then you need a coffee," she said, rinsing out the Thermos cups with her bottled water and pouring the black liquid.

McCasland cradled the gray plastic cup in his hands for a moment before he spoke. "The fall rains came late that year, but when they came they didn't stop. Around 2:00 AM one night the hillside above our house gave way. The neighbors tried to pull Antoinette out of the mud but it was too late."

"And you escaped?"

"I wasn't even there. I was at the office, working on a big shopping centre contract. Our clients were trying to sell a piece of polluted land without being liable for cleanup or future damages. My wife died because of shoddy work like the kind I was doing. The only person who seemed to understand that was the coroner in charge of the case. He didn't shake his head and talk about acts of God. He investigated the site, and when he discovered that the foundation was unstable because the house was built on fill, he recommended changes to the building code.

"That's when I decided to become a coroner," McCasland said, gazing upstream where the swollen river tumbled through a narrow gorge. "Antoinette died because of me, because of my ambition. I thought I could atone by keeping other people from dying."

A seagull shrieked and landed in the water before them, its talons catching at a silver shadow. The salmon rose, thrashing wildly, and then went limp.

Danutia asked, "Has it worked?"

McCasland met her gaze. "Not in that simple way, no. Mostly I've drawn cases of elderly people dying alone. A couple years back, a boy died in a boating accident. I suggested some changes to the boating regulations that might have an effect. And drunk-driving fatalities keep falling, partly because of coroners' recommendations. This is my first homicide, and I don't know where it will lead. So as far as saving lives goes, I haven't accomplished much. As for saving myself—every dead body I see is still Antoinette's and every grieving person is me."

He drained his cup and reached out his hand to return it. Danutia gave his arm a light squeeze before taking it.

"Thanks for listening," he said.

Danutia shook out the last drops of coffee and screwed the cup onto the Thermos. "Isn't that what friends are for?" she asked.

In companionable silence they packed away their picnic things, Danutia wondering about the victim she had nicknamed the Sitting Lady. Did she have a father and mother somewhere, brothers and sisters, grandparents who would mourn her passing? And her killer—did he, like Paul, feel guilt and remorse? Or was her death nothing more to him than a moment's sick pleasure?

Paul slung his backpack over his shoulder and his binoculars around his neck. "Let's walk along the river. You won't see the Potholes, though. The river's too high. In the summer it bounces and swirls over a series of drops where it's carved out huge bowls in the rock, like witches' cauldrons. Of course in the summer we wouldn't have the peace and quiet. Kids leave their radios cranked up while they go off for a swim."

The clouds had thickened and the wind had picked up. As she zipped up her jacket, Danutia tried to imagine coming here in the summertime, plunging into the cold river, and then basking on a boulder warmed by the sun. In another time, another place, the girl she thought of as the Sitting Lady could have been one of those kids, laughing, hanging out with her friends, getting a little sloshed, a little high. She would have looked good in a bikini, with those thin bones.

"I wish we knew her name," Danutia said, half aloud.

Paul too must have been thinking about the girl, for he replied, "Sharma said there was nothing in the suitcase to identify her."

"Nothing," Danutia said, mentally reviewing the girl's meager possessions: a few tops, shorts, underwear, all worn and dirty; a pair of runners with a hole in one toe; a plastic bag of cosmetics. "The only possible lead was a receipt dated 09/02/06 for jeans and a top, presumably the ones she was wearing. Jennifer will follow up when she has the artist's sketch. What are the chances that anyone will recognize her?"

Paul stopped to push up the glasses that had slid down his nose. "I'd say it depends on two things: whether she was known around here, and whether she was good-looking. At the Coroners Service we have files on unidentified bodies going back twenty years. Most of them are men, likely men who had lost touch with family and friends. They were never reported missing, so when the bodies were found where they'd been sleeping rough in the mountains or along the Fraser River, there were no records to make a match. This case is different. From the looks of things, the girl didn't have a lot of money. Yet on the day she dies, she goes out and buys a new outfit. That suggests she was planning to meet someone."

"If it was the murderer, that's no help," Danutia said. "If it was someone else, why hasn't the person come forward?" Scattered drops of rain had followed them down the river; now the rain came more quickly, slanting into the water and ricocheting off the rocks. She scrambled up the bank, Paul behind her, and they headed back towards their bikes.

"The second thing," Paul said as though there'd been no interruption, "was she attractive? If not, it's possible that she would blend into her surroundings, like that creeper over there, and no one would remember her."

Danutia had been vaguely aware of a scratching sound nearby. Now, as her eyes followed the direction of Paul's nod, she saw a long-tailed brown bird inching up the trunk of a Douglas fir.

"But the thing is she was young," Paul said, "and most young girls are attractive enough to catch someone's attention—a clerk, a cashier, a bus driver—and we know she dealt with people like that the day she died. So I'd say the chances of someone coming forward are pretty good."

Danutia was no longer paying attention. She'd halted to study the creeper, which had dropped down and was making its way up the tree trunk again, its long curved bill seeking out insects in the deep furrows, its mottled feathers barely visible against the dark bark. She'd thought Paul might shake up her thinking about Handy Dan, and now he'd done so, quite by accident. Sexual display explained the plumage of some birds. Here, the brown creeper against the brown tree trunk illustrated the opposite principle: camouflage.

Trying to determine how the killer had costumed himself in the past was like trying to follow a bird's flight through the forest. To observe an elusive species, you camouflage yourself, sit quietly, listen, and wait.

She glanced over at Paul, standing silent in the rain, waiting. "How would you like to come with me to a Halloween party on Saturday?" she asked.

PART 3

Halloween/Diwali
October 21-November 3, 1996

. . . if your heart is full of love, then you never ask to
be loved, you never put out your begging bowl for
someone to fill it. It is only the empty who ask to
be filled . . .
—J. Krishnamurti, *Think on These Things*

Eleven

"For years something inside was telling me to get out," the speaker said. "I wouldn't listen. Then one day it was like a light bulb come on and I said to myself, 'All right, time to go.' Packed my clothes, the baby's clothes—she was three by then—and I was out of there. Went back to school, got a job, quit looking for a man to make me feel special." She looked around at the dozen or so men and one woman occupying the folding metal chairs Ritchie had helped set up earlier in the evening. She was a big woman, a bottle blonde with careful makeup and hard blue eyes. Next to her sat her pal, a thin brunette who'd held her hand through the introductions. At the front sat some guys from Leicester and the other halfway house; the facilitator from ReStart; and Ritchie. At the back were the guys from the Head and their volunteer escort. Guys who'd be coming up for release or parole soon, trying to figure out how to have a life outside.

"The point is," the woman said, her hard blue eyes settling on Ritchie, "if I can change, you can change."

Could he though, Ritchie wondered as the meeting broke up and the guys from the Head filed out the door.

"Hey shitheads, stay out of trouble or you'll end up in jail," Ritchie called after them.

"Fuck you, Taylor," someone called back from the sidewalk, but it was dark and Ritchie didn't recognize the voice. Not so long ago he'd known all the guys. It made him uneasy, the sense that he was losing touch with that life. It was one thing to joke about being a free man, another to face a bunch of strangers every day at the Grind. Wondering how they would react if they knew he was an ex-con; wondering how he would react if they gave him a hard time. What do you say when someone asks if you've been in Victoria long, or where you worked before? He didn't want to get caught in an outright lie, so he usually said he'd grown up in Toronto, just arrived in Victoria a few months ago, skipping over the years in between. Always feeling like a fraud, an imposter. In prison you knew where you stood, at least you found out pretty quick if you wanted to stay alive, and then you settled in and did your time. After six years at the Head he'd had a certain position among the staff as well as the population, and now he was shit again.

Upstairs the guys were watching *LA Confidential.* No mindless staring at the tube for him, not tonight. He'd been doing too much of that. Get up, go to work, come home, eat dinner, do his program—AA, NA, ReStart, whatever was on that night—watch TV, go to bed so he could start over in the morning. A routine, like prison. Something you could hold on to.

Only now he could change the routine. If he had the guts. That's what the meeting was about, having the guts to make changes.

Ritchie stopped in his room for his food-spattered copy of *Joy of Cooking,* then headed for the basement kitchen. He'd promised his boss, Elaine, some special baking for Halloween, something Healthy and Wholesome. They'd finally settled on cookies in spooky shapes, as long as he made them with whole-wheat flour and a fruit glaze instead of icing sugar. He could try a batch tonight, make sure the recipe worked. Cooking was soothing—do this, do that, your hands busy, no time for the devil's workshop, and then there it was, a cake or casserole, something you'd made that other people wanted, their words of praise dropping into that empty place inside.

He cracked an egg, watched the broken yolk dribble into the bowl. That's when the blonde's voice came back to him, husky with smoke and anger, breaking as she told about trying to curl up to protect her unborn baby from her husband's work boots, but she couldn't, her belly was too big. That wasn't the part that got to him, though, the violence; he'd seen plenty of that. It was the challenge she'd directed at him: "If I can change, you can change."

Could he though, he wondered again, measuring oil and dumping it into the mixing bowl. He had a job, a place to live, guys around who knew the score. And something inside gnawing at him, like the craving that had got him into this mess. How long before someone offered him a joint, a pipe, a needle, and he didn't walk away from it?

Don't think about it. Stir, stir, stir until you're back with Grandma Stark. You're five and it's your first visit and you're in her kitchen, making sugar cookies. She rolls out the dough and then she brings a heap of little tin molds and says, "Cut any shapes you like." He's so afraid of messing up that he leaves inches of dough between the cookies. Grandma says, "Never mind," and moves his stars and bells to the cookie sheet and then swoops the leftover bits together and rolls the dough out again. When there's only a smidgen left, she shapes it into a heart, saying, "This one is especially for you."

Even at five years old Ritchie knows words can't be trusted. His mom's promises to get up and make him breakfast. His dad's promises to call him. So he lets her loving words pass by. What sticks is that you can shape the dough like clay. On his next visit, he makes cars and buses, big fat cows and skinny snakes—

"Hey man," Chuck said, walking up and sticking his finger into the bowl, "give us a taste."

Ritchie pushed the hand aside. "Fuck off."

Chuck popped his finger in his mouth. "Not bad. Needs more sugar, though. You called Crystal's mom yet?"

"I told you—"

"Don't bullshit me, man; it's all about choices, right? You are *choosing* not to call. What's the worst thing that could happen? Somebody tells you to screw off. What's the best thing that could happen? You get some peace of mind." Chuck pulled a worn black wallet from his back pocket and began to hunt through the cards spilling from their dividers.

"Move it," Ritchie said, nudging Chuck out of the way so he could get to the drawer with the waxed paper. He tore off a piece, dumped the cookie dough onto it, and covered the dough with more waxed paper. The recipe said to chill overnight but he didn't have time for that shit. He picked up the rolling pin.

"Found it!" Chuck exclaimed.

Ritchie looked up. A small blue rectangle dangled in front of his eyes.

"My phone card," Chuck said. "It's yours for the asking. You don't use it now, I'll use it myself. What do you say?"

Rage surged through Ritchie like a jolt of electricity and he felt his hands tighten on the rolling pin. Then his eyes caught Chuck's. Blue eyes like the blonde's at the meeting tonight. Challenging him to stop running away from things like he'd done his whole life. Challenging but not angry, not critical. Gradually his fingers relaxed. Chuck, all these guys, were trying to change their lives. Some of them would make it; some of them might not. But they were trying. He could do that too.

"Thanks," Ritchie said, taking the phone card. He held out the rolling pin. "Make any shapes you like."

At the pay phone in the hall he called directory assistance for Mississauga, writing the number for Kelly's folks on his arm with a pen someone had left lying around. The number was still the same, he half-remembered it, the way he half-remembered the poky little house with the high chain link fence to keep burglars out. "You can never be too careful," Kelly's old man always said, and Ritchie had smiled, knowing he'd already stolen their most prized possession.

The phone rang and rang. Ritchie was about to hang up when the old man's querulous voice, a little shaky now, said, "Don't you know it's after midnight?"

"It's about your granddaughter," he said. "Crystal."

"It's about Marie Wilson," Danutia said when she phoned Pearl Wolf. "I've been put in charge of the case and I'd like to go over your statements, yours and Tanya's."

Danutia had discussed the Castaway connection with Sergeant Lewis and cleared her plans for Saturday's Halloween theme night. Now, armed with the names she'd culled from the military and police files, she would re-interview everyone who'd been questioned in the initial investigation. Marie Wilson's housemates were first on her list. According to her earlier statement, Pearl was a member of the First Nations Songhees band and worked in band administration, though she didn't live on the reserve. She and her white partner, Tanya Moore, lived in Esquimalt in a house Tanya had inherited from her grandmother. At the time of her death, Marie had shared the house with them.

Pearl's only response was a heavy sigh, so Danutia went on. "I'd also like to get in touch with a friend of Marie's you mentioned, a woman named Linda. There's no statement from her in the file. Can you give me her contact information?"

"That one's easy," Pearl said. "Linda, she moved in with us after Marie died."

Danutia suggested meeting at their house the next night; after consulting with her housemates, Pearl agreed.

When Danutia arrived on Wednesday evening, smoke rose from the chimney of the small frame house, one of a handful not yet replaced by apartment buildings. As she made her way up a sidewalk bordered by low shrubs, the porch light snapped on and the door opened.

"I don't see why we have to go through this again," said the young woman who glanced at Danutia's ID and ushered her inside without introducing herself. Tanya—or was it Linda?—was a stick-thin blonde in her early twenties, with a sharp nose and the translucent skin that wrinkles early. Danutia wondered whether the woman's choice of black and white clothing—shiny black leather trousers, white sweater, open black leather vest—reflected her way of thinking. Shoving Danutia's coat into a bulging hall closet, she led her into the living room. Coast Salish art in bold blacks and reds covered its walls. Over the fireplace hung a carving of Raven with the sun in its beak. Danutia wondered whether it was one of Henry Mike's.

A woman with a black braid down her back—Pearl, she assumed—knelt in front of the fireplace, log in her hand. She was wearing well-washed jeans and a navy western-style shirt with red and white embroidery and snaps down the front.

"You can talk to Pearl while I finish up the tea and coffee," said the blonde, and padded off. At the doorway she added, loudly enough to carry down the hall, "Better tell the Drama Queen we're ready."

Pearl tossed the log on the smoldering fire, blew on it until flames appeared, then rose in one fluid motion. She was a little shorter than Danutia, with full hips and bust. "That Tanya," she said with a shrug. "She and Linda, they don't get on so well. Have a seat." She gestured towards a loveseat and two matching overstuffed chairs, their flowered pattern at odds with the First Nations art. Settling into a chair, Danutia wondered whether Marie Wilson, herself a Metis, had come to terms with her less visible mixed heritage.

A door closed down the corridor, slippered feet approached, and a petite woman in a brown suede pantsuit slouched into the room, carrying a box of tissues. She had the kind of ordinary good looks you wouldn't pay much attention to at first glance: regular features, good skin, light brown hair. Like that bird she'd seen with Paul, the brown creeper, Danutia thought, introducing herself.

"I'm Linda," the woman said, curling up in the chair opposite as though trying to make herself invisible.

Tanya bustled in with a tray bearing coffee mugs and flowered tea things (also inherited from the grandmother, Danutia guessed). She plunked the tray down on a handsome coffee table carved from yellow cedar. "There's green tea or coffee," she said, settling beside Pearl on the loveseat. "Help yourselves."

When they'd finishing pouring, tea for Linda and coffees for everyone else, Danutia repeated what she'd told Pearl on the phone: she'd recently been put in charge of the case; there were some possible leads opening up; she had a few questions to ask.

"First, tell me about the night Marie disappeared," Danutia said. Linda sniffed, Tanya fidgeted with a pack of cigarettes, and Pearl stared into the fire, which did little to dispel the damp cold of the room. Danutia waited, curbing her impulse to leap in.

Tanya broke first. "All that's in our statements," she said, straightening the cushion beside her. "Why do we have to go through it again?"

"I realize it must be difficult," Danutia said, gazing around at the three women. "It's six months since Marie was killed. You miss her, but the pain is not so sharp any more, and you're doing your best to get on with your lives." She let her gaze rest on Pearl. "Yet you want closure, and you know you won't have it until Marie's killer is caught. At this distance, when the pain isn't so great, you may remember details that slipped your mind at the time, or that you didn't think were important."

Pearl's eyes met Danutia's; she nodded and then glanced over at Tanya. "It's okay, Babe," she said. "I'll tell her." She leaned forward, forearms resting on her thighs, mug between her hands. "Marie, she wanted to win that trip to Vegas really bad. She looked all over for a grass skirt but couldn't find one, not even in the costume shops. Finally she found a green and brown print skirt at the thrift store. Saturday afternoon, she was in here cutting the top off so it rode on her hips and then slicing the skirt into ribbons, so it'd look like grass, you know? Tanya and me, we were going to dinner at a friend's. Marie made us wait while she got dressed. She put fresh flowers in her hair and those artificial ones around her neck . . ." Her voice faltered; no doubt she was remembering, as Danutia was, that the lei of bright flowers had been used to strangle her friend.

Pearl cleared her throat. "Marie said it was too cold for bare skin, so she put her skirt and bikini top on over a beige leotard and leggings. She said she'd take them off if the DJ was as hot as she'd heard. We laughed when she said that, didn't we, Babe? She looked real good, smiling and happy. We were just going out the door when Linda phoned—"

"I still don't understand how you could cancel out on her," Tanya said bitterly to Linda. "You knew she hated going alone—"

Linda's lips gathered in a pout. "How many times do I have to tell you—"

Danutia turned to Linda. "Let me get this straight. You were supposed to go to the Castaway with Marie that night? There's nothing about that in my files. Why didn't you make a statement to the police?"

Linda put down her teacup and pulled her feet under her. "Nobody asked me," she said.

"Fair enough," Danutia said. "Someone should have. You can tell me as soon as Pearl finishes her story."

But Pearl was silent, staring into her black coffee mug.

Tanya shook out a cigarette and picked up the story. "When we came back," she said, "there was a note on the kitchen table saying 'Aloha, babes.' We figured she'd found somebody else to go with, and so we went on to bed, didn't we, Pearl?" She lit up, took a quick puff and offered the cigarette to her partner.

Pearl shook her head. "You know I'm trying to quit," she said.

Danutia stifled a cough. "When did you discover that Marie was missing?"

"Not till Monday," Pearl said. "This cousin of mine in Port Alberni was having a big bash, so me and Tanya, we left early the next morning, Easter Sunday. We figured Marie must have come in during the night and was still sleeping. When we got home late Monday, the note was still laying there. Marie's bed hadn't been slept in. We heard on the radio coming back that the body of a First Nations woman had been found out at Beecher Bay, but we didn't think about it being Marie. Why would we? She didn't know anybody out there. We were getting worried, though, so we called Linda, then we called some of Marie's other friends. We even called her family in Alberta. Then the news mentioned that skirt she'd made, and we called the police." She glanced up as Tanya's arm slid around her, then her eyes dropped again to her coffee. "It seemed like it took forever for someone to come."

Linda reached for a tissue and blew her nose. "I still can't believe she's dead," she said. "If I'd gone to the dance like I said I would, maybe she wouldn't be."

Pearl raised her head. "Marie was a strong woman. She made her own decisions. You have to stop blaming yourself for what happened."

"Why shouldn't she blame herself?" Tanya snorted. "It's true, isn't it?"

"Bitch," Linda muttered.

Danutia turned her attention to Linda. "Why did you back out?"

"Marie and I went to the Castaway a couple times a month," she explained, twisting a hank of hair around her fingers as though to soothe herself. "I don't like going on theme nights—it's too noisy and it sometimes it gets a little wild. But this time I let Marie talk me into it. The gal she usually went with was out of town for Easter and there was this hot DJ, she said."

"And then you cancelled."

Linda's fingers paused. "I used to work at the travel agency at the base. That's how I met Marie. I'd quit a few weeks before Easter and I had a new job at this high pressure agency. It had been a day from hell, spending hours with clients who walked out without booking anything. Then at quitting time a guy called and yelled at me for half an hour about a mistake in his plane reservation. I wasn't in the mood to play Hawaiian tourist all night."

"Yeah right," Tanya said, leaning over to stub out her cigarette. "You and your moods."

The Drama Queen looked ready to burst into tears, so Danutia intervened. "Tell me what happened on the nights you did go together. That was before you moved in here, right?"

"That's right," Linda said so softly Danutia had to strain to hear. She sighed, reached for a tissue, dabbed at her eyes. "There's not much room to park at the club, so I'd park here and we'd walk," she said. "It's only a few blocks—around the corner and up Esquimalt Road. There's good lighting and lots of traffic, even late at night. In the summer we'd go through the parking lots of the apartment buildings. Marie liked it because it's quicker that way, but I wouldn't do it after dark, it's too spooky, all these sounds and you can't tell where they're coming from."

Here was a possibility Danutia hadn't considered. She'd been so taken with her theory about a costumed killer that she'd assumed he'd either accompanied or followed Marie from the Castaway, though no one who'd been interviewed had noticed her leaving. She mentally reviewed her list of names and addresses from the incident files she'd been working on. Three or four were from Esquimalt, though she wasn't familiar enough with the area to pin down the locations. "Are you suggesting that someone picked her up on her way home?"

"Marie would never have gone off with a stranger," Tanya snapped, and Danutia immediately regretted her choice of words.

Pearl laid a soothing hand on Tanya's knee. "Marie was raped when she was fifteen," she explained, "so she is—was—real careful around men. She liked to dance, flirt a little, have a good time, but Tanya's right, she'd never have gone off with someone she didn't know."

"What about someone she did know?" Danutia asked. "Did she ever mention having trouble with a customer, a run-in at a bar, anything like that?"

The three women exchanged glances and Danutia could sense their ranks closing in defense of their friend. "Like we told the cops before, Marie was a good person," Pearl said. "She didn't have any enemies. And she didn't hang around with bad guys."

"I'm not saying someone had a good reason," Danutia said. "We believe the killer has struck at least once before. We want to find him before there are more victims."

"You mean before any more white girls get themselves killed," Pearl said, setting her mug down with a thump, her self-possession suddenly gone. She stood up, crossed to the basket beside the hearth, and pulled out another piece of firewood. "Couple First Nations women dumped in the bush, who cares? But a white girl, that's different. Cops start jumpin' around like sand fleas." She threw the wood onto the fire and the flames leaped up.

"I know that's how it must look," Danutia said, "and it's true that the investigation at Sitting Lady Falls has opened up new leads. But that's not my job. My job is to find out who killed Esther Mike and Marie Wilson. You can help. Tell me anything that bothered Marie enough to stick in your mind. Even tiny things," she said to Linda, "like that guy yelling at you about an error."

Then she waited. She'd come prepared to test out the relation between eye movements and lying described in the article Alyne had sent. The research suggested that when searching for memories, most people look to the right: right and up for visual memories, right and level for auditory memories. When they are constructing a story—such as a lie—they look to the left.

Tanya stared straight at Danutia, her lips clamped tight. The article didn't mention people who refused to play the game. The other two were doing their best to cooperate. Pearl's gaze, up and to the right, suggested the strong visual orientation Danutia would have expected from the artwork on the walls; whereas Linda's gaze, level and to the right, fit with her sensitivity to sound.

Finally, Linda said, "I remember Marie talking about this guy who started coming into the barber shop not long after I left the agency, must have been late February or early March. Every day he'd come in for a shave and leave her a big tip. He'd joke around, saying he had to tip her like that or someday she might slit his throat. She liked him at first—who wouldn't? Then he started hitting on her, and she didn't like that."

"Did she mention his name?"

Again the search to the right for auditory memories. "No, I don't think so. When we were in the Castaway a few weeks later Marie pointed him out at the bar. She called him the Detroit Dickhead because he was a baseball freak, kept offering to fly her down to Florida for the Tigers spring training camp, like she cared."

"Can you describe him?"

"Sorry," Linda said. "I didn't have my contacts on."

"Surely you have some sense of whether he was tall or short, thin or fat—"

"Sorry," Linda said again. "Without my contacts, anything more than a foot away is just a big blur."

No wonder she relies on auditory cues, Danutia thought. "Did Marie say anything else about him? Was he a sailor?"

Linda's eyes flicked to the right. "No, I don't think so. She said something about some exhibits he was working on, she hoped he'd be finished soon."

"At the provincial museum?" Danutia asked, remembering Henry Mike's comments about the First Nations exhibit there the summer before Esther was killed, and Handy Dan's threat: "They'd better keep their hands off our lands."

"She didn't say."

Danutia turned to Pearl and Tanya. "Do you remember Marie mentioning this person?"

Pearl shook her head. "I didn't pay much attention to Marie's talk. She was always going on about her clients or about some guy she'd met at the bar. But she never stayed out all night, and she never brought a man here. That was the deal we made when she moved in. No men in the house unless they're gay. We get enough shit out in the world, we don't need it in our home, do we, Babe?" she said to Tanya. Tanya's tight lips relaxed into a half smile.

After arranging to walk the two routes to the Castaway on Sunday, Linda's first free day, Danutia took her leave. If the baseball freak that Marie had nicknamed the Detroit Dickhead drank often at the Castaway, either Waldrip or Sybil Swanson might remember him. The nickname stirred something in Danutia's own memory, something she couldn't quite put a finger on. Perhaps she too depended on visual cues. She'd have to test the theory on herself.

So before she drove off she did just that, sitting in the dark car while the warmth of the fire and the smell of wood smoke on her clothes seeped away and the windows fogged up inside. Yesterday's staff meeting, last week's scramble down the cliff face, last year's moonlit pursuit of a killer—her eyes, she noted, shifted up and to the right as the scenes played themselves out in memory.

Further back, to the streets of Winnipeg, her first day of training at the Academy, her last pole-vaulting competition in high school . . . And then, unbidden, the memories she'd been discussing with her therapist. Her coach's hands lingering as he adjusted her position. His arm brushing across her breasts. His face bending over her. Danutia's breathing grew shallow and her stomach knotted. In a momentary flash of consciousness she realized that her gaze had shifted to the left. That's where people looked when they were constructing a story. Was it all lies, then, this secret that had poisoned her life for so many years? A story she'd made up and convinced herself to be true? If she'd been so wrong about her own experience, how could she trust her judgment of other people?

How could anybody drink this shit? Ritchie spat out the coffee he'd drained from the battered aluminum urn. Sweet Jesus Christ. He must be getting spoiled, working at the Grind.

He dumped out the grounds, washed the urn, filled it with fresh water and coffee and plugged it in. That was the rule. You finish the pot, you make a fresh one. No wonder there was always grungy sludge in the bottom.

In the hall the phone rang and then Chuck shouted, "Ritchie! Phone!"

Shit. Must be Elaine, changing her mind about tomorrow's baking. And here he'd just got home. All he wanted was to relax, forget about work, forget about everything.

"Ritchie! Phone!"

Ritchie dried his hands on a kitchen towel and stepped into the hallway. Chuck wiggled the phone around and mouthed something he couldn't make out. He took the receiver and motioned Chuck into the living room. Whoever it was, he didn't want any of the guys hanging around, listening in.

He said hello.

"Ritchie? What's this about Crystal?" Kelly's voice demanded.

"You've taken your own sweet time," he said. "I called Monday night. This is Thursday."

"You know why?" she said. "Because you gave Dad a heart attack, that's why, phoning out of the blue like that. If the ambulance hadn't been two blocks away, he'd have been a goner. We just brought him home from the hospital. He was so agitated when he saw the phone beside his bed I thought he was having another attack. When we got him calmed down, he said you'd called. He'd scrawled this number on his phone pad. It better be important."

Ritchie took a deep breath. "Crystal said she was coming to see me," he said, "only she didn't turn up."

"Why would she want to see you? You haven't had anything to do with her in years. Nothing on her birthday, nothing at Christmas."

"I sent her a locket," Ritchie said. He'd tried to, anyway. A con at Mountain said his old lady had put his picture in one and given it to their daughter to remember him by and on an impulse Ritchie had asked if she'd do the same for him. It cost him six cartons of smokes. The guy said she'd mailed it, but he'd never known for sure.

"That was more than ten years ago," Kelly said, "when Crystal was six. I thought you must be dead."

"Might as well have been. I was in prison. Now I'm out."

"How did you find her, anyway? Had you been in touch with my folks before?"

"Are you kidding? Your dad would shoot me before he'd give me your address or phone number, or I'd have called you sooner." He wanted to think he would have, anyway. "Crystal tracked me down," he said, explaining how she'd phoned the Correctional Service to ask about his whereabouts and been told she'd have to write a letter to be forwarded to him. In her letter she'd said she would soon be leaving to work at a resort on Lake Temagami and he should write to her there.

"So I did," he said. "I told her I'd be getting out on parole soon. She answered straightaway, saying she'd meet me at the bus station in Victoria."

"When was that?"

He braced himself. "Her birthday," he said. "She wanted to be here for her birthday." He hurried on, before she could say anything. "I waited at the station all day, but she never showed up. Cold feet, I thought, but then I got worried." He didn't say why. He also didn't say: She'd found an old photo of me you'd hidden and cut out my head and put it in the locket. She said I was a hole in her heart, like that hole in the photo.

"That was almost two months ago. And you're just now getting worried?"

"Look," Ritchie said. "I just want to know she's okay."

"Far as I know, she's still up North with that asshole boyfriend of hers," Kelly said, her voice carrying a hint of the jealousy he'd sensed long ago when he was making the baby laugh and Kelly would snatch her away for a diaper change or a feeding. Who was she jealous of now, him or the boyfriend, or both? Any other time he might have felt jealous himself, some young smartass pawing his little girl, but now he felt nothing but relief. Crystal was safe. That's all he wanted to hear, Crystal was safe.

Down the hallway Chuck was tapping his watch and motioning Ritchie to come on. Was he wanting the phone or what? Ritchie waved him off and turned his back. When Ritchie tuned in to Kelly again, she was saying, "Still, it's been a long time since I heard from her."

Ritchie felt himself go numb. "How long?" he asked, willing her to say yesterday, last week, and last month. Any time as long as it was after that girl died at Sitting Lady Falls.

"Beginning of August," Kelly said. "Before she left."

Anger churned in his belly and he felt himself tossing aside the inner constraints he'd been wearing like shackles. "You haven't talked to her since? What kind of a mother are you?" That's it, give it to her, if she was here you'd smash her head in, and then you wouldn't feel the cold prickles of fear.

"We had a big fight," Kelly admitted. Ritchie could imagine how it would have been, Kelly banging around, saying all the hurtful things that came to mind. "My good jewelry and my watch went missing. She denied taking them, of course, but who else could it have been? I told her to get out. I figure she's trying to get even. You know how kids are. Or maybe you don't. Anyway, I'll see if I can find out anything from Brad's folks and let you know."

"Fuckin' right," he said, and slammed the phone down. He felt a hand grab his elbow and flung it off. "Get away from me."

"Man, you gotta come see the news," Chuck said, his eyes shiny with fear and excitement.

Farrell glanced at the television suspended above the bar. "It's still fifteen minutes before the press conference comes on," she said, pushing away her empty beer glass. "How about a quick game of pool?"

"I haven't played in a long time, but why not?" It would be better than trying to make small talk while they waited, Danutia thought as she followed her colleague through the noisy after-work crowd at Schooners, a brewpub about halfway between their detachments.

The table was full size and not in bad shape. Danutia rolled a couple of cue sticks across the green surface, selected one.

Farrell won the break and put down two stripes. Danutia lined up, stroked quickly, and sank the 11. She didn't get good shape, though, and so she sent the 5 wide of the side pocket.

Farrell sank two more. Danutia walked around the table, hunting her shot. "Nine in the corner," she said, tucking her thumb under, taking her time, feeling the returning oneness of eye and hand. The 9 dropped neatly, followed by the 7 into the side pocket, and then the elusive 5. She didn't have a good shot on anything else, so sent the cue ball where it would do no harm.

Farrell moved into position. "I thought you said you hadn't played much."

"We had a table at home when I was growing up. Dad thought it would keep his kids out of mischief."

"Did it?" Farrell asked.

"Most of the time." Danutia grinned, remembering the endless games she and Andrew had played in the old barn while Alyne made out with her boyfriend in the hayloft. Then Andrew died, and Danutia stopped playing. She didn't tell Farrell about that. Instead she told her about battling her siblings for the evening's prize, a homemade sundae in summer, a chocolate bar in winter.

A couple of turns later she sank the 8 ball.

"Right on!" Farrell said.

"What's my prize?" Danutia said, pleased that Farrell was a good sport about it.

"Chicken wings!" Farrell said, ordering some when they regained their stools.

Maybe redheads aren't all bad, Danutia thought.

On the television set above the bar the West Shore staff sergeant was already talking, his face as expressionless as a robot's. She strained to hear over the hubbub around her as he described the body found at Sitting Lady Falls. Then the screen filled with the artist's sketch of the girl, reconstructed from the partially skeletal remains.

A polka-dot bandana held straight dark hair away from a narrow face. High cheekbones, short straight nose, a small mouth with lips that pouted a little, as though disappointed in what the world had to offer. Eyes like two black marbles, the artist's hand unable to conjure the spirit that had animated them.

The image faded. "If you can help us identify this girl, or if you saw anyone matching her description in the Metchosin area on the Labor Day weekend," the staff sergeant said, "please call Crime Stoppers or the West Shore RCMP."

Six weeks she had lain in the forest, and no one had missed her.

As the newscaster wrapped up the interview, Danutia let the bartender refill her coffee cup. Times like these she wished alcohol didn't give her a headache. She could use a little social lubricant. She still felt uneasy around the attractive redhead, though she'd been pleased when Farrell suggested getting together to watch the press conference. Maybe Farrell felt as isolated as she herself did. Not knowing how to move into that territory, she fell back into shop talk. "What did you think?"

Farrell drained her half-pint and signaled for another. "Staff handled the questions well enough, but the sketch was fuzzy. The image should be better in tomorrow's paper. We'll have to see what happens."

"Did you get a report back on that pink purse?"

"I bugged Sharma about it today. Tomorrow, he says. Vancouver's promised. Again. You making any progress with Handy Dan?"

"Maybe. I have my eye on the Castaway Club. There's a Halloween party on Saturday night. Paul and I are planning to do a little undercover work."

Farrell's blue-green eyes crinkled mischievously. "Paul? You mean

Paul McCasland, the coroner? I wouldn't have thought he was your type."

"He isn't my type," Danutia said. "He's a friend. Or becoming one."

"Whatever you say." Farrell played with a wisp of auburn hair that had strayed from her tightly wrapped bun. "You remember Mike, the dog handler? He's coming over to see me this weekend. Why don't we come along to the Castaway? I love dressing up."

"Why not?" Danutia said, and told her the plan.

Twelve

Ritchie was lying in bed staring at the darkness when Nancy knocked on the door.

"Phone. She says it's an emergency."

He'd heard the phone's faint ring, heard Nancy's heavy footsteps in the hallway above as she'd moved to answer it. Before that he'd heard Chuck fumbling around in the dark, heard the sighs and groans and snores of a house full of sleeping men, heard the house creaking, the mice or rats scrabbling in the walls, the distant buzz of traffic, a siren shrieking. Through it all he'd lain on his bed, fully clothed, waiting for this call. He'd been waiting ever since he'd seen that girl's picture on the television last night. Except for the dark eyes and long hair, it could have been his own youthful face staring back at him.

His clock said 6:10. He padded upstairs in his socks and picked up the receiver. He cleared his throat. Kelly didn't even give him a chance to say hello.

"Brad just got back from Temagami yesterday. He stayed on after the lodge closed to help get the place ready for winter. He says Crystal left at the end of August. You know why? Because she had a letter from her father."

She said it "faa-ther," like something nasty you'd poke with a stick. He stared blankly down the long corridor to where a sliver of light shone under the kitchen door. The smell of burnt toast seeped out. He should be hungry—he hadn't eaten since lunchtime yesterday except for those day-old muffins on his way home—but the smell made him want to throw up.

"I'm going to the police," Kelly hissed. "If something's happened to Crystal, it's all your fault. Why didn't you stay out of our lives?"

Ritchie replaced the receiver and trudged towards the light. He closed the kitchen door behind him. Chuck sat hunched over a plate polished clean: one hand held a half-eaten slice of toast and jam; the other lay on an open book, the index finger extended like a kid learning to read. Ritchie would have razzed him about that, but he didn't have the energy.

As though reading his mind, Chuck closed the book. It was that twelve-step book, Ritchie could tell now, with those goody-goody sayings that drove him crazy.

"You look like Lazarus before he was raised from the dead," Chuck said.

The kitchen was cold. Ritchie turned on a burner and held his hands over the slowly warming ring. "Nobody's seen Crystal since the end of August," he said. "Kelly's going to the police."

"Good thing, too," Chuck said around a mouth full of toast. "It's what you should have done weeks ago."

"And then what?" Ritchie said. "End up back in the pen? I go to them with this story about a missing kid and what are they gonna think? You know how it is, happens over and over. Some kid goes missing; the nice respectable parents have this sob story, and the next thing you know they're being charged with murder. So what's gonna happen when the dad isn't some high-flying lawyer or techno freak but a guy out on parole? 'Go directly to jail, do not pass Go, do not collect two hundred dollars.'" He touched a finger tip to the red-hot ring. How many movies had he seen about guys frying in the chair? If only the pain was over that quick, like lightning striking. He turned on the tap and ran cold water over his throbbing finger.

Chuck brought his plate to the sink and shoved it under the tap. "How much worse is it going to look if the cops come to you?" He glanced at the stove clock. "Look, I gotta get to work. You do too. Let's talk tonight."

"Yeah, sure," Ritchie said. But he didn't go to work, didn't even call Elaine until almost noon, and then said he'd been too sick to get out of bed. She'd been good to him, he owed her that much. Afterwards he had a smoke on the back porch and crawled back under the covers. All day he listened to the rain drip from the eaves and splat against the broken concrete path outside the curtained window.

The wind blew a light rain across Danutia's windshield, making it hard to spot the boundary of the Beecher Bay Aboriginal community. On the main highways, you could tell when you hit First Nations lands because they were plastered with billboards—white-owned businesses taking advantage of the only loophole in the provincial ban. East Sooke Road was too lightly traveled for billboards. When she spotted the Beecher Bay sign, Danutia slowed to a crawl, watching her odometer and scanning the roadside for the place where Marie Wilson's body had been dumped in dense undergrowth, 1.1 miles inside the boundary.

She needn't have bothered to measure. A roadside cross decked with artificial flowers stood back from the verge. Most passersby would assume it marked a fatal traffic accident.

She stopped, although she didn't expect to find anything. The Ident team would have gone over the ground thoroughly; any traces they'd missed would have been swallowed up by the burgeoning vegetation. Still, she could pay her respects. As she stood trying to imagine Marie in her bikini top and homemade grass skirt, she noticed a tarnished silver chain looped around the arms of the cross. She bent to examine it. Half of a broken-heart pendant inscribed *Always, Linda*. She thought back to the single item of jewelry Linda had worn Wednesday night. A pendant on a silver chain, too small for Danutia to identify from where she sat. Now she felt sure it was the other half of the pendant she held in her hand. It was true the death of a friend could break a heart as surely as any other loss.

Drawn into contemplating her own losses—her brother, two grandparents—Danutia missed the number she was hunting and had to double back. The rutted driveway led to a mobile home surrounded by vehicles in various states of disrepair. Danutia parked behind a dusty black car, license number WAM 453. The car, a Plymouth Fury, obviously hadn't been anywhere in a while. The back left bumper was smashed, the tail light dangling, the tire flat. Danutia was here to investigate its whereabouts on the Easter weekend,

A renewed appeal for information about the earlier murders had gone out with the artist's sketch of the girl at Sitting Lady Falls, though the press releases were carefully worded so as not to suggest the cases were related. West Shore would check out the flurry of calls from people claiming to have seen the unidentified young woman. Danutia was following up an anonymous tip to Crime Stoppers about a suspicious car parked near where Wilson's body was found. The tipster wasn't sure of the make—Ford, Chevy, something like that—but had noticed the letters WAM in the license plate because they were her own initials. The DMV listed five vehicles with WAM license plates in the Victoria area. One registered owner she'd talked to said he'd given his black Plymouth Fury to a nephew, Nathan Barnes, who lived out at Beecher Bay.

As Danutia opened her car door, a large reddish brown mongrel came barreling out of the trailer. A young man stepped out and spoke sharply. The dog halted six feet away from her, panting heavily. The young man snapped his fingers and the dog slunk back to sit beside him.

Trying to calm the adrenaline racing through her veins, Danutia shut the car door behind her and took a step forward. "I'm looking for Nathan Barnes," she said.

"That's me." He was tall and slim, in his early twenties, Danutia guessed, dressed only in baggy jeans and a thin tee shirt despite the wind and rain. Unmarked car or not, he would assume she was Government, Danutia knew, if not police then social worker, or public health nurse, or Indian Affairs bureaucrat. Strange white women did not come to make social calls.

She pointed to the Plymouth. "Is that your car?"

"I guess you could say that."

Danutia explained her business and the young man invited her inside. There she found a cheerful blaze in the woodstove, no more clutter than in her own apartment, and a pregnant young Aboriginal woman curled up on a blue couch, leafing through an *Island Parent* magazine. Danutia introduced herself when it became clear that Nathan wasn't going to, and the young woman nodded, though she didn't give her own name.

Nathan sat down at the kitchen table and Danutia followed suit. The dog curled up at their feet.

After a few preliminary questions about the car, Danutia asked about Nathan's whereabouts on the Easter weekend. The young woman, who'd been ignoring them, looked up sharply from her magazine. "He was screwing that bitch."

Nathan opened his mouth, revealing teeth much in need of fillings and braces, and closed it again.

"Well, it's the truth, isn't it?" she demanded, flinging her magazine onto the coffee table. "What's this all about, anyway?"

Danutia asked, "What bitch was that?"

"Annie Miller, that's who. She kicked him out and he moved in with me, and then she found out she was pregnant and she's been harassing us ever since. She's trying to get him into trouble, that's what."

"Do you know for a fact that they were together on the Easter weekend?" Danutia asked.

"Oh yeah. There was a big party at my uncle's place and they came out for it, crashed with me. I could hear them going at it. Three nights I had to listen to that. There were other people here, you can ask them."

Nathan's exact movements might be harder to pin down than his girlfriend imagined. Still, it seemed likely that the tip that had brought Danutia here, like so many tips to Crime Stoppers, would prove to be a dud: Annie Miller turning out to be Wanda or Wilma or Wynette Ann Miller, WAM, out for revenge.

Nevertheless, Danutia took down the names and contact information of everyone at the party. They had been in the area when Marie Wilson's body was dumped and Danutia now had a reason for getting in touch with them. People who would never volunteer information to the police would sometimes cooperate when questioned. With luck, her trip would not be a complete waste of time.

As she packed away her notebook and rose to leave, a sleepy-eyed toddler wandered into the room, his diaper bulging and a baseball cap many sizes too large askew on his head. "Firsty," he said.

Nathan scooped him up, nose wrinkling as he lugged the boy to the fridge and pulled out a sippy cup half full of milk. Embroidered in orange across the back of the navy cap was the word Tigers. Danutia moved where she could see the front. A Gothic D, embroidered in white. A Detroit Tigers ball cap, like the one Tom Selleck wore in the Hawaiian Luau poster.

"Cap looks a little big for him," she said to Nathan. "Is it yours?"

"Naah, the dog drug it in a few months back," he said. "Phoenix here's been wearing it ever since. Throws a fit if we take it away."

"Well, prepare yourselves," she said. "I'd like to borrow it for a while."

As she climbed into her car, ball cap in hand, she could still hear the little boy howling.

Sunil edged the Honda forward until the ferry worker signaled him to stop, inches from the station wagon in front.

"See, I told you we'd make it," Leanne said, opening her door to the damp night air, heavy with the smell of gasoline.

"Last car on," Sunil grumbled as he squeezed past tightly packed vehicles. "We'll be lucky to find seats." Ahead of him, Leanne made for the stairs to the passenger deck, paying him no attention.

If they'd left earlier, like he'd wanted, they could have huddled out of the wind on the sundeck and watched the islands go by in the daylight. He'd gladly have skipped his biochem lab, but Leanne wouldn't cut her painting class. That meant they'd hit the worst of the Friday afternoon crawl through the Massey Tunnel and barely made the seven o'clock sailing. He should have left her in Vancouver.

Even though tourist season was over, the ferry was crowded. After a long search they finally found seats behind some noisy kids. Sunil dumped his coat and headed to the snack bar for some fries. His mom would have saved dinner for them, but that was two hours away. He didn't know why she'd insisted that he bring Leanne over for tomorrow's Diwali celebration, after that fiasco at Dussehra. Maybe she thought the big illustrated *Ramayana* she'd sent back with Leanne at Thanksgiving would make her more sympathetic to her Hindu heritage—and her Hindu relations. Mom was like that, big on family. He'd hoped Leanne would refuse, but she'd jumped at the chance to do more Carr research. As for himself, he planned to sneak out for a few beers with his friends.

Fries in hand, he settled in to read the Victoria newspaper he'd snagged from the blue recycling box. He was halfway through the recap of the Canucks' win over the Flames when Leanne poked him with her pencil.

"Will your folks think I'm being sacrilegious?" she asked, thrusting her sketchpad in front of his eyes. He put down his newspaper to take it.

"Don't touch," she said, "your fingers are greasy."

It was too late. He'd already left a greasy thumbprint on the edge of the pad. The sketch showed a monkey in a skullcap holding open a short, tight-fitting jacket to reveal a portrait of a woman Sunil now recognized as Emily Carr. Glancing over, he saw the *Ramayana* open on Leanne's lap. She'd copied a pose of Hanuman, the monkey god, baring his chest to reveal Rama's face imprinted there as a sign of his loyalty. He didn't know whether to laugh or get angry.

He handed back the sketchpad. "Don't show it to them," he said.

"But why?" she asked. "I'm trying to understand, but I can only do it through my art."

Sunil contemplated his cousin's puzzled face. She'd stopped spiking her hair, and honey-blond curls lay softly around her ears and along the collar of her rain jacket. The bright contempt he'd so often seen, or thought he'd seen, in her gaze had given way to earnest questioning.

"Look," he said, "did you grow up with any religion at all?"

She shook her head. "My Nana took me to church with her once when I stayed overnight with them. When Dad picked me up that afternoon, I asked about the sad man with blood on his face. He got really mad and wouldn't let me spend the night with them for a long time, and never on a Saturday. So Nana never took me to church again, but once in a while a Bible story would pop out and then she'd say, 'Your dad doesn't like these stories, so this is our little secret, okay?' I couldn't see the problem, but I promised. When I was older, he told me about having to say prayers for hours when he did something wrong, and being strapped by the nuns at school. He calls himself a recovering Catholic."

Sunil thought about his own dad, who would have been up at sunrise performing the Agnihotra ritual, as he did every morning. "My dad's the one who told us stories," he said. "After our baths, Mom would tuck us into our bunk beds. If Dad was home, he would come in and sit down cross-legged on the floor, put his hands together, and bow to us, saying, 'Whoever hears the story of Lord Rama will be blessed with success in this life and peace in the next.' It was a tradition from his childhood in India, before television. We would bow back, trying not to giggle. Then he'd tell us the story of how Rama and his brother Lakshmana killed the demoness Tataka, or how Hanuman leaped across the ocean to find Sita."

He paused, searching for words that would make sense to her. He wasn't good at this kind of stuff—his world was made up of figures and formulas and quantifiable data. That other world, of gods and heroes and miraculous deeds, lived in his bones but not on his tongue. Finally he said, "For Rajit and me, Rama and his friends were like the heroes on the Saturday morning cartoons, you know, Batman and Superman and Tarzan. Especially Tarzan, because he was friends with the animals and lived in the jungle, not in a modern city. We liked the fights and the battles and the magical powers."

Leanne had turned to a new page in her sketchbook and her pencil moved across the surface, though Sunil couldn't see what she was drawing. She'd lost interest, it seemed. So he was surprised when she asked, "And the festival this weekend—what's it called? How does it fit in?"

"Diwali? Have you read the *Ramayana*?"

"Bits here and there. I was more interested in the pictures."

"What else," he said, eyeing the toddler in front, who'd turned around in her seat and was blowing wet, buzzing raspberries at him and grinning with delight. He pursed his lips and blew some back. The mother glared at him and told the little girl to sit down in her seat and stop that, she was getting her pretty shirt all wet and nasty.

"So tell me about Diwali. I don't want to make a fool of myself this time," Leanne said.

Reluctantly he turned his attention back to his cousin. "Diwali means 'festival of light,'" he said. "You remember when we were over here at Thanksgiving, and we acted out Sita's trial by fire? Well, after Rama and Sita are reunited, they travel back to the kingdom of his birth, which he'd left many years ago. I won't explain why, it's too complicated. When he reaches Ayodhya, Rama dresses in magnificent finery and enters the city in a triumphal procession. The lights and fireworks of Diwali celebrate Rama's defeat of Ravana, the monster who abducted Sita. When we get home tonight, you'll see that Mom and Ajji have turned on all the lights, inside and out, and lined the sidewalks and the garden paths with tiny oil lanterns. Mom will have cleaned the house and bought new clothes for everybody, including you, so be prepared. Tomorrow you'll be expected to wear them to the Diwali celebration. It's a lot of fun. The women will bring lots of food—no meat, by the way—and lots of sweets, like rice pudding and custard. Then there'll be singing and dancing."

"I guess I can handle that," Leanne said. "But what about Halloween? Tomorrow's the last Saturday of October—there must be some Halloween bashes around."

"Lots of clubs have Halloween parties. We can go after Diwali. Why don't you check out the entertainment section," Sunil said, passing over the newspaper. "I'm going outside. Want to come?"

"Too cold," Leanne said, rustling the pages.

She was right. The wind was strong, with fine sharp rain like sleet. No moon, no stars visible. He did a quick turn around the deck and returned, shivering, to his seat.

Leanne was intent on the front page and didn't even look up. "Did you see this?" she asked.

"What?"

"Sitting Lady Falls," she said, pointing to a sketch of a young girl. "Remember the police barricade when we went there at Thanksgiving? That's where they found this girl's body. They still haven't identified her." Leanne held out the newspaper. "Anybody you know?"

"Why would I know her?" Sunil said, pushing her hand away.

"I don't know, she looks a little familiar, like I might have seen her on the street or somewhere," Leanne said, studying the image closely.

A chime sounded and a recorded message informed them they were nearing Swartz Bay.

"Time to head back to the car," Sunil said, taking the newspaper from her and bundling it up to return to the recycling bin. They followed the herd down to the lower car deck, squeezed their way past milling passengers and open doors, found the car, and buckled themselves in.

As they waited in the dark for the ferry to dock and the cars ahead of them to unload, Sunil thought about the coming celebration and how he'd described it to his cousin. He'd told her what to expect, all right, but he hadn't said anything about its meaning. Like asking a Christian about Easter and hearing about decorating eggs and eating chocolate. He thought of his mother, setting up her books for the spice shop so that her business year ended at Diwali, and a new one began. Settling accounts, starting fresh. That's what Diwali was about, knowledge triumphing over ignorance, light over darkness. Leaving the old self behind and beginning again. He thought about his own life, the drinking, the partying, the girls. Cutting classes, not studying for exams till the last minute. His grades were slipping. If he wasn't careful, he'd lose his scholarship. What would his dad say to that? It was time for a new beginning.

After Diwali.

Thirteen

"You haven't heard from me for a while. But you will. Soon."

The voice stopped but the tape hummed on as Danutia pulled into the parking lot of the Castaway Club. She clicked off the hand-sized tape recorder that lay on the seat beside her and tucked it into the pocket of her voluminous skirt. The muscles in her body hummed too, taut with the possibility that tonight she might encounter Handy Dan.

She wiped her foggy windshield and peered out in search of Paul McCasland. She'd told him about the call to Crime Stoppers, offered him the chance to back out. He'd insisted he'd do anything he could to prevent another death. He owed it to his wife. What could she say to that?

The pulse and glow of strobe lights spilled out of high windows and a heavy bass line pounded against the car, the fine rain distorting both light and sound. Though it was nearing ten o'clock, the parking lot was almost empty. The club wouldn't start hopping until midnight, Waldrip had assured her. A couple in his-and-her tango costumes strolled towards the canopy-covered stairway leading to the entrance. Two masked men in cheap nylon costumes, one a pirate and the other Frankenstein's monster, glanced around nervously as they passed. Not Handy Dan's style.

Then a masked devil with angel wings and a halo above his red horns paused under the canopy and a lighter flared. McCasland's signal. So this was what he meant when he said he'd come as a Hell's Angel. Danutia liked his droll sense of humor. She hadn't been so inventive, hadn't even considered dressing as a biker babe. She'd dashed into Island Masquerade, explained her needs to the owner, and come away with a gypsy outfit complete with long, dark wig. She checked the wig in her rearview mirror, gathered up her skirt and shawl, and, taking a deep breath, stepped into the damp chill air.

Danutia hadn't been in costume since the night in Winnipeg when her lover—a fiftyish doctor with an erection problem and, as she had discovered, a penchant for young girls—had dressed her up to look like a child she'd told him about, a child who had been raped. Tonight, as she pulled on her scooped-neck gypsy blouse, the remembered pain of that experience had forked through her head and neck until she'd thrown off all her clothes and climbed into the shower. While the hot water cascaded over her tense muscles, she'd cursed the lover, cursed the coach who'd abused her (for at that moment she was convinced it *had* happened, she hadn't just made it up, and it *was* abuse, even if she'd liked it), cursed all who exploited and hurt women and children, until the pain left and she felt powerful and exhilarated. It was a remedy suggested by her therapist, and it had worked much better than Oma's silver knife and dark room, better than yoga. Afterwards she had darkened her eyebrows and rouged her cheeks and lips without a twinge. Now to put her gypsy costume—and her wits—to the test.

She locked the car and paused, fingering the tape recorder in her pocket and thinking about the Smith & Wesson she'd left at home. Should she have strapped it on? No, she'd done the right thing. She was here for information, not a shootout.

Hurrying towards the club, she called out, "Paul! Is that you?" He nodded and put out his cigar. Then she hooked her arm through his and they joined the ragged lineup.

Half a dozen people were bunched up ahead of them at the entrance, where a dispute had erupted. Some underage kid with a fake ID, Danutia surmised, moving to the side for a better look. A bouncer in a gorilla suit was closing in on a heavyset guy wearing a chef's cap.

"This *is* a costume," the guy insisted, but the Tarzan at the door shook his head.

"He doesn't have the ten bucks for the cover," Tarzan said to the gorilla.

"Look, my friend's already inside, I saw him go in. He'll lend me the money. Just let me go ask."

"Hey buddy, come back when you've got the money or a costume," the gorilla said, taking the guy by the arm and forcing him to turn back down the stairs.

"Fuck off," the guy muttered, stumbling down the steps.

Danutia recognized both the voice and the acne-pitted face burning with shame. It was the busboy from the Crossroads Café, the one with the drunken mother. Out from under her thumb and still he couldn't do anything right. As they waited to have their hands stamped, she told Paul about the boy and his mother. "She kept complaining about a ring that was stolen while she was in the hospital," Danutia said. "Said West Shore RCMP never investigated. They probably figured the son had something to do with it and she wouldn't press charges."

Finally they were inside. She headed for the high table she'd picked out the day before, luckily still empty. She'd turned down Waldrip's offer of sticking a Reserved sign on it, not wanting to call attention to herself. It was too far from the action to attract the early crowd, as she'd hoped, but perfect for surveillance. From there she could monitor the entrance, the bar, and the adjoining pool room. Until the crowds poured in, she'd also have a good view of the dance floor. Then she'd have to rely on Farrell and her partner, who would keep watch from the back bar. Paul went to the bar to order, a virgin Caesar for her, a pint for himself. She settled in to wait.

"What are you waiting for? Bhangra!" Sunil shouted over the din to the half dozen friends, some Anglo, some South Asian, gathered around the table, all in costume. He didn't often wear traditional garb in public, but tonight his Diwali clothes had become a costume like any other. He'd left his turquoise stole in the car and thrown off his embroidered sherwani in the hot press of bodies inside. If he had a few more drinks, he might throw off his kurta too, he thought now, though he liked its silky feel against his chest.

"Bhangra! Bhangra!" he repeated, pushing back his chair.

"To this music?" someone shouted back.

He was already moving towards the dance floor. Punjabi folk tunes, heavy metal, what did it matter, as long as there was a beat. Earlier tonight he'd danced while the Diwali candles burned brightly, danced clutching a handful of sweets from his mother's shop, danced to purge the darkness within, and still the music surged in him.

When he turned to look back, he saw that the others had followed, all except Leanne. She sat alone in the new sari Yasmin had given her to greet the triumphant Lord, scarlet with a gold thread for prosperity. The matching scarf was gathered loosely around her shoulders, the veil dangling. Her head was bent, her hand moving. What, was she drawing again? Anger surged through him. Why couldn't she go along with something he suggested for once? Hadn't he spent half the day touring the Emily Carr house with her and then traipsing through the Ross Bay Cemetery in the rain, looking for the artist's gravesite?

A vampire had walked up behind her and was leaning over her shoulder. That's it, suck her blood, Sunil thought, then she raised her head, her look so confused and defenseless that he regretted the notion. He remembered how she'd abandoned her usual brusqueness when they'd finally located the modest granite plaque, brushing aside the sodden yellow leaves to read the simple epitaph: "Artist and Author. Lover of Nature." Diwali, as his father had reminded him this morning, was also a time for brothers to show affection for their sisters; lacking sisters, he could treat his cousin more kindly. He sighed and made his way back to the table, the vampire retreating as he approached.

"Come on, dance," he said, reaching out his hand. "It's simple. Just do what I do."

"No thanks."

"You want these guys hitting on you?" He gestured through the smoke haze towards the men perched on bar stools like hungry vultures. He didn't come to the Castaway much, but she'd seen the ad and insisted.

She'd flipped her papers face down when the vampire spoke to her. Now she turned them right side up again. "I'm busy."

Sunil looked down at the napkins she'd been drawing on. Beside them lay a rectangular clipping from the newspaper. He picked it up. It was the sketch of the dead girl. "What are you doing?" he asked.

"That murdered girl—I think I know who she is. Remember that day you took me out to Metchosin—Labor Day? She's the girl who got off the bus."

Sunil's mouth went dry. "That's crazy," he said. "What makes you think that?"

"Remember I said last night that she looked familiar? But there was something wrong with that sketch; it was like something a computer would generate, not a real person. So I've been experimenting—changing the jaw line, the shape of the nose, the eyes. It was the eyes that threw me. In the sketch they're dark and make her look native, but she wasn't, her eyes were blue. The eyes and the bandana. It wasn't around her neck, it was covering her hair. Have a look." Leanne picked up the top napkin and held it out to him. "That's her, isn't it?"

Sunil wiped his sweaty palms on his trousers and took the flimsy square of paper. The lighting was too dim to make out the lines, even if he had wanted to see them. He longed to wad the napkin into a tiny ball and eat it, eat them all, like a drug dealer swallowing his stash, but the image would simply flow again from Leanne's hand. So he pretended to study what she'd drawn. "Hard to say. I didn't get that good a look at her."

"Wait a minute," Leanne said. "I remember now. You went back to give her a ride."

Sunil swallowed. The strobe lights shifted from red to blue, the music's heavy beat faded into a slow ballad. Costumed revelers washed to and fro. He hardly noticed them, surrounded as he felt himself to be by the faces of his family: his mother's sorrowful, his father's resigned, Rajit's scornful, Nandi's pained, little Kumala's puzzled, Ajji's horrified by this tragedy engulfing her favorite grandson, as he knew himself to be. Then they coalesced into this one face before him, her eyes wary as she waited for his reply. Would she believe him?

Sunil swallowed again. "When I went back," he said, "she wasn't there."

Leanne's mouth tightened into a thin line. "Then what happened to her?"

Sunil glanced over his shoulder at the dance floor, where his friends were. "How would I know?"

Leanne rose, adjusted her shawl and veil, and swept past him, towards the dance floor. "As soon as we get home," she said, "I'm telling your dad."

Sunil trailed after her. What else could he do?

His feet were leaden at first, his body a sack of potatoes that he heaved around the floor. As he gave himself to the beat, he felt his worries recede. Through him danced a poor farmer, plowing the earth, sowing the seed, reaping the harvest, the cycles repeating while the drums beat and the flutes wailed and a figure like a darting flame shadowed his every move.

At the first bars of "Macarena" Danutia leaped to her feet. Enough sitting.

"Dance?" she said to Paul, though with the "Macarena" you didn't need a partner. She wormed her way through the crowd and onto the dance floor, where lines were already moving, forward, back, pivot to the right. She fell in behind a shambling bear that didn't know right from left, the line dancing she'd done at school dances and country bars saving her from his mistakes, though not from his big feet when he stepped backward instead of forward. A few lines over, Paul's wings were shaking, his halo wobbling. He spied her and waved, throwing off his moves. Oh well, give him credit for trying. It was so hard to get guys to dance, especially guys her age. Maybe that's one of the reasons—a healthy reason—she liked older men; they weren't so wrapped up in protecting their egos.

And Paul? What if he asked her for a dance later on, now that she'd broken the ice? Paul is here as a decoy, not as a date, she reminded herself. You've sworn off men. The "Macarena" is fine, no body contact, no hands to set your blood tingling, not even eyes across from you to meet or avoid. No distractions. Remember why you're here.

Sunil and his friends were on the dance floor, she noticed. Like many heavy people she'd known, he was a good dancer. Danutia had been startled when he and his cousin showed up, both in Indian dress. She wasn't concerned about them recognizing her—they'd met her only once, as Sharma's blond colleague. Sure enough, they'd walked past without a glance. But what were they doing in a place like the Castaway?

It was nearing midnight and so far there'd been no activity except by the drug dealer, a scrawny man with a sharp, wasted face. He hadn't bothered with a costume, or maybe his black cowboy hat and boots were his costume. She'd watched him working the crowd: sidling up to guys hunched over the pool table, exchanging a few words with drunken women who grabbed at his arm, then wandering out for a smoke, the buyer following. Once a nerdy guy in glasses had stopped him, but the dealer shook his head and moved away.

As the "Macarena" gave way to Sarah McLachlan's "I Will Remember You," Paul appeared at her elbow. "Dance?" he said, holding out his arms.

He'd been such a sport this evening that she could hardly say no. At this kind of dancing he wasn't clumsy at all; his lead was gentle but sure, despite the trailing bed sheet and drooping wings. She could feel her body yielding and kept her eyes away from his. Before the song ended, she broke off, muttering "Ladies."

It was midnight, the time she'd arranged to meet Jennifer Farrell. Farrell had arrived around eleven, looking stunning in a long white Princess Leia dress, with her auburn hair twisted into buns over her ears and a Darth Vader escort. Now she stood in front of the cracked washroom mirror, putting on fresh lipstick. Beside her, a chick in dominatrix gear pushed at her lacquered hair.

The chick left and Farrell said, "So you're a gal with moves, and not just with a pool cue. Who would have thought it?"

Danutia could feel herself blushing. "Any problems on the dance floor?"

"Nothing much so far," Farrell said, stroking on fresh mascara. "Between sets, a guy in a cheap pirate outfit tried to hit on Catwoman. The bouncer was right there, so I didn't intervene. I'll keep an eye on him."

"Shit, I hadn't even thought of her as a possible target. Is she native?" Danutia said, trying to remember what Waldrip had said about there never being enough women to go around, so he hired an exotic dancer to keep the loners entertained.

Farrell leaned forward, the mascara brush in her hand and a smirk on her face. When Danutia caught her eyes in the mirror, she said, "No, but my informant is."

"You didn't say anything—" Danutia broke off as two women barged in, one talking loudly about her ex's shortcomings, the other, glassy-eyed, heading straight for a none-too-clean toilet.

Farrell dropped her makeup into a small white purse. "Give me a call sometime," she said, and wandered out.

Fuming, Danutia headed back to her perch near the entrance. What did Farrell think she was doing, anyway? This was *her* case, *her* setup, and now she was losing control. Through the crowd, she could see Paul at their table, signaling for another beer. When she arrived, a server was setting out a pint of Granville Island and another virgin Caesar. The server was Sybil Swanson.

"On the house," Sybil said with a smile and a wink.

Smiling back, Danutia dropped a generous tip on the tray. The tip wasn't exactly hush money; still, she hoped that Sybil would take the hint and leave.

Instead Sybil leaned closer. "I figured you might be here tonight," she whispered. "When you were in yesterday, you asked about a guy Marie Wilson called the Detroit Dickhead who had a thing about baseball. Like I said then, I don't remember anybody like that about the time Marie was killed. But that guy over there—" she glanced towards the bar—"the vampire, he was trying to get up a bet with the bartender on a football game Monday night, and guess who's playing. The Detroit Lions and the New York Giants. It may be nothing, but I thought I'd better let you know." She finished clearing their empty glasses and turned away.

Danutia glanced back at the man she'd indicated, one of the dozen or so male vampires tonight, some dressed like Lestat in the movie,

some in the more traditional Dracula costume. This man was a tradi-
tionalist. Danutia was reminded of the men in the film *Moulin Rouge*.
Take away the jeweled medallion, the fangs and dripping blood.
Replace the black cape with a dinner jacket. Then you would have
a Victorian gentleman with his starched white shirt and vest, black
pants, black shoes. A man like Esther Mike's killer.

The vampire moved next to the young Aboriginal woman two
stools away. She'd come alone not long after Farrell, wearing a Coast
Salish cedar bark hat and a button blanket that she'd quickly removed
in the heat. Under the blanket, she wore a black T-shirt proclaiming
"Custer Died for Your Sins." At the time, Danutia had wondered
what Pearl would think of the woman. Now, she wondered whether
this was Farrell's informant, blatantly offering herself as bait. She'd
danced with a vampire earlier, Danutia remembered, but who knew
whether it was the same one.

She needed to be closer. "Stay here," she whispered. Paul nodded,
though whether he'd heard her over the din, she couldn't tell. Then
she picked up her glass and, pretending to drink, poured virgin Caesar
down her front. She didn't have to pretend disgust as the cold, viscous
tomato juice slid down her chest. She jumped up and hurried towards
the bar, hoping Paul wouldn't follow.

She took the towel the bartender handed her and stood turned
away from the oblivious pair, mopping her skin and blouse and trying
to overhear their conversation. It seemed to be innocent enough,
light-hearted banter about which costumes might win prizes. She was
wondering how much longer she could remain without drawing their
attention when she heard the vampire say, "Give me your hand and
I'll tell your fortune." Something—the voice, the word "hand"—sent
cold shivers down her spine. She punched the Record button on her
tape player and stole a quick look at the man who might prove to be
Handy Dan.

He was of average height and build, with a slight paunch that the
cape didn't quite conceal. Beyond that, it was hard to tell whether his
features were his own or part of his costume, and even his height and

paunch could have been augmented. He looked like everyone's idea of a vampire, and no one in particular. If this was the same man, no wonder Linda hadn't been able to describe him. He was making a game of the palm-reader's usual patter, nothing suspicious in it, and Danutia was about to decide he was harmless when she caught the words "... make you famous. Soon."

Some verbal tics are as individual as fingerprints. Something about the way he said "soon" matched the word she'd heard on tape only hours ago, though the caller to Crime Stoppers had done his best to disguise his voice. She glanced up.

Dracula was staring straight at her, his eyes narrowed. He murmured a few words to the Aboriginal woman and disappeared into the crowd around the bar.

Danutia tossed the towel onto the bar and hurried towards her table. Paul was nowhere in sight. He must have gone to the Gents. No time to contact Farrell. The vampire was heading towards the door. She was only a few steps behind him when she was blocked by a half dozen new arrivals. The vampire had slipped through. What if this was indeed Handy Dan, and she had let him escape?

The crowd loosened and Danutia squeezed past. She spotted a black cape among the lounging smokers, but it wasn't him. Then she spied a long cape with a stand-up collar towards the back of the parking lot. That must be him. She rushed to her car but the caped figure continued on, up the hill and into the warren of low-rise apartment buildings that surrounded the Castaway Club. Tomorrow she was supposed to walk that route with Linda. Why hadn't she insisted that the woman take time off work to show her before tonight? Too late for regrets. Danutia hurried after the disappearing vampire. Soon the darkness swallowed her up.

As the night wore on, Ritchie felt more and more like a fool. Why had he let Chuck talk him into coming?

"Hey man, what you need is to get *out*, have some *fun*," Chuck had said last night when he came into their room to find Ritchie lying on his bed in the dark, wondering whether Kelly had gone to the police yet, how long it would take for them to come after him. Wondering if the face that stared back at him from the morning paper, a face like his and yet not like his, was that of his daughter. If only she'd sent him a photo, he'd know. But he couldn't bear knowing.

"I know this club that's having a Halloween party tomorrow night. Hold on," Chuck had said when Ritchie started to object. "You're thinking what if we get caught, we'll be in deep shit, but the beauty of this place is that we go all dressed up, dance with some chicks, nobody's the wiser. You don't even have to drink, if that's what's bothering you." He'd held up two costumes he'd lifted from the storeroom at work, damaged ones, he'd assured Ritchie, they would have been sent back anyway. "So what do you want to be, a pirate or a monster?"

So here he sat in his thin nylon monster suit and plastic mask, drinking ginger ale while everyone around him, Chuck included, was getting plastered. So much for AA and reforming his old man. Oh, Chuck had ordered straight tonic water the first couple rounds, but then he'd switched to vodka tonics, and now he was pissed and refusing to leave. Ritchie checked his watch again, the figures swimming in the pulsing strobe lights, red and blue like a cop car flashing. Shit. Twenty to one. If they were going to make curfew, they'd have to take a cab, and pronto. If they had enough money.

He turned to where Chuck hunkered on the last stool, his hands in his pockets and his eyes glued on the dancer gyrating on her little platform not two feet in front of them. She was dressed like a cat, with little ears sticking up from smooth dark hair, a tail that kept getting in her way. Older than she'd like to let on, Ritchie guessed, older or sicker, from the raspy way she was breathing. Between sets she'd pranced off to the alcove behind them, separated from the dance floor by a black screen. When Chuck tried to follow, the Tarzan bouncer had planted himself in the doorway until Chuck slumped back onto his stool. Now she stretched long claws towards them.

Ritchie leaned over. "We gotta go," he said. "You got a five?"

Chuck shook his head, his eyes never leaving the dancer. A veiled woman in a red sari passed in front of them, making for the can around the corner. Chuck flapped his hands as though shooing her on. He must have touched her or something, because she took another step or two and then wheeled around, eyes blazing, and threw a punch at Chuck's head.

"C'mon, let's get outta here," Ritchie said, but he was too late.

Chuck grabbed her arm. "What the fuck's going on?"

The woman's veil fell away, revealing a wide soft nose above inviting lips and cheeks as soft as butter, with barely a hint of bone underneath. It was the face he'd once thought he'd buried forever.

Fourteen

Dracula was nowhere in sight. The mist had thickened into fog that lay over everything like a blanket of cotton wool, muffling the music from the club and the voices of revelers outside. The short street up from the Castaway Club dead-ended in fenced parking lots for a cluster of low-rises. She'd never find him now.

Danutia made her way along the chain-link fences, searching for an opening. Metal clattered to her left and she paused. A cat's yellow eyes stared back at her and the damp cold reached for her bones. At least her head was warm and dry, protected by the wig that earlier had been hot and itchy. Gathering her shawl more tightly about her, she moved on. Linda had mentioned a shortcut through here, so there must be one somewhere.

On the other side of the fence, muffled footsteps approached, a car door opened and closed, headlights came on, an engine turned over; the headlights cut an arc through the fog as the car backed out. The driver had been no more than a blurred outline, a thickening of the air. What was the point of trying to pursue Dracula in this? He had only to remove his cape and fangs to be unrecognizable.

Slowly Danutia retraced her steps, wondering what to do next. She could return to the club, admit defeat to Paul and Farrell, say goodnight and go home by herself, or invite Paul to go home with her. And then what? How would she ever sort out her feelings about men if she gave in to the least hint of attraction? And she'd never been good at admitting defeat. Surely there was some way of pursuing her hunt for Marie Wilson's killer. From what Danutia had observed tonight, the Castaway attracted a lot of regulars, and, like the Dracula she had vainly pursued, many of them came on foot. Marie's house-mates were sure she wouldn't have willingly climbed into a stranger's car. Would she have been so careful about someone who lived in the neighborhood and offered to walk her home?

Remembering the lists of military and police personnel who'd been in scrapes recently, Danutia strode quickly to her car. Grateful that the car was dry, if not warm, she climbed in, turned on the map light, and pored over the lists and her map of the area. Several lived in Esquimalt, three nearby. Two of them had connections to the base, not surprisingly, since it was only a few miles away. The third was an Esquimalt police officer who'd been caught with a prostitute. Despite the hour, she would check them out. One of them might be Dracula.

She should let Paul or Farrell know what she was up to, but that would require too many explanations, too much delay. If she needed backup, she could radio in.

According to the map, Wardell Thomas, a mechanic with Fleet Maintenance who'd been charged with drunk and disorderly in July, lived closest to the club. In fact, his building backed onto the cul-de -sac across from the club, she discovered, though she'd had to wind through several streets to reach it. If there was a way through the parking lots, Thomas would know about it. She pressed the buzzer of Apartment 8.

Almost instantly a man's angry voice barked, "Whadda fuck?" In the background she could hear a baby's cries and a woman's soothing sing-song.

Time for a little improv. "Paul babe, let'sh have a drink," Danutia said, slurring her words. It was an offense for a drunk to impersonate a police officer, but not, she hoped, for a police officer to impersonate a drunk.

"Hey mon, you come de wrong place. Now fuck off." The intercom went dead.

She believed him, so she did. Thomas might have been able to disguise his looks, but not his heavy Caribbean accent. Had he been celebrating his child's birth when he was arrested, Danutia wondered? If so, he didn't seem so happy about it now.

Richard Hawkins, a consultant at the base, lived in a small frame bungalow off Lampson Road. A motion sensor light came on as she approached, but no one answered the doorbell. Scratch two.

The Esquimalt policeman who'd been caught soliciting sex on

duty lived the other direction, in a duplex near the harbor. Again the house was dark. No answer. Where were these people anyway? Then she remembered. This was the Saturday before Halloween. People who liked to have a good time were out having a good time. She was turning away when the headlights of a passing car caught a Canucks sticker in the window. There'd been stickers at Hawkins' place too, she realized. Stickers she should have observed more carefully. She should have another look.

Danutia decided to park at the Castaway and walk to the Hawkins place, following the route Linda had said she and Marie always took after dark. A few people in costumes lounged around the club, smoking. Rock music blasted out as the doors opened, then dropped to an insistent bass line when they closed. She considered checking in with Paul and Farrell but rejected the idea. If she told them her plan, one of them would insist on accompanying her, and she didn't want that. She wanted to experience the walk as Marie would have, a woman alone at night. And if they wondered what had become of her, surely they could trust her to take care of herself.

The music faded away as Danutia strode off down Esquimalt Road. The street was well lit, the Saturday night traffic light but steady. A vehicle slowed behind her; she kept walking and it roared away. A guy in a pickup on the prowl. At Lampson she turned right. At the end of the block, another right would have taken her to Marie Wilson's house.

Danutia carried on up Lampson, and then turned left onto Hawkins's side street. She hadn't realized how close this house was to Marie's. How easy it would have been for Hawkins to follow Marie out of the club, catch up with her seemingly by accident, offer to walk her home just when she began to feel uneasy about being on the street by herself. Perhaps they'd danced that evening, she in her fake grass skirt and plastic lei, he with his Detroit Tigers ball cap and flowered shirt, like Tom Selleck in *Magnum PI*. Perhaps he'd been charming, like Dracula tonight, and when they reached her corner, he'd invited her to his place for a nightcap. Perhaps she'd decided she'd misjudged him, owed him at least a drink.

The only problem was that Hawkins didn't fit the profile she'd been looking for, violent crimes and offences against women. A complaint had been lodged by a car rental company, alleging that Hawkins had falsified information on the rental contract and refused to pay for damages to the vehicle. Hawkins must have decided to pay up, because the charges were soon dropped. It was the date that had caught her attention. The complaint was filed on April 22, the alleged accident having occurred on the Easter weekend. The weekend of Marie's death.

Danutia walked past Hawkins's bungalow. Still no lights on. She turned, wishing now she had her handgun in her pocket, instead of the tape recorder and a packet of Fisherman's Friends. On foot, she had no way to radio for backup. Still, she wasn't here to confront anyone. All she wanted was a good look at the stickers she'd glimpsed earlier, on the mailbox to the right of the door. She debated whether to sneak up from the side and hope not to trigger the light, or to carry on with the drunken gypsy act. Better to stay with the gypsy routine, she decided; it would arouse less suspicion if she was spotted by a wakeful neighbor, and might even convince Hawkins if he happened to answer the door. Besides, she needed the light to see the stickers.

Smear her lipstick. Tousle the wig a little more, though not enough to dislodge it. Arrange her blouse and shawl to reveal bare neck and shoulders. Suck on a Fisherman's Friend—the smell was vile, even if it wasn't alcohol. When she was as ready as she'd ever be, Danutia sauntered down the sidewalk, singing off-key.

She could have saved herself the trouble. No one answered the bell and she heard no movement inside. If the Dracula she'd spooked had been Hawkins, he'd had plenty of time to make it home. She knocked loudly and shouted "Hey babe!" She was beginning to understand the lure of acting, she thought, this license to become someone totally different. Still, she mustn't forget her purpose. The motion sensor light would soon dim and be gone. She moved closer to the mailbox.

Sports logos. Not just any logos, though, she noted with rising excitement. The gothic letters she'd seen recently on the Detroit Tigers cap. Next to that, the winged helmet of the Detroit Red Wings, familiar from the years she'd watched hockey with her dad, and then two she didn't recognize. She memorized the shapes; sure they'd turn out to be other teams from Detroit.

By the time she returned to her car it was past 2:00 AM and the Castaway was dark. Now she felt less sure about not letting the others know what she was doing. She wondered how long they'd stayed. Farrell was a police officer; she was used to long hours and fruitless stakeouts. Paul was a different matter. He'd come along as a personal favor, and probably thought she'd ditched him. She discovered she didn't want to lose his good opinion.

She drove home, her clothes damp and her teeth chattering. By tomorrow she'd likely have a nasty cold. Serve her right. She turned on the taps to run a hot bath and then checked her messages.

The first voice was Paul's. "Call as soon as you get this message, no matter what time it is," he said.

Danutia punched in the number he'd left. When he picked up, she could hear classical music playing in the background. She imagined herself in the room the music conjured up for her, then put the fantasy aside. "Did you wait up on purpose or are you an insomniac?" she asked without preamble.

"A little bit of both," he replied. "What happened to you?"

"Sorry about that," she said. "I tried to follow the vampire who was putting the make on that Aboriginal woman at the bar, but I lost him. I'm pretty sure he was the Detroit Dickhead who was hassling Marie Wilson before she died." Briefly she recounted her evening's adventures. "Now all I have to prove is that Richard Hawkins is Handy Dan."

"You'd better talk to Farrell," McCasland said. "You may have your sights on the wrong guy."

"Why, what did I miss?" Though in truth she was too tired to care.

"You mean besides me winning second prize for Best Costume? All I know is there was a dust-up of some kind. Farrell called in reinforcements and hustled some people out the back way."

"Okay, I'll call her. You can go back to your Bach—"

"Sibelius, actually."

"Whatever. Thanks for coming tonight. I enjoyed our dance." Danutia put down the phone, turned off the taps—who knew when she'd get a bath—stripped off her damp clothes, and wrapped herself in her bathrobe. Then she called West Shore. Farrell was in an interview, she was told. She would call back.

Her answering machine showed one message remaining. Maybe it was from Farrell. Danutia pushed Play.

The caller sounded agitated. Not Farrell, another woman. She mentioned Sharma. *Yasmin, of course, I should have recognized the voice.* "You must help me," she said. "I don't know what to do. Sunil has been arrested."

Sunil stared at the phone on the duty constable's desk. He should call his parents, he knew he should. It was almost 2:00 AM. They might be asleep. Worse, they might still be awake, drinking Ovaltine and wondering what had happened to him and Leanne. Better to call now, when he could explain about the guy in the bar. But his dad would want to know where they were, why they were at the West Shore RCMP detachment instead of the Esquimalt Police Station. But if he waited . . . He thought about Leanne, closeted with that cop in the Star Wars getup. What was she saying? If only she'd shut up when he told her to, hadn't said anything about the dead girl.

"Hey, my dad's a cop," he said to the duty constable, a grim-faced guy pecking at a computer with two fingers.

The guy looked up. "So?"

"Mind if I use your phone, give him a call?"

The guy nodded and went back to his pecking.

Sunil's hand shook as he punched in the familiar numbers. It would only ring once before his dad picked up, awake or asleep; middle-of-the-night calls were so common. He heard his dad's sleepy, "Sharma here."

"Dad, I'm in trouble," he blurted out, and then hurried on. "Nobody's hurt, it wasn't an accident or anything like that—"

"Where are you?"

"West Shore RCMP. This female corporal, Farris, Farrell, something like that—"

His father didn't wait for him to finish. "I'll be there in twenty minutes."

Sunil hung up, relieved at not having to explain over the phone, but puzzled by his dad's response. Surely his mother would want to know . . . Only that they were alive, unharmed. His dad could tell her that much.

He headed towards the plastic molded chairs that lined the reception area's back wall, glancing around for a newspaper or magazine, anything to pass the time. The room was bare except for posters advertising things he didn't want to think about: missing children, women's shelters, crisis lines. He slumped onto a seat, suddenly feeling queasy. It wasn't just the alcohol, though he'd probably had more than he should have. He'd heard his mother talk about being sick with worry, and now he knew what she meant.

He must have made some sound, for the duty constable peered over at him.

"You about to barf?"

"I'm fine," Sunil said, straightening himself.

"You feel like tossing your rocks, you let me know," the constable said. "The janitor phoned in sick tonight and we've already had a bunch of drunks. I don't fancy doing any more mopping up." The phone rang and he picked up.

Sunil's sweaty kurta clung to his body and he was shivering. Not from the cold, he realized, but from fear. How easily his dad had discovered the perpetrator of all those childhood crimes Sunil had been so quick to deny. Stealing money from his mother's purse. Eating a whole banana pudding she'd made for Diwali. Kicking a soccer ball through the neighbors' window. Getting drunk and sideswiping a car. And what he'd done this time was so much worse. It didn't bear thinking about. Sunil stretched himself across half a dozen chairs and tried to forget it all.

A hand shook him out of a troubled doze.

"Sunil. Sunil." His dad's voice as distant as when he'd called to him across a soccer field. Reluctantly, Sunil dragged himself back to the present. His dad, as neatly dressed as ever in a dark suit and necktie, guided him into a small room and set a paper cup of coffee in front of him.

"What's this all about?" Sharma asked.

Sunil stared at his hands. "Leanne wanted to go to a Halloween dance after the Diwali celebration," he said, letting it sound like a spur-of-the moment decision. "We ended up at the Castaway Club."

"The Castaway? That's no place for your cousin or you either. What were you thinking? Where is your cousin?"

"Dad, you never lectured, so please don't start now. At least let me tell you what happened."

"I've never had to see my son when he's been drinking and driving, and endangering people's lives, including his own. If you could see yourself," Sharma said, gesturing.

"Dad, just listen, please. I didn't drink and drive, not this time. That's not what this is about. We were all up dancing. The floor was so crowded I didn't notice that Leanne had left to go to the washroom. Then one of my buddies tapped me on the shoulder and pointed to where Leanne was arguing with a guy in a pirate outfit. A couple of bouncers had gathered around, and some other people. I went over to see what the problem was. Leanne claimed that the pirate had grabbed at her as she walked past; the guy said he hadn't touched her until she threw a punch at him."

His father looked at him quizzically. "And someone called the police? Usually clubs like that don't bother."

"Yeah, the bouncers were about to hustle the guy out when this Princess Leia chick whipped out her RCMP ID," Sunil said. "She radioed in a check. It turned out the guy was violating his parole conditions, so the Esquimalt police came to pick him up."

"Then what are you doing at the West Shore Detachment?" Sharma asked.

"Princess Leia works out of here. Name of Farris, Farrell, something like that." He saw his father's face tense up at the mention of the name, so he hurried on. "She wanted to make sure Leanne was okay." The explanation sounded lame, even to him. He braced himself for the next question.

"She wouldn't have brought Leanne all the way to Langford for that. There must be something more to it. Sunil, what are you not telling me?"

Sunil glanced around the small room. They were sitting at a long table. In front of them there was another table and a whiteboard covered with writing and photographs and a poster. The face of the dead girl— the face from the newspaper—stared at him accusingly. He nodded towards the poster. "Leanne thinks she knows something about that."

Sunil saw his father's worried eyes go blank and his face close into a mask. It was no longer his dad who sat beside him on a hard metal chair but RCMP Corporal Surinder Sharma, Forensic Identification. Again the chill crept over him. He felt as he had when he was a boy hiding in his closet, waiting for his father's heavy footsteps, the creak of the bedroom door, his father's quiet voice saying, "I know what you've done." He forced himself to continue.

"Dad, we saw her. We were out in Metchosin on Labor Day. She was trying to hitch a ride."

"And did you give her one?" Sharma asked, his voice so gentle Sunil could feel the tears welling up. His eyes dropped to his dad's necktie, charcoal gray with tiny elephants marching across it. Like a whole herd of Ganeshes, he'd said proudly when he'd presented it on Father's Day, how many years ago?

Sharma leaned forward and asked again, "Did you give her a ride?"

Sunil looked up into his dad's face. "Leanne didn't want to, so I dropped her at Witty's Lagoon and went back. But the girl wasn't there." His stomach heaved as Sharma leaned back, his face closed again. "Dad, don't you believe me?"

Sharma fiddled with his tie, as though it was suddenly too tight. "I would like to believe you, son," he said at last.

The door shut on the darkness, and Sunil was lost.

The porch light was on at Leicester House. Ritchie dragged himself up the stairs and rang the bell. Nancy was expecting him, but still he could sense her peering out the spy hole. Good thing he'd ditched the monster suit and mask at the police station.

Nancy let him in and locked up behind him. The guys were always making jokes about the locks being on the wrong side, but tonight Ritchie wasn't laughing.

"I made some coffee," Nancy said after he'd signed in.

Ritchie followed her into the kitchen. He sat at the table while she poured two coffees and dumped cream into hers. Nancy was a favorite around the house, a big-boned woman in her forties maybe, quick with a joke and a smile, though tonight she wasn't laughing either.

"So tell me again what happened," she said. She had dark circles under her eyes and Ritchie remembered something about a druggie daughter with an FAS baby. Maybe that's why she wasn't so quick to judge, like some of the others.

"I fucked up," he said.

"You're here, Chuck's in Wilkie Road," she said. "Seems to me like he's the one with the problem."

The table was cheap pine, scored with crisscrossing lines. He ran a finger over the grooves as though he were reading a palm. "I should never have listened to him. We had no business being in that club, and I knew it."

"You can beat yourself up on your own time," Nancy said. "Just tell me what happened. Chuck got drunk and grabbed a girl, is that right?"

He'd been trying to blot it out, but suddenly there it was again, that face caught in the pulse of the strobe lights, young and scared and full of bravado. Hot coffee slopped over his shaking hands. He set the cup down.

"He grabbed a ghost," he said, and then he told her the story he'd never told anyone, a story he'd done his best to forget.

This was back when I wasn't much more than a kid, living in Toronto. I used to tell myself it wasn't my fault, it was the bike. A 1972 Harley Sportster this guy traded me for my old Mustang and a steady supply of weed. The Ford needed tires and a brake job that would have cost me a bundle, so I thought I'd made a great deal. Turned out the bike was a piece of shit.

I made the deal on a Wednesday and rode the bike around town a couple days. The engine cut out at a light a time or two. The guy who'd owned it said all it needed was a good run on the road, so late Friday morning I headed out on Bayview Avenue. I was planning to cut back to Highway 11 and head north. I had some business that night in Sudbury. That's less than two hundred and fifty miles, no big deal. In Richmond Hill I whipped into the Steerburger and parked my bike. I didn't have a helmet and my hair was blown every which way, so I took off my gauntlets to smooth it down. These two chicks were giving me the eye through the window. Chicks always seem to go for guys in leathers. I pretended not to notice. Inside I ordered a double cheeseburger with fries. While I'm waiting, this blonde comes up and starts talking about the bike, how much she's always wanted to ride one. Would I take her around a block or two?

The blonde wasn't my type at all, too tall and wholesome-looking, with an accent and braces on her teeth. Her friend was a different story. She was East Indian, long hair tied back in a bandana and huge dark eyes. Even from a distance I could feel a spark leap between us. I gave the blonde a ride first, and then asked if her friend wanted to go for a spin.

"My name's Sita," she said, "and yes, I do."

I liked the feel of her arms around me and I didn't want to take her back. At the first red light I twisted around and said I was going out on the road, did she want to come. She said sure, as long as she was back by three thirty. That gave us a couple of hours, long enough to run up to Lake Simcoe and back. I would still make Sudbury before midnight.

She was wearing Levi's and an embroidered blouse with puffy sleeves, not ideal but it was a warm spring day. I warned her I didn't have any protective gear for her, not even any goggles, but she said no problem. "I'll just close my eyes," she said, and let her eyelids droop. She looked so vulnerable I couldn't stand it. How could she trust some guy she's never met before?

"Better keep your mouth closed as well," I said. "Else you'll be eating bugs."

She laughed and whipped that bandana off her head and tied it around her face like a bandit. "How's this?"

Soon as we were out of town she snuggled up real close and it was like I could feel her heartbeat through my jacket. The warmth of her was driving me crazy, but at first I took it real easy. I wasn't used to having a rider. We were traveling through rolling farmland, green tops coming up through soil that was covered with snow a week earlier. Before too long we were running alongside these rows upon rows of red pines, in lines as straight as soldiers on a parade ground. Vivian Forest, it's called. I remembered it had some great off-road biking trails and a big pond in the middle, where it was quiet. My buddy's dad used to take us fishing there. I kept thinking about her arms around my waist and that quiet pond in the middle of the forest.

When I turned off the gravel road and into the forest I could feel the back end of the bike wobble. Her hands dug into my chest. I slowed down and everything seemed to be okay for a while, just the two of us sliding through these red pines. Then I crested a rise and the trail dropped away below me. I couldn't see the sharp curve at the bottom. When I hit it I jerked the front wheel around, fighting for control. The back end slid over and I felt her fingers let go. She screamed and then I heard a sickening thud. I jumped off the bike and raced over.

She'd been thrown against one of those red pines. I could see blood coming from her head and running into the needles on the ground, almost the same color. She wasn't making a sound and I couldn't tell if she was breathing. What could I do? I didn't know shit about first aid and there was no one else around. I'd have to go for help, and the nearest hospital was miles away. I picked up the bike and turned the key. Nothing happened. Again. Again. Then the smell of gasoline—I'd flooded the carburetor. I waited a few minutes and tried kick-starting it. Nothing. A piece of shit, that's what it was. I kicked the bike a few times and then pushed it out to the road, where there was a downgrade. I ran alongside the bike until it started to sputter and then I hopped on.

I opened up the throttle and flew down the road. Without a passenger the bike cornered like a dream. Signs flashed by.

STARLIGHT MOTEL

PETRO-CANADA

HAPPY TIMES CAFÉ

BARRIE

HOSPITAL 2 KM

HOSPITAL

HOSPITAL EMERGENCY

I turned north and kept going. It's too late, I told myself. If she didn't die instantly, she must be dead by now. There's nothing I can do.

I kept going until I reached Sudbury. That night I got plastered and picked a fight in a bar. The police threw me in jail to sober up. I went kind of crazy after that, drinking, doing dope, robbing convenience stores. That's how I finally ended up in prison. I was living common-law with this chick named Kelly. We had a kid and I couldn't hold a job, so I started hitting the all-night Mini-Marts. Then one night this dumb-ass clerk wouldn't hand over the money and I beat him to a pulp. Something came over me; it was like I couldn't stop. Now I figure it was like you say. It was myself I was beating. And then tonight in that bar I saw Sita's ghost, or someone who could be her double. That girl Chuck grabbed.

Ritchie told his story staring out the kitchen window into the darkness beyond. When he finished he went on staring, conscious of the dripping tap and rain on the porch roof, the whirr and blast of warm air as the furnace came on, the lingering smell of the fish and chips they'd had for dinner. Nancy had sat quietly while he emptied himself out, and now he waited for her words of judgment.

She gathered up their empty coffee cups and carried them to the counter. "That's a lot of shit to carry all these years," she said. "Did you ever find out what happened to Sita?"

"I was too chickenshit. I stayed away from Toronto for months, wouldn't watch TV or listen to the radio or pick up a newspaper. I told myself somebody would have found her and taken her to the hospital. I put her out of my mind, and before long it was like it never happened. To me that clerk I beat up wasn't a person; he was just another fucked-up guy like me who probably deserved to die. Not once did I think about his family, or Sita's family, what they were going through. Until tonight, when Sita came back to tell me it's my turn to suffer."

Nancy had rinsed out their cups and now stood with the drying towel in her hand. "Sounds to me like you've suffered plenty."

Ritchie shook his head. There was one last thing he needed to say but the words were buried so deep he didn't know if he'd ever find them. He was scrabbling around in his mind, looking for them, when the words of the blond woman at the meeting came back to him: "If I can change, you can change." Suddenly the walls he'd built to hide the knowledge from himself fell away. "You know that girl they found out at Sitting Lady Falls?" he said. "I'm pretty sure that's my daughter."

Fifteen

Ritchie watched the door of Leicester House close behind the blond RCMP constable.

"Bitch," he muttered, turning away. She'd kept after him for an hour, like Crystal's death was his fault.

"She's just doing her job," Valerie said, her steely blue eyes meeting his. "I'd better do the same. I have to write up a report about Chuck. I'll take you to West Shore to make a statement about your daughter in an hour or so." She must have been up half the night but she didn't look it, every permed gray hair in its place and her face on, as his grandmother would have said. She went into the office with the Executive Director sign and closed the door.

Hard as nails, Valerie was, but fair. She spent a lot of time trying to get guys out of one kind of trouble or another. Last night it was his and Chuck's turn. She'd come down to the Esquimalt Police Station, listened to their stories, studied the results of their breathalyzer tests. Ritchie was clean, so she'd signed for him and sent him back in a cab. Chuck was way over, and it wasn't his first violation. He hadn't come back.

Ritchie stood alone in the hallway, wondering what to do with himself. He was too restless to sleep and Nancy, the one person he could talk to, had gone off shift at 7:00 AM. After he'd finished telling her about Sita, they'd sat at the kitchen table talking and smoking. Just before she left this morning, she'd picked up the phone and handed it to him, saying, "Might as well get it over with. Call your ex-wife." So he had. He told her about the picture in the newspaper. She said she'd book a flight.

Then Valerie had arrived and he'd had to go through the part about Crystal again, and then she'd phoned the RCMP, and he'd waited, and then the questioning. The RCMP bitch wasn't too bad at first, but it tore him up to talk about Crystal, and then when he mentioned the Castaway, she'd gone all cold, and the emptiness inside spread like a pool of black water.

Ritchie lifted his jacket from the row of pegs beside the door and shrugged it on, then reached for his runners.

Frenchy sidled into the hallway, stretching and yawning as though he'd just woken up. Ritchie knew better, though, he'd heard the soft murmur of the television from the living room.

"Hey Ritchie," he said, "where you goin', eh?"

Ritchie finished tying his laces. "Don't know. I gotta get out of here."

"Can I come along?"

"Suit yourself." Ritchie yanked open the door and clattered down the steps, pulling out his smokes as he went. At the street he paused to light up. Maple leaves littered the lawn and sidewalk, as they did every morning now, and would until the tree stood naked. Somebody should rake them up.

Frenchy eased the door shut and limped towards him, his left foot dragging through the leaves. He was a scrawny guy with bad teeth, but he also had a quiet dignity that Ritchie envied. Frenchy had ended up inside after a series of burglaries to support his crack habit. As he came near, Ritchie held out his pack of Du Mauriers.

Frenchy waved it away. "I quit smokin', crack, everyt'ing, except in the sweat lodge. It's been five days, two hours, and—"glancing at his watch—"eighteen minutes since my last one." His eyes dropped to the moccasins he'd made last week. "I was just listenin' to the news, eh? They're trying to make out like Chuck, y'know, like he killed them women."

Ritchie took another quick puff, then pinched out the flame and stuck the half-smoked cigarette back in the pack. It was still five days till payday. When he was younger he would have thrown it away, like the rest of his life. "They're crazy. Chuck didn't kill nobody." He glanced up and down the street, the low-rises full of losers, the decaying houses full of old people waiting to die. He thought of the forest out at the Head, where he could lose himself for hours, chopping wood.

Frenchy seemed to read his mind. "How about we go down to the

Gorge," he suggested. A few houses away a heavyset guy in a hoodie got out of an old Ford Escort parked across the street and stood as though waiting for them. As they approached, Ritchie could see it was the pimply guy with the dimple in his chin, Mitch, Trav, whatever his name was. He hadn't been in the Grind since the storm, more than a week ago now. Probably wondered why Elaine had never called about his application. The rage Ritchie had felt as he wadded up the piece of paper and threw it into the garbage bubbled up in him again.

"Hey Zitface, what the fuck you doing here?" he demanded.

The guy hunched his shoulders as though protecting himself from a blow. "I crashed last night with that friend of mine I told you about, the one that lives over there," he said, waving vaguely at a low-rise. "I was just leaving." He reached for the door handle on the driver's side, and then turned to face them again. He was wearing black pants looked like they'd been slept in, and Ritchie would bet he had on a white shirt under that hoodie, same condition. Seems like that's all the kid ever wore.

"No offense," the guy said, "but me and my buddy were hanging out at the Castaway last night. I saw you getting into that cop car. Everything all right?"

There was something about the kid he didn't trust, but Ritchie didn't have so many people in his life he could throw them away. "This here's Frenchy," he said finally. "We're going to the Gorge."

It wasn't exactly an invitation, but the kid fell in beside them, and he didn't object. For a block or so they walked in silence through the cool morning air. By the time they reached Gorge Road the Sunday traffic was picking up, without the weekday frenzy. A bus rumbled past, belching acrid smoke. After years out at the Head, Ritchie found the city noise and bustle overwhelming. Still, he spent a lot of time walking the streets. Walking away his anxiety about Crystal, yes, but also trying to connect to the world he'd known before things started going wrong.

This morning there was no walking away. The girl's face from the television hurried along beside him, the bleeding face from the past lay under every tree, Chuck's face swam in front, lecturing him about giving handouts. Past collided with present. It was Zitface, bumbling along behind now, who'd been asking for money that night they'd gone to the falls. He'd been dogging Ritchie ever since. What the fuck was going on?

Ritchie wheeled around, but before he could say anything, Frenchy asked, "You guys ever seen them falls at the bridge? Some Songhees brothers were telling me about them the other night. The falls and the legends about them."

"Can it for a minute, will you? I gotta get rid of this shithead." Ritchie stopped and the guy almost ran into him. "Hey Zitface," Ritchie said. "What is it with you? You following me or something? Get lost."

The guy's pudgy face wrinkled up like a kicked puppy's, but he didn't move.

"Ah, what's the problem, eh?" Frenchy asked. "He ain't hurtin' nobody."

Ritchie shook out his half-smoked cigarette and lit it. After a couple of puffs he turned on his heel and set off again, fast. When the butt burned his fingers he chucked it into the street. At the corner of Gorge and Tillicum he stopped and waited until he heard the uneven scuffle of moccasins behind him. Then he turned around.

Frenchy was hurrying to catch up, his limp more pronounced, his lumberjack shirt flapping open. Ritchie could see the black T-shirt underneath with its stylized silver bear, insignia of the native brotherhood at the Head. The kid plodded along beside him.

"Ah shit," he said.

Soon all three stood on the bridge where a couple weeks ago he'd stood with Chuck. The water was calm today, only a string of bubbles suggesting the rocks that lay hidden under the surface. Rocks that can snag you drag you down, like the booze did Chuck. Today he was sitting in a cell out at Wilkie. If he was lucky, he'd go back to the Head. If he wasn't, he'd be shipped off to Mountain.

"Chuck told me his dad used to scare the bejesus out of him, going through these rapids," he said.

Zitface dropped a rock into the current. "At least he had a dad."

Ritchie heard the bitterness, felt his shoulders sag under the weight of the kid's unspoken needs. He remembered what the kid had said that afternoon of the storm, about his mom telling him he didn't have a dad, just a sperm donor. Is that why he kept hanging around, hoping Ritchie would turn into the dad he never had? *Too bad, kid. I'm running on empty.*

"Them rocks, they were just doing their job, eh?" Frenchy said, gazing into the water swirling past. "This Songhees brother told me a story about how they came there. The way I heard it, in the old days a young girl named Camossung and her grandfather lived up the Gorge, where the old Craigflower School is. That was Songhees land, y' know, before the whites came and moved them onto reserves. Anyway, a flood came along and Camossung and her grandfather were starving. They wandered down this way, looking for food, but they couldn't find any, eh. Finally Camossung pleaded with Halys the Transformer. 'We're starvin', give us food.' So the god said, 'You like fish?' but no, she didn't like fish. 'You like cranberries?' but no, she didn't like cranberries. Halys was gettin' fed up, so he asked, 'What do you like then?' 'I like duck and herring and oysters,' Camossung said. So the god made plenty of them things along the Gorge. But then he punished her for bein' greedy, eh. He turned her and her grandfather into stone and put them into the river to protect the Gorge for the Songhees people. And that's what made the falls, this big submerged rock under the bridge. It drowned a few whites, but that didn't keep you guys from taking over, eh?" Frenchy grinned, exposing his crooked and rotting teeth.

Ritchie, who'd been drawn into the story despite himself, shook it off. "A little blasting powder and bam! It's gone," he said, cuffing Frenchy on the shoulder.

The kid leaned over the railing, staring into the depths below. "When the rock was blasted, what happened to Camossung?"

"She copped it," Ritchie said, the tide of sorrow sweeping in again. "That's what happens to young girls." Sita, Crystal. How many others?

Frenchy ignored him. "You know, that's what I asked the brother. I said, what happened to the spirits, did they rise into the air and float off? He said no, the power is still there, deep in the rock. If you dive into the rapids and hold on, Camossung will guide you. She learned her lesson, eh, so she can help others. I think about that sometimes, when I'm itchin' for a pipe. But I can't swim, so I stick to the sweats."

That's what he needed, Ritchie thought; something to hold on to, but what?

What a loser, Danutia thought as she turned away from Leicester House. She should have felt sorry for Taylor, a guy whose only child had been murdered, but something about him creeped her out. And it wasn't just the way he'd plucked the raisins off the face of one of those pumpkin scones he'd offered her, first the eyes, then the nose, then the mouth, leaving the scone itself uneaten, though that was bad enough. There was a hollowness to him, a lack of backbone, that made her want to shake him. His daughter had gone missing almost two months ago. Why hadn't he called them sooner? Or his ex-wife? Though in all fairness, she had to admit to herself as she climbed into her car, it wouldn't have helped Crystal. By then, she was already dead. Danutia had told him that, but it didn't seem to matter. He knew as well as she did that any delay made it harder to catch a killer.

She hadn't told him about Sunil Sharma. He would find out soon enough that Sunil had been questioned and released. She still couldn't believe Sunil had murdered the girl she'd thought of as the Sitting Lady. The girl now had a name, an identity. Crystal Angela Taylor, nicknamed Cat by her dad.

By the time Farrell had called last night, Sunil had been released, with instructions not to leave the island. Though he'd admitted going back to the bus stop without his cousin, he'd stuck to his story that the girl was no longer there. With no evidence to tie him to the crime scene, Farrell had been forced to let him go. Now she would send out her team to track his movements on Labor Day, trying to determine whether he was telling the truth or lying. This news had disturbed what little sleep Danutia might have had last night. She wanted the killer caught, but she didn't want Sunil to be the culprit, to be the cause of so much suffering.

Danutia radioed West Shore to let Farrell know that she was on her way. The duty constable asked her to hold. It was still early—early for a Sunday morning in this neighborhood, anyway, the inhabitants being the type to party late and sleep in. A couple of early-morning dog-walkers were out, that was all. A light flicking on drew her attention back to Leicester House. It was a large, rather ramshackle two-story affair with high basement windows, yellow siding, and brown trim. On the covered front porch, a tub of winter pansies shared space with several bicycles.

Taylor came out the door just as Danutia's radio crackled into life. The duty constable reported that Farrell was about to meet with the CO. She'd join Danutia at the coffee bar down the block from the West Shore detachment as soon as she could get there. "She says to order her a big breakfast and a 3-3." Danutia ended the call and pulled out.

The coffee bar was half-full of people reading the Sunday paper and talking in hushed morning-after tones. Danutia ordered three breakfast bagels with ham and scrambled eggs—two for Farrell and one for herself—and two coffees, then carried the laden tray to a corner where they wouldn't be overheard.

She had finished her bagel and was writing up the interview with Taylor when Farrell sank into the chair across from her. She'd changed out of the white Princess Leia dress into navy trousers and shirt, but Danutia doubted she'd slept: her hair was still coiled into buns over her ears, though the braids were threatening to unravel. Dark freckles stood out against a face white with fatigue.

Farrell emptied the three sugar packets and creamers into her coffee. "Guess everything's cold by now."

"You're welcome," Danutia said, and went back to her writing.

"Sorry. Thanks." Farrell attacked a bagel with knife and fork. "Too bad about losing Handy Dan last night. Tell me about Taylor while I eat. What've you got?"

"We have a name," she said. "Crystal Angela Taylor. Born September 3, 1979, in Toronto. On or about August 8, she wrote a letter to her father, Ritchie Taylor, from Temagami Lodge in Ontario, where she was working, in care of Corrections Regional Headquarters. Taylor received the letter on August 15. He had been incarcerated for fifteen years, the last eight of them at William Head. He hadn't seen Crystal since she was a toddler and hadn't been in contact with the mother for years. Crystal said she wanted to meet him, wherever he was. He wrote back immediately, telling her that he was being released on parole on September 3 and suggesting that they get together later in September, after he had settled into Leicester House. On August 30 he received a postcard from Thunder Bay, saying that she'd be arriving by Pacific Coach from Vancouver at 4:00 PM on September 3—"

"Her birthday, right?"

Danutia nodded. "She said that would be the best birthday present she'd ever had. Taylor arrived at Leicester House about 11:00 AM on the third, dumped his stuff, and parked himself at the bus station in case she came in earlier. He stayed until the last bus came in around 11:00 PM, and then raced back for curfew. She didn't show. He went back the next day, and the day after, and then he gave up. I checked the dates on the letter and postcard, and the Executive Director of Leicester House vouched for his release date. She'd picked him up out at the Head herself. By the time he got out, Crystal was already dead."

Farrell's fork paused in mid-air. "How did he expect to recognize her, did she send a photo?"

"I asked the same question. No, she wanted to surprise him. She said he didn't have to worry, she'd know him anywhere. Seems she'd found a photo of him in a locket he'd sent when she was little. The locket hasn't turned up, has it?"

"If it had, and their pictures were in it, we'd have ID-ed her a lot sooner." Farrell fished in her jacket pocket and brought out a folded sheet of paper, which she smoothed and passed over. "Sharma's niece drew this. It's way better than the sketch in the newspaper, isn't it?"

Danutia drew in a breath as Crystal Angela Taylor came to life on the page before her. A teenage girl sat on a boulder, thumb out for a ride. A polka-dot bandana covered the top of her head; straight dark hair and bangs framed her face; a girl with attitude—mischievous and defiant and vulnerable. No question that Taylor was her father: They had the same slender faces with high foreheads and high cheekbones, deep eye sockets, dark hair—Crystal's dyed from a lighter brown, according to the autopsy, presumably to heighten the similarity to the photo in the locket. Time had made some changes: Taylor's hair was receding now, with the beginnings of a bald spot, and his blue eyes were haunted, not bright and full of mischief like his daughter's.

"Crystal was right," Danutia said. "She would have known him anywhere, and he would have known her."

Farrell spread jam on half her remaining bagel. "Leanne showed me one she'd drawn on a napkin last night at the Castaway, but it wouldn't photocopy, so I asked her to draw it again. Took her about ten minutes, can you believe it? Besides leaving off the bandana—something most people would notice—the police artist got the eyes all wrong, she said. They made the girl look native, and she wasn't. Leanne wasn't sure of the eye color—she was too far away."

"Blue, like her dad's," Danutia said. "That's the one thing he remembered. Mind if I keep this?"

"Go ahead," said Farrell. "I've sent copies out with the uniforms, along with a photo of Sunil. What I need now is to find someone who saw them together."

Danutia refolded the sketch and tucked it in her handbag. It was so easy to focus on finding the killer, feeding off the adrenaline of the hunt and in the process forgetting the victim, all the victims. The sketch would remind her.

"What I can't understand," Farrell said, "is why nobody reported her missing."

Danutia shrugged. "That's what I asked Taylor, again and again. He says he figured she got cold feet, decided she didn't want a con for a dad. Then when the body was found at Sitting Lady Falls, he started worrying, he says, but he doesn't seem to have done much. If he was scared of getting involved with the police, he could have contacted the lodge where she was working. He did track the mother down, finally. She thought Crystal was still working up in Temagami with her boyfriend. They'd gone up there together early in August and the mother hadn't heard from her since. You'd think she would have been worried by that, but she and Crystal had had a fight over some jewelry Crystal had stolen from her. When the mother talked to the boyfriend, he said Crystal had left on August 28, taking most of his money with her. From the sound of it, she was no angel, our Crystal."

"Stole her mom's jewelry, did she? That may solve one mystery," Farrell said, pushing back her chair and picking up her coffee cup. "Refill?"

Danutia shook her head. "I'm already swimming in caffeine. What mystery?" It was too late; Farrell was already halfway to the counter. When she returned, Danutia repeated, "What mystery?"

"Just as I was leaving the detachment a fax came through from Vancouver on that pink purse you found. The purse had been emptied, but there was an inside zippered compartment with a hole in it. A ring had slipped down between the lining and the outer plastic. A big diamond surrounded by rubies, worn platinum band, size eight and a half. That would be about your size," Farrell said, glancing at Danutia's large hands, which she resisted shoving under the table. "Too big for the girl, and too expensive," Farrell went on. "Did you get contact information for the mother?"

"Taylor called her this morning. She's arranging a flight out and he will let us know when she's arriving."

"Good," Farrell said. "I'll pick her up at the airport. We'll need her to ID the body and the ring."

Chairs scraped as tables near them began to fill up and the noise level rose. Farrell inched her chair closer and leaned forward. Her face had regained some of its color, but the worry lines across her forehead and around her eyes had deepened. "My turn, I guess."

This is it, Danutia thought, feeling her own muscles tighten, the sick feeling in her stomach she'd so far kept at bay. The case against Sunil.

"What Taylor told you fits in with what we've pieced together," Farrell said. "The girl arrived at the bus station on Labor Day—a day earlier than expected. She bought new clothes to meet someone we now know to be her long-lost dad. She left her belongings in the bus station locker and took a bus out to Metchosin. Leanne says she was sketching the poplars at Lombard and William Head Road and saw the Taylor girl get off the bus. The girl didn't speak to Leanne or Sunil. His Honda was parked across the road. When Leanne returned to the car, Sunil suggested they should give her a ride. Leanne wanted to do some more sketching, so they agreed that he would drop her at Witty's Lagoon and meet her again in an hour."

"Not much time to pick up the girl and murder her," Danutia pointed out.

"True, but I don't think that's when it happened. Labor Day was hot and sunny and the park would have been full of people. Here's how I figure it. No one answering her description turned up at the prison that afternoon. Either visiting hours were over by the time he picked her up, or she'd decided to follow the original plan and meet Taylor downtown the next day. But she didn't have any money, so Sunil put her up somewhere and arranged to meet her later on. The beach at Witty's Lagoon is a nighttime hangout spot for young people. He parked at the beach, they had a few beers, and eventually they wandered over to the Sitting Lady. There they went skinny-dipping in that pool below the falls—there was mud and bits of vegetation on the inside of her clothes—and drank some more. Remember those beer bottle caps Sharma found? There were traces of the girl's nail polish on a couple. Sunil made a pass, she tried to run away, he followed her and strangled her."

"You suggested something like that when we searched the area, but do you have any evidence?"

Farrell drained her coffee cup. "I will," she said. "I located the bus driver and had him brought in this morning. Most of his passengers are regulars, he said, so he remembers strangers. I showed him Leanne's sketch and he recognized the girl, though he wasn't sure of the date. He dropped her off at the last stop on William Head Road at about 3:10 PM. He said she was asking how to get to the prison and pissed off that the bus didn't go any closer. He also saw a young woman with a sketchpad and a white Honda parked on the other side of the road."

"Did he see Sunil?" Danutia asked.

"No, he must have been in the car at that point," Farrell said. "You know what else they found? Fingerprints on the purse. But there's no match on file. I wish I'd fingerprinted Sunil before I turned him loose."

"You can't do that without charging him, and there's no evidence to warrant that," Danutia said.

"Look, whose side are you on, anyway? You know it happens all the time."

"With people who don't know any better, maybe. That doesn't make it right," Danutia said.

Farrell scraped back her chair and stood up. "I thought you wanted to catch this killer, but it seems you're more interested in protecting your pal's son. Well, here's another piece of news for you. Sharma's been suspended. A lot of evidence in this case has already gone through his lab. If he's been tampering with it, the two of them may end up sharing a cell."

Farrell stalked out. Danutia sat on in the noisy coffee bar, thinking of her friend with the wise words and sad eyes. If he had to choose between his son and his duty, which would it be?

A hand shook his shoulder and from far away a voice tight with anger called his name. Sunil half-opened his eyes and tried to get his bearings. He was lying face down on a hard futon couch with a striped Hudson's Bay blanket thrown over him. The floor was moving side to side. He thought he must be drunk or stoned but then he recognized, beyond the edge of the couch, the wooden planks of the houseboat. He groaned and tried to push himself up but he was like a beached whale; gravity sucked him down and the waves lulled him once more.

"Sunil! You must wake up! Why are you sleeping the day away? We have only one hour."

He pulled the blanket over his head and tried to squirm away. No use. Fingers sharp as an eagle's talons dug into his shoulder muscle. "No," he said. "Go away."

"Come," said the voice, which he now recognized as his brother's. "Papa-ji promised. If you aren't there in an hour, the police will issue a warrant for your arrest."

"Arrest? Me? What for?" Sleep fled as he sat bolt upright, running his fingers through his matted hair and patting at his wrinkled clothes. There were stains on his new kurta. He wondered how they'd got there, and then remembered asking his dad to pull over while he barfed. Slowly the night's events came back to him—the bright Diwali lights, the throbbing music of the Castaway Club, Leanne making a scene, the West Shore police station, his dad's distant face . . . That's why he was here instead of at home. Because he couldn't bear the way his dad had looked at him, the doubt in his eyes. Luckily he'd had the key to Roger's houseboat, entrusted to him when his friend went off to school in Montreal. He'd made his dad drop him off at the marina and collapsed on the couch, and now Rajit was saying something about his dad having him arrested.

"What did you say about Dad?" he asked. His tongue felt thick and he needed a piss but not here, with the houseboat rocking, what if he missed the tiny toilet . . . It was different at night, when you could piss off the side with no one the wiser.

"I said he promised you'd be at the West Shore detachment by five o'clock. That's an hour from now. You have to talk to the lawyer before then. He'll go with you."

"What lawyer? I didn't call a lawyer. Why do I need a lawyer?"

"You tell me. Anyway, it's somebody Dad knows; he's taking a float plane from Vancouver. Dad's picking him up in the Inner Harbor and bringing him here. So you'd better get cleaned up."

Sunil flinched as Rajit tossed a duffel bag towards him. It plopped at his feet like a giant black slug. He toed it gingerly. "There's no shower here. Why can't we go to our place?"

"Because it's crawling with reporters and camera crews. I had to sneak out through that broken fence at the back. Nandi picked me up a few blocks away."

Sunil chuckled. "We used to do that, remember, and sneak out after the folks were in bed?" He stripped, shivering in the unheated air, and wet a clean T-shirt from the bag to use as a washcloth. "You were going to see Nandi and didn't want your kid brother tagging along, but what could you do? You bought me soda pops and I sat on the beach drinking them while you and Nandi made out."

Rajit didn't laugh. "I should have walloped you in the head with a piece of driftwood," he said. "Then there wouldn't be all this trouble. All day Ajji is on her knees making puja, crying and pulling out her hair. Mama-ji is rushing around, doing this, doing that, making food nobody wants to eat. And Papa-ji, what do you think he has been doing while you lie here sleeping like a dog? He's calling this lawyer and that lawyer until he found someone willing to fly over on a Sunday to try to save your sorry ass."

Sunil couldn't bear to think of his family's distress, so he seized on this last detail. "Why Vancouver?" he asked, stepping into clean briefs. "He knows lots of lawyers on the island."

"Because this time, it's not just you in trouble. Because of you, Dad has been suspended. Can you think what that means?"

The thud of footsteps on the dock outside spared him the effort, and his brother's anger. As he hurriedly pulled on jeans and a turtleneck sweater, Rajit opened the door to the cries of seagulls, cold air tainted with rotting fish, and two large men who filled the tiny space.

"Mr. Grimes, my sons Rajit and Sunil," his dad said.

"Call me Ed," the man said, giving Rajit a quick handshake, then gripping the hand Sunil reluctantly held out. "Son, we have some talking to do, and quick."

Sunil wanted to retort that he had a father, thank you, but in the circumstances he wasn't so sure, so he kept his mouth shut.

The lawyer released Sunil's hand and consulted his watch, then turned back to the other two. "It's ten past four. I understand the West Shore RCMP detachment is about a ten-minute drive from here. That gives us about forty minutes. Why don't you two find a coffee bar somewhere and bring me a double shot espresso when you come back. What will you have, son?"

Sunil muttered, "Nothing for me."

"Fine then," Grimes said, and in another few minutes they were alone, Sunil sitting on the futon couch, now restored to its upright position, the lawyer across from him on a wooden kitchen chair he'd moved over from the table. He was bald with a fringe of gray hair and piercing blue eyes, like Patrick Stewart on *Star Trek*. Juries would trust his calm manner and smooth voice, his expensive but conservative clothes. He folded his arms over his chest, examining Sunil like he was some deadly virus.

"Okay, son," the lawyer said, "pretend I haven't heard anything about what happened. I want to hear what you have to say. Tell me the story. From the beginning."

So Sunil told him the same story he'd told his dad and the RCMP corporal in the Princess Leia costume: about driving Leanne around Metchosin, about sitting in the car while she sketched the poplars, about the bus arriving and the girl getting off, about feeling sorry for her when she stuck out her thumb, about Leanne not wanting to give her a ride, about their deal, about dropping Leanne at Witty's Lagoon and going back for the girl. "Except when I arrived, she wasn't there," he concluded.

The lawyer pulled at his ear. "You know, son, I believe every word you've said."

Sunil sighed and closed his eyes in relief.

"Except for that last bit," the lawyer added.

His eyes popped open again.

"Don't try to bullshit me, son. Someone saw that girl in your car. A jury won't like it if you're caught lying." He glanced at his watch. "We have thirty minutes. Let's have the truth this time."

So Sunil told him.

Sixteen

Danutia almost missed the call. She was filling the coffeepot with water. When she turned off the tap, she heard the message machine click on and Alyne say "Catch you later." Danutia snatched up the receiver and said hello.

"You are there! I didn't wake you, did I?" Alyne rushed on. "I have to leave in a minute to take Jonathan to school. I've just found out I'm presenting at a family therapy conference in Vancouver on the Remembrance Day weekend. I could pop over to Victoria on the Monday. It'll just be me. Can you book the time off?"

"I don't know," Danutia said, heading back to the kitchen, cordless phone in one hand and coffeepot in the other. "I'm in the middle of this case—"

"That's what you always say. I'm going to come anyway, even if we only manage lunch. How's your therapy going?"

Danutia cradled the phone under her right ear, leaving her hands free. The way this conversation was going, she would need her coffee. She wrestled a filter out of its packet and into the basket. "I cancelled my appointment this week."

There was a moment's silence during which she imagined her sister counting to ten. "Did you feel you weren't getting anywhere?" Alyne asked, her voice tinged with disapproval. "Or were you getting too close? And don't give me that business about being too busy. As I tell my clients, you're making a choice. At least own up to it."

Danutia took ground coffee out of the freezer and dumped four spoons into the basket, then two more. "Okay, here's why. All those stories I've been telling my therapist about being molested? I must have made them up."

"What makes you think that?"

"That article you sent on eye movements. You know, if your eyes go to the right, you're remembering. If they go to the left, you're lying. That's what the article says. I tried it out on myself. When I thought about Coach molesting me, my eyes went to the left." She punched the button on the coffeemaker and moved away from its sudden gurgle.

"That's you, always making things black and white. It's more complicated than that. If you read the piece again, you'll see it says that looking to the left means that the person is constructing a memory. That could mean lying. It could also mean piecing together fragments of memory to try to make sense of them. It could mean lots of things. The observer has to pay attention to the whole context, test out various possibilities. If you'd been lying all this time, your therapist would have figured that out."

"Are you sure?" Danutia asked.

"I'm sure. I'm a psychologist, remember? I deal with clients all the time. Anyway, I have to take Jonathan to school. See you Remembrance Day."

Turning over her sister's remarks, Danutia bundled into a warm jacket and high-top sheepskin slippers, bought in Winnipeg three years ago and now falling apart, and carried her coffee mug onto the balcony. Only her face and hands were exposed to the early morning chill. The sky had cleared, the temperature had fallen. A faint moon hung above dark streets stretching downwards to the strait, punctuated by streetlights and the flash of headlights.

Did she think in black and white? She remembered the shame that had washed over her, sitting outside Marie Wilson's house, when she'd concluded that she'd made the whole thing up, and then the relief that had quickly followed. Because if her coach hadn't molested her, she could let go of the guilt that had eaten away at her all these years. But if he had molested her, she must have been asking for it, right? Wait a minute; she'd never think that about a teenage girl abused by someone in a position of trust and authority. Why would she think it about herself? Was she equally judgmental about other people? She thought of her parents, how their grief over her brother's death had hardened into bitter anger at themselves, at each other, at the world. As her grief had hardened into anger against them. Is that why she'd felt so little sympathy for Ritchie Taylor yesterday—was she protecting herself lest his grief touch her own?

And what about Sharma and his family? After the first message about Sunil's arrest, Yasmin had left another saying that her son had been released from custody. Danutia hadn't answered either call. Perhaps she had unconsciously accepted Farrell's judgment that the boy was guilty. Her earlier qualms about Sharma's objectivity made it easy to assume he'd tampered with the evidence to protect his son. And so she'd avoided any contact. Yet what evidence was there for either conclusion? She should call them, see how the family were coping. Her hand reached for the phone.

She hesitated. Her first responsibility was to the law she had sworn to uphold. If she called Sharma, would she compromise the investigation? Finally she punched in numbers. Not Sharma's but her therapist's. Then she had work to do.

An hour later she stood behind two businessmen at the airport car rental agency. The file on Richard Hawkins was in her hand. When the men departed, she identified herself to the cheery agent and explained her business.

"I'm investigating a complaint your company filed against Richard Hawkins," she said. "According to the complaint, Hawkins rented an Oldsmobile Achieva on March 18. On April 8, he used the express check-in to drop off the keys without reporting damage to the vehicle's right front fender and headlight."

"You're in luck," the agent said, opening and closing drawers. "I handled that rental myself. The name's Jason, by the way, Jason Turnbull. It was all a big mistake, which didn't surprise me. He'd rented from us several times before, never any problem. I tried to tell the business office he'd be back and we could straighten everything out, but they wouldn't listen to me."

"The complaint was filed June 15. Apparently Hawkins hadn't returned the company's phone messages or responded to letters mailed to his Esquimalt address between April and June. How was the matter resolved?"

Turnbull fanned a stack of Special Offer flyers across the counter. "A month or so later I saw him coming out of Arrivals and waved. He said he didn't need a car that trip, a friend was picking him up, but then I explained about the Achieva. He hadn't even realized the car had been damaged—it was raining and still dark when he drove out that day. He figured somebody must have clipped it in the parking lot where he was staying. Since he'd been away, he obviously hadn't received our letters and phone calls. He was so apologetic, you wouldn't believe."

Whatever Turnbull's other virtues might be, he was no judge of character. From the photos of the Achieva, it was clear that Hawkins' story about the parking lot was a lie. If he'd pulled into a spot, another driver couldn't have hit the front headlight. If he'd backed in, he couldn't have missed seeing the damage the next time he drove the car. Nor was it likely that the accident had occurred on the quiet residential street where Hawkins lived: the right side of the car would have been against the curb. Danutia had spent enough time in Traffic early in her career to know that the driver of the Achieva must have hit something.

Frustrated by the agent's gullibility, Danutia asked, "And so the complaint was dropped on July 20? What about the Visa card? Hawkins claimed he had insurance coverage on his Visa card, but apparently the card belonged to somebody else. Why wasn't he charged with fraud?"

"Oh, that," Turnbull said. "He'd been out to dinner with a friend the night before and they'd somehow switched cards. He didn't realize it till he got to Toronto, and by then he'd forgotten that he'd used the card here. He wrote out a check for the whole amount, rental and repair, no problem. Soon as the check cleared, the company dropped the complaint."

Danutia refrained from pointing out that the Visa card would have been swiped when the car was rented, not when it was returned. If Turnbull had stopped to think, he would have caught Hawkins in two lies. Instead, he'd been blinded by his preconception of the man as a "good customer."

Hawkins had returned the car on Easter Monday, the day Crime

Stoppers received the tip about Marie Wilson. If it had been used to dispose of her body, it could still contain trace evidence. She had one more question. "We have reason to believe the Achieva may have been involved in another incident we're investigating. Could I have a look at it?"

"Hey, you're talking six months ago," Turnbull said. "That car's long gone to a used car lot somewhere. It would have been even without the damage. Nothing we rent is more than six months old. You want to know what happened to it, you'll have to check with the main office."

The phone rang and the clerk picked up. Danutia leafed through Hawkins's file. When the call ended, she said, "Can you tell me what Richard Hawkins look like?"

Turnbull didn't hesitate. "Oh, you know. Short, heavyset. Wears glasses."

"Beard? Mustache?'

"I'm not sure."

Danutia folded the photocopy of the Ontario driver's license that Hawkins had given the car rental agency on March 18 to hide the name and showed it to Turnbull. "Is this the person you know as Richard Hawkins?" she asked.

A confused look crossed Turnbull's face and his eyes moved down and to the left. "No, I don't think so."

Her suspicions confirmed, Danutia thanked Turnbull and walked away. The thumb-size print showed a broad-faced man with bushy eyebrows and a neat mustache, no glasses. It gave Hawkins' weight as 195 lbs, his height as 5' 10". To Danutia, those figures suggested a man of average build. To the agent, a skinny beanpole, Hawkins looked short and fat. His Hawkins wore glasses and was clean shaven. Like most people, Turnbull saw only what he expected to see. To fool them, Handy Dan wouldn't even need a costume.

Ritchie sat on the front porch of Leicester House smoking and waiting. His muscles ached to do something—rake leaves, replace the cracked stair board, anything—but he didn't want to get his jeans and shirt dirty, so he smoked instead, half a pack already, while a varied thrush turned over soggy maple leaves, hunting for worms. When he went to the Head he didn't know fuck-all about birds, but he'd had plenty of time to learn. He'd made a feeder once but he got tired of trying to keep the squirrels out of it, so then he just watched; mostly chickadees, juncos, robins. His favorite was the varied thrush, which was like a robin, only robins go around in bunches and the varied thrush is a loner. He liked its orange eye stripe and the black band across its chest, made it look like a bandit.

A ghost car pulled up out front—like everyone who'd been on the wrong side of the law, he could spot them a mile off. Nothing happened at first and he waited, his legs refusing to move. Then the front passenger door opened and Kelly got out, her black dress sliding up her legs. She was heavier than he remembered, or maybe that was the puffy coat, her eyes hidden behind sunglasses though there was no sun, just heavy gray cloud. The cop stayed in the car. He wished the cop would get out, make it all official. That would be easier. What was he supposed to say to this woman he'd loved so long ago, this woman whose little girl had died because she wanted to see her daddy?

About halfway to the porch Kelly stumbled. There was a crack in the sidewalk, under the leaves he should have raked. Or maybe she'd been drinking. Who could blame her? What else was there to do, flying through the darkness with no one to talk to, no one to notice the tears running down her cheeks, no one to hold her hand. She'd cut her hair and streaked it and it fit around her face like a helmet. He wondered if she still used that hairspray to hold it in place. He'd hated the feel of it but she said in her job—she was a manicurist then—she always had to look good.

She'd taken off her sunglasses and she didn't look so good now, her face puffy and her lipstick smeared. She stood there wobbling on black high heels, waiting for him, expecting him to do something, like she always had, even when he didn't know what to do. When she phoned last night he'd expected her to rage at him, tell him what a shit

1e was. All she did was sob, her voice so choked he could hardly make
)ut the words: "I can't do this by myself." Like a chump he'd said he'd
;o to the morgue with her.

Now she said, "Ritchie?" Her voice was uncertain, as though she
Jidn't recognize him, and maybe she didn't, it had been a long time
1go.

He stood up and brushed off his jeans, wishing he'd had some-
ching better to wear. When he reached her, he took her hand. This
time she slid into the back seat and he sat beside her, holding her
hand, while the words gushed out of her.

"I'm so tired, I didn't sleep a wink last night. I just missed that
direct flight to Victoria I told you I was taking. I was already at the
airport and I had to do something, I couldn't just go home and stare
at the walls all night, so when I heard there was a flight to Edmonton
with connections here I took it, I didn't register that the connecting flight didn't leave till this morning. Anyway, there I was in the
Edmonton airport at midnight, not a soul around after everyone else
got their baggage, nothing open, no coffee even, though that was just
as well, I didn't need anything to keep me awake. It was freezing, I
tell you, minus 25 the pilot said as we were coming in, and not much
warmer inside, and me with nothing on my legs." She ran a hand
down her skirt and rubbed her calf in its black pantyhose, for warmth
or comfort, he couldn't tell which, waiting for him to say something.

"Okay, maybe I should have worn pants and boots," she said, as
though defending herself from a comment he hadn't made. "But it
just didn't seem right."

He couldn't find the words he thought she wanted to hear and so
he just sat there, holding her hand. One nail was rough where she'd
broken or chewed it and her skin was cold, cold. Nothing would have
helped, he wanted to say, but that wouldn't help either. So they sat,
silently staring out the windows as around them the good people of
Victoria went about their everyday business.

The ghost car pulled up at the hospital and the cop turned around
in her seat. It was the redhead who'd been at the Castaway, her hair

pulled back in a bun now, not over her ears. "This is it," she said. "Are you ready?"

Kelly nodded but when the cop opened the back door, she didn't move. Tears brimmed in her eyes and the makeup that held her face together threatened to crack. Not now, he thought, don't say it now. But she did. She turned to him and said, "Who would want to kill my baby girl?"

He didn't want to think about it. He'd killed a girl by accident and beat a man to death and wanting didn't enter into it, it happened. That's the way it was for a lot of guys. That blond cop yesterday did tell him something, and now he told Kelly.

"Whoever it was," he said, "he didn't rape her." He didn't mention the other thing the cop had told him, that it wasn't the sicko who'd done in the two native women. No point in dragging that in, Kelly would only worry more.

"Is that supposed to make it better?" Kelly snapped, and climbed out, dabbing at her eyes with her fingertips.

He followed the two women through glass doors and down long corridors stinking with disinfectant. An old guy in a blue hospital gown shuffled past, IV stand in one hand and a pack of smokes in the other. Ritchie felt a sudden spurt of anger at him for throwing his life away, which must have shown, because the guy stared at him with watery blue eyes and said, "Up yours, mate," and hobbled on. And then he knew it was himself he was seeing in twenty years, thirty years.

Or tomorrow. He'd already thrown his life away, hadn't he? What was the point of hanging on?

The cop led the way through white double doors into a cold space heavy with the smell of disinfectant. He could feel Kelly dragging on his arm now, the click-clack of her heels slowing down, like a horse shying.

"It's all right," he whispered, but it wasn't, how could he say such a stupid thing, it would never be all right.

A guy in a white hospital coat came out of an office and the cop talked to him in a low voice. "This way," he said and they followed. The man said more and the cop did too but it was like he was walking underwater, the sound washed over him, only a few words bobbing to the surface: "sorry . . . bad condition . . . tattoo." He'd never gone in much for tattoos himself, not like a lot of the guys who were walking tattoo parlors, just the one on his chest.

They stopped in front of a stainless steel wall like a giant filing cabinet and the man pulled out a drawer. The cop said something else and the man turned back a sheet. He didn't look, how could he, he'd never seen her living since she was a baby and he didn't want to see her dead, but he caught a glimpse of dark hair as he turned away.

Beside him Kelly had buried her face in his shoulder but then the cop said, "I need you to take a look at this" and so she took a half-step forward.

"Three needles," she gasped, squeezing his hand real hard, "just like yours." And then he had to look, not at the shattered face thank god but at the fragments of skin stretched over the ribcage. And there they were, the three tailor's needles he'd had tattooed on his chest when she was born, one for each of them, the Taylors. His eyes were hard and dry but his hand reached up and rubbed his chest until his flesh burned.

Then the drawer slid back in and it was over.

A few minutes later they were standing beside the cop car and the cop was saying something about Crystal's effects. Some word, eh, effects. As though you could put the effects of Crystal's death into a box and mail to the right person.

"I understand she took some jewelry from you," the cop went on. "Was there a ring?"

Kelly nodded, gripping his hand so hard her nails bit into his palm. "A platinum band with four small diamonds."

It was the ring he'd given her, though they'd never made it to the justice of the peace. He was surprised she'd kept it, hadn't sold or pawned it herself years ago, or had it reset to something more her taste. She'd been disappointed at the time, had wanted a flashy engagement ring she could show off to her clients and girlfriends. He was putting together part-time work here and there, no way he could afford two rings, so he'd figured better the one that counted, the one that said till death do us part. But it didn't work like that, they'd parted anyway, and now death had brought them back together.

The cop frowned and Ritchie could tell the answer wasn't what she'd expected. "No, it's nothing like that," she said, taking out a card and handing it to Kelly. "When you've had a chance to recover a little, I'd like you to come to the station and give us a description of the missing pieces."

"It doesn't matter," Kelly said. "I don't want them back."

"But you do want us to find the killer, don't you? This information may help us with the investigation. So let's say this afternoon around three. A car will pick you up. I'll also get you to look at a sketch by an artist who thinks she saw your daughter the day she was murdered. If it's a good likeness, we'll release it to the media. Someone may recognize the clothes she was wearing. The press conference is scheduled for five. That will give you time to notify other members of the family, won't it?"

"Don't ask me to talk to reporters," Kelly said. "I couldn't do that."

"Don't worry, I'll make sure you are safely away before then, and we won't give out your names," the cop said, eyeing Ritchie like he'd be lynched if they did. "In the meantime, where can I take you?" She turned to open the back door of the car.

Kelly plucked at his sleeve. The face she held up to him was splotched and puffy, as though she'd taken a beating; her hazel eyes were dull with sorrow and defeat. He could feel a wrenching inside, like a rusty gate slowly opening.

"Nowhere," Ritchie said, for once knowing what to do. He took Kelly's hand, tucked her arm in his. "We need to be alone for a while."

Seventeen

The sky had clouded over and now a light rain fell as Ritchie trudged the few blocks to Kelly's motel, his mood as gray as the day. It was his day off and he had better things to do than play tour guide to his ex. He didn't know what he'd expected—that she'd do her business here and go home, he guessed. Instead she'd booked for a week, which he'd paid for, two hundred bucks, when her credit card was declined. "Guess I maxed it out for the flight," she'd said, explaining to the manager why she was here and fretting that the police might keep her longer. The manager had tut-tutted and thrown in another week if she needed it—what the hell, the motels along the Gorge were empty most of the winter. So who knew how long she'd be here, expecting him to hop every time she said jump.

The time they'd spent together yesterday, after the cop left, was all right, Ritchie had to admit. Hard to take, some of it, but all right. At first they'd circled each other like strange dogs, Ritchie pressing to hear all about Crystal, Kelly backing off.

"I don't know you anymore," she'd said. "I only know the man you used to be. Maybe you've changed, for better or worse."

"What is there to say? I've been in prison," he'd responded.

Kelly wasn't buying that. "Crystal died trying to find out what kind of man she had for a dad. So I figure I better find out for her. If I like what I hear, I'll tell you about her. If I don't, I'll keep her to myself."

He'd thought for a minute, and then said, "I'll tell you what kind of man I am. I'm a piece of shit. If I hadn't written back, Crystal would be alive and happy."

They were sitting in a dumpy little café having burgers and fries. Kelly had reached out and wiped ketchup from his cheek.

"The truth is," she said, "she might be alive, but she wouldn't be happy. Crystal hadn't been happy for a long time. Ever since she clued in to the fact that some kids had daddies who stayed around for more than three months. She tried calling a couple of my boyfriends

Daddy, then she stopped talking to them at all. It wasn't my fault you weren't around, but I was the one she blamed. By Grade Seven she was cussin' me out and threatening to run away to live with her real dad. Believe me, if I'd known how to find you, I'd have told her."

Ritchie's image of Crystal had shattered into a million pieces. In his fantasies she'd sometimes appeared as a sturdy blonde like her mom and sometimes as thin and dark like himself, but always she'd been laughing, surrounded by friends. Instead she'd become a sullen, angry, rebellious teenager. Why should that have surprised him? That's what he himself had been, for much the same reasons.

Sick with the pain of it, he'd pushed his plate away. "You want to know about me? Let's get out of here and I'll tell you. I'll start with a girl before your time, a girl named Sita."

So he'd told her, and now he regretted it. Last night she'd gone all quiet and patted his hand in an absentminded sort of way, said, "That was a long time ago." That was last night. Now, knowing her, she'd use what he'd done as a stick to beat him with whenever he got out of line. He'd have to put up with it for today, at least. He wanted to see the photos she'd brought. She wouldn't unpack them last night, said she was too tired. He wondered whether she'd kept any of him with the baby.

The flashing red Vacancy sign was the only moving thing at the Value Inn, twenty decaying rooms ranged around a central courtyard. Its chief attraction was the kitchenette. He'd bought her fifty bucks worth of groceries and carried them back for her.

"Come for breakfast whenever you get up," she'd said. "I'm still not much of a cook, but I can scramble eggs."

He was ready for something to eat. He crossed the courtyard, the grass greening up now that the rains had set in. There was a pot of winter pansies outside Number 17 and a note taped to the door, the ink already running.

> Its almost 2:00 pm Toronto time and Im starving. Try the
> Chinese place down the road. K

The Imperial Garden, she must mean. They'd passed the restau-
ant last night on their way to the grocery store. *So much for doing
jour own cooking.* He should have known. She'd always claimed she
was too tired to cook after working all day, so on her way home
she'd pick up burgers, pizza, fish and chips, Chinese. Nothing fancy.
Nothing to come home to. Maybe that's another reason he'd signed
up for chef's training, searching for that magic recipe for home,
family.

It was raining steadily now and he hurried along the wet sidewalk, the dampness seeping through his thrift store ball cap and
denim jacket. He was late, and Kelly was pissed off, and so was he.
So what's new?

The Imperial Garden was across the road, a brick shoebox with a
hand-lettered sign. The place looked dark but a sign in the window
said Open, so he crossed and went in. The walls were covered in
flocked red wallpaper, the light bulbs concealed within paper Chinese
lanterns. From the back came the sound of running water.

A cold breeze entered with him and Kelly looked up from her
newspaper. She'd fluffed her hair, and the pale light from the picture
window picked up the blond streaks. She'd traded the black dress for
a navy track suit and a polar fleece vest. She looked like an ordinary
woman, Ritchie thought, a woman who's gotten the hubby off to
work and the kids off to school, taking a little time for herself. Not
like a woman whose child has been murdered.

He ditched his wet jacket and pulled out the chair across from her,
the scrape of metal on tile loud in the empty room.

"Where've you been?" Kelly said, shoving the newspaper at him.

He ignored it. "What does it take to get some food around here?"

He could feel the fight brewing, like thunder rumbling before the
lightning hit. That was the way it had always been. Words sharp as
knives making a little cut here, a jab there, until the blood was flowing
like water. Like a distant echo, he could hear a man and woman going
at it in the kitchen, the man's scolding voice jabbering away in Chinese,
followed by a soft, high-pitched reply. A moment later a slight Asian

girl glided through the swing door carrying a tray laden with steam ing dishes. She should be in school, not slaving away in a dump like this. He caught Kelly's gaze, saw her jaw soften, tears rise, and his own irritation slipped away. *Life's too precious*, he wanted to tell the Chinese man. *Treat her gently. You never know when you may lose her.*

"You like to order?" the girl said, setting down shrimp fried rice a glutinous sweet and sour dish, limp vegetables swimming in soy sauce. The mingled odors reminded him of the worst meals he'd had in prison.

"I'll stick with tea," he said, pouring himself a thimbleful of weak green stuff.

Kelly fished the newspaper out from under the rice bowl and handed it over. "Take a look at the front page."

The paper was open to an inside page so he refolded it and there was his daughter on page one. He had to fight back the lump in his throat. The cop had shown them the sketch yesterday, the one showing her hitching a ride, but still it took his breath away.

"Read the caption," Kelly said, so he did.

West Shore RCMP released this drawing of the young girl whose body was found on Thanksgiving Day at Witty's Lagoon Regional Park in Metchosin. Leanne Perry was sketching the historic poplars on Lombard Drive when the girl, who has been identified as Crystal Angela Taylor, age seventeen, of Toronto, disembarked from a Number 54 bus about 3:10 PM on Labor Day, Monday, September 2. Perry and her cousin Sunil Sharma, who was with her, are the last people known to have seen the girl alive. Sharma is the son of RCMP Corporal Surinder Sharma of the Island Headquarters forensics unit. Anyone with information about this case is urged to call Crime Stoppers or West Shore RCMP.

The door of the Imperial Garden banged open and Ritchie looked up.

Zitface lumbered towards them, holding up a soggy newspaper. "Did you see this?" he asked from halfway across the room.

Ritchie refolded Kelly's paper and tucked it under her purse, as though that would do any good. "What the fuck are you doing here?"

"I went to the house but Frenchy said you'd gone to the motel, and then I saw the note and came here," the kid said, as though that explained anything. The dark hoodie he always wore was wet and mud-stained, and the sores on his face were worse than ever, raw and bleeding.

"You look like you been in a catfight and lost," Ritchie said.

"It's the stress," the kid said, his face getting redder. "My mom's cancer and all."

"You poor kid," Kelly said. "Is she going to be okay?"

Now he'd have to introduce them. "This is Kelly," he said, and stopped. What more could he say?

"I'm sorry about your loss," the kid mumbled, and Ritchie wondered how he knew, then figured Frenchy must have told him.

"Thank you," Kelly said. "And what's your name?"

"You don't want to know," he said, coloring again. "My friends call me Mitch."

"Well, Mitch, don't just stand there, have a seat," Kelly said, handing Ritchie the things from her chair.

"I'd better be going," the kid said. "I just wanted to tell Ritchie here that the cops came around last night, asking whether I'd seen your daughter or this guy—" he tapped the paper in his right hand— "and you know, I did. I live out there, see, at the top of that row of poplars, and I saw him in that white Honda and a girl with him, only I couldn't see her bandana and all and I didn't know it was your daughter until I saw that drawing."

White Honda. Something stirred in Ritchie's memory. On Labor Day he'd split wood and stacked it and imagined her turning up at the Head—she'd promised to surprise him, hadn't she?—watching every car that came and went. There'd been one that turned around without stopping. It was white, wasn't it? He wasn't sure about the make, but it could have been a Honda. Yes, it must have been.

"I saw him too," Ritchie said. "The bastard murdered my daughter."

At ten o'clock on Friday morning Danutia showed her ID at the gate of CFB Esquimalt and followed the blue lines on the road that would take her to the Naval and Military Museum. Earlier in the week she'd been tied up in court. On Thursday afternoon she'd picked up the threads of her investigation into Richard Hawkins.

None of his neighbors remembered having seen Hawkins for several weeks. The elderly woman next door gave her the name and number of the owner, a former neighbor who'd moved into a condo when his wife died. When Danutia reached him, the owner said that Hawkins had leased the house for two years in May 1995, explaining that he would be working on a project at the base and needed space to store materials. He'd been a model tenant, paying by post-dated checks and never complaining, so the landlord had had no occasion to speak to him since, or to go inside. Danutia wondered whether he'd be so content if he'd seen the mailbox plastered with logos from Detroit sports teams, but she didn't mention them. If her suspicions were justified, the mailbox would be the least of his worries. So far, she had no grounds for obtaining a search warrant.

A phone call to the base revealed that Hawkins had been hired as a consultant to the museum, which was undergoing a major expansion. The personnel officer didn't know his exact duties. Knowing she would have a better chance of picking up stray bits of information in person, Danutia declined to have her call transferred. Instead she'd asked for the museum's hours, determined to be there when it opened the next morning.

The blue lines ended at a rectangular parking lot lined on two sides by historic red brick buildings with wide verandahs and freshly painted gingerbread trim. A flag flew above them, cracking like a whip in the cold, blustery wind. Beyond lay the choppy waters of Esquimalt Harbor and in the distance, the Western Communities. Danutia parked and, tucking her notebook into her jacket pocket, went in search of the curator, Joseph Horowitz.

A signpost pointed to Museum Administration in Building 37. Horowitz wasn't in. Claire, his assistant, directed her to a nearby warehouse. On the second floor, a handful of women sorted through boxes while three men made miniature battle scenes. Danutia asked for the curator and a woman led her towards the back, where a man with thick, rimless glasses stood flicking through a rack of naval uniforms. She introduced herself and presented her ID.

"Sorry you had to come looking for me," Horowitz said. "Someone called wanting to borrow a uniform and so I popped over to see whether we could lend him one. He's out of luck, I'm afraid. We don't have a duplicate, and he's not about to walk out with the only one we have." He peered around. "I assume this isn't a social call. Perhaps we should go somewhere more private. Not the office, the walls are like tissue paper."

Leading her outside and across the parking lot, he unlocked the door of one of the other red brick buildings, ushered her into a room furnished with a huge oak dining table, and motioned her to take a chair. "These exhibits aren't finished yet," he said, "so no one will disturb us here. Now, what can I do for you?"

"We're trying to locate Richard Hawkins in connection with a car accident a few months ago," Danutia said. "His landlord referred me to you."

"Dick?" the man said. "I thought he'd settled with the rental company."

"There seems to have been more damage than was apparent at the time," Danutia said, staying as close to the truth as she could. "The company hasn't been able to contact him, and so I'm helping out." She put on her best Girl Guide smile.

Horowitz stared at her over the top of his thick glasses. "The taxpayers would be delighted to know their money is being spent so wisely," he said wryly. "As far as I know, Dick is back in Kingston. I have his contact information at the office. But if that was all you wanted, you would have called."

"I do have another question or two," Danutia said. "I understand that the museum—that's presumably you—hired Hawkins as a consultant. What is his job, exactly?"

"I'll show you," he said, leading her to another small room where a mannequin in a frogman suit stood rigid.

Even at a glance it was obvious to Danutia that, mustache and beard notwithstanding, the face behind the mask was female.

"Took a good bit of sawing to get her flat enough to fit, I'm told," Horowitz said, "though that was before my time. That's your standard department store job, no expression, not much range of movement, costs maybe four hundred bucks. Now take a look at this." He moved aside to reveal the figure behind him.

A weather-beaten helmsman of the Royal Navy leaned forward over the wheel of a sailing vessel, his brow furrowed, his eyes intent upon the horizon, his feet braced against a gale.

"That's amazing," Danutia said. "I can almost feel the ship pitch and hear the wind whistling through the rigging."

"Hawkins is a genius," Horowitz said. "Makes a big difference to how visitors respond, as you can imagine. Last year we got a government grant to expand our displays. At five thousand to fifteen thousand dollars each, we can't afford many of Hawkins's creations. So we have to decide where they'll have the most impact. When we think we have a room worked out, I give Hawkins a call and he flies out, we spend a week or two hashing things over, then he goes away to make the figures and sends them to us. This guy," he said, adjusting the hand position slightly, "got here before his ship was ready."

Danutia studied the helmsman's slightly crooked nose, heavy brow ridges, and pale blue eyes reddened by the wind. The eyes were so lifelike she felt her flesh crawl. With this level of craftsmanship, Hawkins, if indeed he was Handy Dan, would have had no trouble disguising his own identity. No wonder it had been so hard to get a fix on the man. Another thought occurred to her. "Where does he get his models?" she asked.

"Friends, neighbors, people he sees walking down the street. Men, anyway. He says it's harder to find women."

Danutia felt a tingling down her neck. Maybe her idea wasn't so wild after all. "Why, what's involved?"

"You know alginate, the stuff that's used to make casts? He covers the person's head, or whole body, or whatever he's modeling in that goop and wraps it in plaster bandages. When the alginate dries, he cuts the cast away and he has a perfect mold. I guess women don't like being wrapped up like mummies. He tried to get Claire, my assistant, to model for him, but she wouldn't do it, not even for a hundred bucks."

Making a mental note to speak to Claire, Danutia asked, "Can you tell me the exact dates Hawkins was in town?"

"No problem. Claire will have that information."

When Danutia turned for a parting look, the helmsman's pale blue eyes seemed knowing and slightly sinister. She hurried after Horowitz, who locked the door behind them. Dark clouds scudded across the sky and whitecaps raced to shore.

"Here's something that should interest you, being in law enforcement and all," the curator said as they crossed the parking lot. "This used to be the parade square. You know how it was made? Convict labor. Leveled it with fill, dumped cinders from the boilers and coal fires on top, and brought out the guys in the brig to pound away till it was smooth. Best parade square in the navy." He shook his head, and the sun glinted off his glasses. "That's what we need these days, more convict labor. Those guys out at Club Fed have it made."

"No need for fancy weight rooms then, eh?" Danutia said. As they entered Building 37, a phone rang and Claire called out, "Ottawa for you."

Horowitz shook hands briskly. "Excuse me," he said. "Just ask Claire for whatever you need."

Danutia made her way to the assistant's desk and asked for Hawkins's contact information in Kingston and the dates of his visits.

"That's easy," Claire said. "He's paid a per diem, so I'll just pull up his time sheets." She entered a few commands and then rattled off six sets of dates over the last eighteen months. As Danutia wrote them down, she realized with a sinking feeling that none of them coincided with the dates when the two Aboriginal women were murdered. She'd let her imagination get the best of her. Still, she couldn't quite let go of her gut feeling that Hawkins was not what he seemed.

"How have you found Hawkins to work with?" she asked Claire, keeping her voice and expression neutral.

"I'll be glad when the exhibits are finished," Claire said, leaning back as though ready for a gossip. "That man gives me the creeps."

Danutia slipped her notebook into her jacket pocket. "Why is that?"

"You know how some guys come on to you but inside alarm bells are going off? They act like studs, but they don't really like women. Well, Dick's that kind of guy. A girlfriend of mine used to call him the Detroit Dickhead, even though he was from Windsor."

Danutia felt her pulse quicken. That was Marie Wilson's name for the guy who was pestering her.

"Seems he was crazy about all the Detroit teams, even wore these goofy caps," Claire went on. "Pretty good, eh?" She picked up a pen and drew what seemed to be heavy T's on her notepad. "Marie and I used to have a lot of laughs about him. Only she's dead now."

Not T's, Danutia realized. Crosses. "Marie Wilson?"

"Yes, I guess you'd know about that, wouldn't you." She laid down the pen. "Marie worked at the base barbershop, and before I knew better, I'd sent the Dickhead to her for a haircut."

"Mr. Horowitz mentioned that Hawkins wanted you to model for him and you refused."

"Damn right I did. I'd already turned down a date or two, so you'd think he'd get the idea. Then one day he asked me to model, said I'd make a perfect CWAC radio operator, you know, the Canadian Women's Army Corps. When I said no way, he said too bad, I had that ball breaker look, just like the CWACs in the photos he'd seen. A few days later, I found one of his fake eyes in the desk drawer, staring up at me. He said it was just a joke, but it creeped me right out."

The remark was one any sexist might make. The eye seemed

more sinister. A violation of Claire's personal space. A warning that she was being watched? Marie too had spurned him. Had he been watching when she set off from the Castaway to the home she never reached?

Danutia kept her speculations to herself. "Did he ask Marie to model as well?"

"If he did, she never mentioned it," Claire said. "When he first came he was looking for a model for a new First Peoples exhibit somewhere. He made it clear that only a Coast Salish woman would do. I suggested he get in touch with the people up at the Royal BC Museum. They were organizing an exhibit of Esquimalt and Songhees landmarks around Victoria. Mind you, that was before I figured out what a creep he was. He never mentioned it again, so I don't know whether he did or not. If it was Coast Salish he wanted, he wouldn't have asked Marie. She was Metis. You could see the French and Anglo in her bone structure and blue eyes. But then, I don't know what other projects he might have been working on. I'm certainly not First Nations."

As Claire talked, Danutia considered the possibility that Hawkins had talked Esther Mike and Marie Wilson into modeling for him. For Esther, a hundred dollars would have been a lot of money. Marie might have needed money enough to agree even though she disliked the man. Had alginate been mentioned in the autopsy reports? She'd have to check. If not, the Detroit Tigers ball cap was her last hope. If she could link it to both Hawkins and Marie Wilson, she'd have solid grounds for searching his house. She'd have to put pressure on the lab for some results.

As soon as she was back at her desk she called Forensics. Carl the technician answered on the sixth ring.

"Any results from Vancouver on that Tigers ball cap?" she asked.

He blew up. "Look, we've got three major investigations going and with Sharma out, I'm it. We're getting a new guy sometime next week, but until then you'll have to do your own follow up."

"Okay, okay," Danutia said. "It's not my fault you're short-staffed."

Though in some obscure way she did feel responsible. Her call to the Vancouver lab was not much more productive.

"Monday for sure," the Vancouver tech said when she stressed the urgency of the case. "Sooner if I can get to it. I'm working all weekend as it is."

She hesitated before making a third call. Now that the girl had been identified, she didn't have any reason to get in touch with Paul McCasland. Then she tapped in his number anyway. She couldn't talk to Sharma directly without jeopardizing both the investigation and her career, but he had been suspended and his son was under suspicion of murder. She wanted to find out how the family was coping. Paul was Sharma's friend, he would know.

McCasland answered just as she was about to hang up. She could hear classical music playing in the background, something slow and melancholy. "What's happening with Sharma and his family?" she asked after they'd exchanged wary greetings.

"I was wondering if you'd get around to asking," McCasland said. "I offered to call you earlier in the week, but Sharma wouldn't hear of it. 'We must not interfere,' he said. 'We must let her find her own way.'"

"What the fuck am I supposed to do?" Danutia demanded, stung by the condescension. "This is Corporal Farrell's case, as she made quite clear. She doesn't want me second-guessing her decisions and messing up her investigation. Fair enough. What's your problem with that? I'm not a television PI hired to prove some poor slob innocent, I'm a cop bound by strict rules of procedure."

"You are also Sharma's friend, or at least I thought you were. Nobody's asking you to *do* anything. But you could let the family know you care. You could let Sharma know you believe in his integrity."

But did she, that was the question. Or did she believe him capable of tampering with the evidence to try to save his son? Why would she believe that? He was always scrupulous in his work, careful about the inferences he drew, slow to make judgments. Yes, but those cases didn't involve a family member. Would she feel herself less bound by rules if it were her sister suspected of murder? The very thought of her sister being treated like a criminal made her stomach knot with fear. You see things in black and white, Alyne had said. She'd admitted to her therapist that Alyne was right. Yet now she had to confront the possibility that if someone she loved were in danger, her certainties would crumble.

"I'll see what I can do," she said slowly.

Eighteen

Ritchie flipped back through the last album, its final pages forever empty. "Which birthday did you say this was?" he asked, pointing to a photo of Crystal on rollerblades. She was bending low, her arms poised to take off, her eyes and wide grin barely visible under her helmet.

"Twelfth," Kelly said. "I bought the skates and my folks chipped in for the helmet and knee pads. We got them wrist things too, but she wouldn't wear them, not even after she got a bad sprain."

Ritchie wished he'd been there to comfort her when she fell, but at twelve she might have already been too old for that, might have pushed him away. There weren't many photos afterwards, except for the ones of a sulky Crystal at her Grade Nine graduation. By then she was pushing everyone away, it seemed. He closed the album and handed it back to Kelly. An awkward silence fell, increasing the tension he'd been able to ignore as long as he kept his mind on the photos and the stories Kelly told about them. Every day after work he'd drop by, they'd make instant coffee and eat the day-olds he brought from the Grind, then they'd leaf through the pages, Kelly would cry, and they'd go out to eat.

Now it was over, and he didn't know what to do. He pushed himself off the bed and picked up his cigarettes from the worn Formica table.

Kelly looked up at him, dry-eyed. "Ritchie, I want to see where she died," she said.

"Jesus, it's like an oven in here." Ritchie strode to the motel room door and threw it open. "Why do you keep the heat cranked up so high?"

"Please don't change the subject," Kelly said from behind him, her voice roughened by time and booze but without the hard edge he remembered. There'd been no booze since she arrived—not while he was around, anyway. That had been his condition and she'd

218

agreed. Too easy to end up as Chuck had, back in the slammer. No sex either—that had been her condition. As though he could get it up, that dead thing curled between his legs. And no television news or newspapers while they were together. This time was for sharing Crystal's life, not her death. And now Kelly wanted to rip apart this fragile space they'd built.

"I want to see where Crystal died," she repeated.

"That's crazy. Why would you want to do a fuckin' thing like that?" He flicked his half-smoked cigarette onto the wet asphalt and watched the tip flare and sizzle out. The rain shower that had begun the minute he stepped out of the Grind had ended, and the freshly washed street glinted in the fading sun. He took in big gulps of the soft, moist air and felt it soothe his dry throat.

"Because—hell, I was never any good at this," Kelly said. He heard a rustle as she took a tissue and a snuffle as she blew her nose. "Come sit beside me. If you'll try to listen, I'll try to explain."

He wanted to get the hell out and never come back, but instead he found himself turning towards the bed, where she had propped herself against the fake wood headboard and drawn the comforter up to her chin. The red album lay at her feet. He picked it up and carried it to where the others were stacked on the dresser. The white baby album was on top, the one with the newborn Crystal on the cover, her eyes squeezed tight. There was a bruise on her forehead from the forceps. He'd worried about it, he remembered, worried whether she'd always have that scar. She'd been scarred all right, only it wasn't the forceps that did it. Gently he laid the red album over the white one, and then perched on the foot of the bed.

"That's better," Kelly said. She'd stopped bothering with makeup and her hair lay in loose curls around a face that looked tender to the touch.

"All the way here from Toronto I kept thinking about the highway running along thousands of feet below, a highway I couldn't see in the darkness," she said. "I kept thinking about Crystal's journey along that highway, wondering what had happened to her along the way.

Brad said they hitchhiked up to Temagami, and I figure that was safe enough, he's a big guy. He said she left the same time as a guy from Thunder Bay that was staying there, so maybe she got a ride with him partway, and maybe he didn't take advantage. Maybe he even gave her bus money to get here, who knows. Brad says she took some money from his wallet, but it wouldn't have been enough. That part of her journey will always be dark, like that highway I was flying over.

"It was dark when I left Edmonton Monday morning, and still dark when I arrived in Vancouver. But by the time I'd changed onto the dinky little plane that flies to Victoria, the sun was coming up, making a path over the water. That's when I thought, now I can see the road Crystal took, and I want to follow it to the end."

Kelly threw back the comforter and swung her feet around. As she pulled on her runners, she said, "I've done my part. I've told you about Crystal's life. Now it's your turn. She came here because of you, and she was killed out there near that prison, trying to find you. I want you to show me where she died."

Ritchie felt like he'd been punched in the stomach. "You think I know how to find the place, even if I wanted to? We didn't exactly get day releases to picnic at the local parks."

Kelly looked up from the shoe she was tying. "That friend of yours, the one with the horrible acne, he lives out there, he said. I bet he could take us. You could ask him."

"He's no friend of mine," Ritchie said, reaching for his jacket, "just some punk that keeps following me around, who knows why. You want to go, you ask him."

"He's lookin' for a daddy," Kelly said. "Anybody can see that. Just like Crystal was." She planted herself in front of the motel room door. "I want to see where she died. And you need to. Not just for Crystal, but for that other girl who died, Sita. Maybe she was already dead, or would have been by the time you got back with an ambulance. You'll never know. What you do know is that you didn't go back for her because you couldn't face what you'd done. Well, here's your chance to face what's happened. It won't be easy. But how easy do you think it's been for me to look at these photos and tell you how my baby made me laugh and how she made me so mad I smacked her one, and all the time knowing I'll never see her again?"

Ritchie stared out the room's one small window. It had fogged over and there wasn't much to see outside except the encroaching darkness and the blinking Vacancy sign. He thought about the twelve-step programs he'd sat through over the years, resisting the idea that he could somehow make amends. How can you give back a person's life? You can't. But maybe, like other debts, you could pay forward what you can't pay back. When he was young, he'd been a coward. That didn't mean he had to be a coward all his life.

"The kid dropped off his resume at the Grind," he said. "Maybe I can find his number."

This time Danutia spotted the number beside the rutted driveway on the first try. Wood smoke curled from the chimney and scented the air, but no barking dog raced out of the trailer when she parked. Maybe no one was at home. No big deal. She could hang the gift bag on the door handle.

The Plymouth Fury still sat where Danutia had seen it last, rust beginning to show around the dangling tail light. On her previous visit, she'd been investigating a tip to Crime Stoppers that put Nathan Barnes's car in the area where Marie Wilson's body had been dumped. She'd checked out Nathan's alibi and eliminated him as a possible suspect. Since then, she had learned about Richard Hawkins and the accident to his rented white Oldsmobile Achieva.

Careful not to touch anything, she inspected the damaged rear fender. Flecks of white paint clung to the crease where it had been clipped by another car. Though the Achieva had been scrapped, the traces of paint could tie Hawkins to the vicinity on the Easter weekend. Her excitement mounting, she retrieved the happy face gift bag from her car and strode towards the mobile home.

Lights were on inside and as she knocked, she could hear the mechanical laughter of a sound track. She wouldn't have thought they'd get much reception out here, but then she remembered the satellite dish on the roof. Finally the door opened, releasing a wave of heat and the smell of burnt toast. Nathan's pregnant young girlfriend stood there, toddler on her hip, his face covered with jam and his fingers clutching his last morsel of bread.

"You want Nathan, he's out with the dog," she said.

"I have something for Phoenix," Danutia said. The youngest in her family, Danutia didn't have much experience with small children. She shoved the bright yellow bag towards the boy. "This is for you."

Face puckering, the boy grabbed his mother's loose smock. His bread fell to the floor. He hadn't howled yet, which Danutia took as a good sign.

"Come in then." The young woman turned back into the room, leaving Danutia to close the door. She slipped the tiny Tigers cap out of its bag and held it where he could see it, then put it on his head. "Look, it's just your size."

The toddler looked dubious at first, then, crowing with joy, he grabbed the cap off his head and stuffed it in his mouth.

Footsteps clattered on the stairs outside and the door banged open, admitting Nathan Barnes and a wet, smelly bundle of brown fur that sniffed at Danutia's hand before curling up under the kitchen table.

Giving her hand a quick swipe on her pant leg, Danutia nodded towards the cap. "There's no telling when Phoenix would get the other one back, so I brought him a substitute. While I'm here, I'd like to ask a few more questions about the Plymouth."

The young man didn't respond, so she plunged ahead. "It looks like it's been in an accident. What happened?"

"It was night time," Nathan said. "I saw a deer's eyes shining on the side of the road and slowed down. This guy behind me was going too fast. He pulled around me but didn't clear my fender. Bam and he was gone. Almost knocked my car off the road."

"He didn't stop?"

"Nope."

"When did this happen?"

"I was coming back from that party I told you about. It was Easter Sunday, must have been midnight, one o'clock, something like that."

"Were you alone?"

"No." He glanced over at the pregnant woman, who was picking up scattered toys and pretending not to listen. "Annie was with me."

"Ah yes, Annie." The former girlfriend who'd reported his license plate number to Crime Stoppers. Danutia had threatened to arrest her for obstruction of justice. Yet without her mischief-making, vital evidence might have been lost forever. Maybe Sharma was right, and she should learn to take things as they unfold, without judgment. "Did you report the accident?"

Phoenix had discarded the cap and stood tugging at Nathan's jeans. The young man bent to pick him up. "Nope."

"Why is that?"

"The insurance had expired."

"And that's why it's still sitting there?"

"That's right."

"Then you won't mind if I have it towed," she said.

He didn't howl, and Danutia was glad of it.

Danutia radioed in for a tow truck. No telling how long it would take Forensics to get to it. Short-staffed as always, the unit was now without Sharma's services as well. The best Danutia could hope for was an eventual match between the white flecks on the fender and the factory paint used for the 1996 Oldsmobile Achieva. Still, if the paint did match, it would be one small step towards building a case against Richard Hawkins. She headed back towards Victoria along Rocky Point Road, pleased with her morning's work.

Except for the nagging voice reminding her she'd done nothing about Sunil.

Paul McCasland, who had a buddy at West Shore, was keeping her posted about developments in the case, such as they were. Officers who'd canvassed the Metchosin area on Sunday with Leanne's sketch in hand had turned up a witness who reported seeing the girl getting into Sunil's car. Accompanied by a lawyer, Sunil had gone to

Farrell on Sunday afternoon and changed his story. He had dropped
Leanne at Witty's Lagoon to do some sketching at about 4:00 PM, he
said. Figuring the girl might be hungry, he had then stopped at the
Crossroads Café for takeout burgers, fries, and a six-pack of beer. He
hadn't noticed the time, but it must have been about half an hour
later when he reached the bus stop. The girl was stretched out on the
big boulder by the mailboxes, sunning herself. She'd quickly devoured
her share of the food, not saying much. She was obviously underage,
so he hadn't offered her a beer.

When she finished eating, Sunil had offered to take her wherever she was going. She refused and he left. He'd arranged to pick up
Leanne at five thirty, so he had about an hour to kill. He'd found a
deserted strip of beach where he had a couple of beers and a nap. His
cousin was waiting at the Witty's Lagoon Information Centre when
he arrived about five forty-five. He hadn't been down to Sitting Lady
Falls, had no idea where it was. He hadn't seen the girl again. She'd
never mentioned her name or her destination. He hadn't told the
truth at first because he didn't want to get into trouble, his dad being
RCMP and all. He'd readily agreed to surrender his car for inspection
and to have his fingerprints taken for purposes of elimination.

There had been some corroboration of his story. A server at the
Crossroads had identified Sunil's photo—though she couldn't say
exactly when he'd been in. Then later in the week Paul had phoned
again. A report had come back from the Vancouver lab—Sunil's fingerprints matched ones on the pink plastic purse.

When she'd heard about the fingerprints, Danutia had been
reminded of Sharma's odd behavior when she'd asked about the
purse. At the time, she'd put his delays down to overwork and the
echoes of his sister's death. Perhaps the truth was that he'd been covering up evidence that incriminated his son. She hadn't voiced her
doubts to Paul.

"They picked up Sunil and questioned him again," Paul had
told her last night. "He said he didn't remember handling the girl's
purse." Maybe it had been lying on the boulder and he'd moved it to

sit down. He hadn't looked inside, knew nothing about a ring. He didn't remember exactly where the beach was where he'd napped. He didn't remember seeing anyone else while he was there. Why hadn't she accepted his offer of a ride? He didn't know, he guessed she didn't like his looks.

"Farrell didn't have enough to hold him, so he's been released pending results of the vehicle inspection," Paul had said.

Last night, Danutia hadn't known what she should think or do.

Now, seeing the sign for Lombard Drive fly past, she braked and consulted her map. As the name suggested, this was the avenue of poplars Leanne had sketched; it connected the road she was on with William Head Road. Directly below her, then, was the bus stop where Sunil had allegedly picked up Crystal. Turning the car around, she stopped at the intersection to take in the lay of the land.

There were no cars in sight. It was mid-morning on a gray November Sunday, with little to draw inhabitants from their houses, and less to attract the outdoor types who flocked to the area on sunny summer days. Through the tall spires of poplars, bare now except for a few yellow leaves, she could make out scattered buildings, green fields of winter pasture, and the road below, running south to William Head Institution and north to the Crossroads.

She set off down Lombard Drive, which soon narrowed to one lane with occasional pullouts. When she reached the bottom she turned left and parked on the shoulder. From the accounts she'd heard, this must be close to the spot where Sunil had waited while Leanne sketched. Gazing up the hill at the leafless poplars bending in the wind, she could almost imagine how they would have appeared in their late-summer glory. She zipped her jacket against the chill wind and crossed the road for a closer look.

Three feet or so beyond a set of rural mailboxes was the flat boulder from Leanne's sketch. A blackberry thicket ran along the fence behind it, the last berries shriveled, the leaves blackened from frost. In early September the berries would have been plump and juicy, a tart sweetness on the tongue. A good place to wait for a ride.

She returned to her car and checked her watch: 11:53. She would time the drive from here to Witty's Lagoon and back, not forgetting to stop for takeout burgers and fries. It was almost lunchtime anyway, and she could save the leftovers for dinner. Afterwards she'd scour the countryside for the secluded beach Sunil had mentioned. She could do at least that much.

As she pulled out, she saw a city bus approaching from the north. Given the low levels of service in rural areas, chances were good that this would be the driver who had brought Crystal here. Danutia felt a powerful impulse to stop him and question him. Perhaps there were other vehicles, cyclists, who knows what, that Farrell, in her zeal to implicate Sunil, had failed to ask about. Farrell wouldn't welcome her interference, but the universe had put the bus in her way, so why should she hesitate? As the bus slowed, she jumped out of her car and ran back across the road, waving.

The bus crunched over the gravel shoulder and rolled to a stop near the mailboxes. The door swung open and the driver shouted, "Car trouble?"

"Nothing like that," Danutia said. "I'm RCMP and I'd like to ask you a few questions."

"No need to act the lady in distress, then," he said. "I would have stopped anyway. Come on up so I can close the door. You're letting the cold air in."

"We'll be more private in my car," Danutia said.

"I reckon this is about that girl. My only passenger's George here and he rides with me every day. He knows all about it. That right, George?" he said over his shoulder.

A cackle came from somewhere behind the fogged windows. "You better believe it."

"Better make it quick," the driver said, motioning Danutia up the stairwell. "I only got three minutes." Bill Poteet, his name tag said. He was balding and gray, like the uniform he wore, and his stomach drooped over his belt.

Danutia slid into the seat behind him. Across the aisle sat an elderly man gripping a white cane. George, she presumed. He was enveloped in a black duffle coat, with a black Greek fisherman's cap pulled low to his ears, so that little of his face was visible except for his bulbous nose; even so, she had the sense he was following her exchanges with the driver with rapt attention.

She dug a pencil and notebook out of her shoulder bag, and then flipped a few pages as though hunting for her notes on the case. "First I'd like to confirm the times the girl boarded and left the bus," she said.

"No doubt about that." Poteet unscrewed a Thermos and took a swallow. "The Number 54 leaves the CanWest Mall at 3:20, arrives here at 3:52, and leaves again at 3:55."

"And this is the girl, dressed as you remember her?" Danutia said, showing him her copy of Leanne's sketch: Crystal in jeans and a halter top, with a bandana over her hair. Lucky she had kept it with her.

"That's her all right," Poteet said, putting away his flask and taking out what seemed to be a log book.

"Did you notice any other items in her possession," Danutia asked, "such as jewelry or a backpack?"

Poteet looked up from his record keeping. "She took her transfer out of a little pink handbag. That's all."

"You forgot the chain!" George wheezed, turning his milky blue eyes towards Danutia. "She had a chain with something on it."

"I didn't see anything like that, and anyway, how would you know?" Poteet said. "She was sitting behind you. Not that you could see anyway."

George rubbed an ear with a liver-spotted hand. "I may be blind, but I can hear, can't I? Though the hearing seems to be going, like everything else. Anyway, she kept fiddling with the chain, running some doodad back and forth. A cross, maybe. You know why Bill here didn't notice? He was too busy staring at her boobs." George guffawed, a phlegmy rattle. The white cane beat a soft tattoo against the floorboard. "No bra, you said, just little titties like lollipops under a pink napkin."

"A little young for you, I'd have thought," Danutia said to Poteet, then wished she hadn't. She didn't want him to clam up on her.

Poteet shoved his logbook into its compartment and cranked open the door. "I'm going out to clean the mirrors. George here can answer your questions."

"Bill doesn't like my little jokes, do you Bill," George said when he finally caught his breath.

Neither did Danutia, but this was new information, and it might be important. Taylor had mentioned sending his daughter a locket. If that's what Crystal had been nervously playing with on the bus, she would likely have still been wearing it that evening. The killer could have taken it, either because it was valuable or because it held photos that would identify him or his victim. It was also possible that the dogs and the forensics search had missed it. Who knows what Penny Pinscher had smelled under the earth at the old bridge site, before the rainstorm closed the dig. She would stop by the Witty's Lagoon Information Centre and ask whether anything had turned up.

"You seem to have an excellent memory, George," she said. "Let me get your name and address, then you can tell me everything you remember about the girl."

Danutia made hurried notes as George recounted not what he had observed—he would be no help there—but what he had heard, smelled, intuited. He said that when the girl got on in Langford, she stumbled a bit, like she wasn't comfortable in her shoes. That would be the pink high-heeled sandals. She asked whether the bus went to William Head; George thought she sounded tired and nervous. When Bill said yes, she took that seat—here George half-turned and gestured behind him. She must have been leaning forward most of the way, because he could smell cheap rosewater soap and hear that chain sawing back and forth. She didn't say anything till Bill announced, "Last stop on William Head. You getting off here, Miss?" Then she stepped forward, her jeans brushing against his seat. On the second stair she stopped and asked, "Where's the prison?" Bill said coupla miles up the road. "You said you went to William Head." "Sorry Miss, I must have misunderstood you.

I thought you asked if I went up William Head Road. This is William Head Road." "So what am I supposed to do?" "I don't know, Miss. I guess you could walk." He mimicked the two voices, Bill's wearily polite, the girl's puzzled, then petulant.

"She stamped her feet at that, I can tell you," George went on, "saying that would take forever and she didn't have much time. Then she asked, 'When's the next bus?' and Bill said, 'About three hours.' This isn't the city, you know, buses going every which way all the time. Four a day, if we're lucky, that's what we get out here. That's when she let loose with a few fine words that would have got her mouth washed out with soap in my day, I can tell you."

He leaned towards Danutia, his eyebrows raised and his lips pursed with the excitement of what he was about to say. "Old Bill must have been feeling sorry for her, though, 'cause he said, 'Look, there's a car across the road, maybe they'll give you a ride.' Now you know who that was, dontcha? That feller that killed her, that's who."

Danutia resisted the impulse to defend Sunil. "Did she say anything in response to Mr. Poteet's suggestion?"

George huffed a little, and then tried again. "She said her mama told her never to take rides from strangers unless they were white, rich, and handsome, and a Honda didn't qualify. Bill tells me the guy's a Paki and ugly as sin to boot. I'da liked to heard what she said to him, I tell you. 'Course, maybe that's why he killed her."

People killed for less reason, Danutia had to admit. She remembered her initial uneasiness about Sunil, her sense that his charm covered a less easy-going temperament. His story was that he'd offered the girl a ride and she'd refused, though he insisted he didn't know why. What if she'd taunted him about his looks or his skin color? Would he have forced her into the car, held her captive somewhere until he could return later that night? But in that case, why would he have taken her to Sitting Lady Falls to kill her? It didn't make sense. Someone else must have picked her up.

"Were you aware of any other vehicles on the road, cyclists, horseback riders, anything like that?" she asked.

George shook his head. "Nothing and no one."

Danutia thought back to her conversation with Farrell. The corporal hadn't mentioned other passengers; if there'd been any, surely they would have been interviewed. But then, no one had interviewed George. She'd better check. "From what I understood Mr. Poteet to say, you were the only other passenger on the bus. Is that right?"

"As usual, Bill's got that wrong," George said. "He must have forgot about Trav. He was asleep in the back. He hasn't been riding with us for a while, but during the summer, he took the bus back and forth to the Crossroads most days. He was a busboy there, went to work early in the morning, before I got on, and came back on this afternoon run, so tuckered out he snored. Stank to high heaven, too. He was heavy on his feet, so I reckon he carries some extra pounds, and Bill said his face was all broke out in pimples."

Trav. The name nagged at her, then clicked into focus. The kid who'd dropped the tray of glasses when she'd identified herself as police. She'd seen him again at the Castaway the night of the Halloween theme party. Crystal's dad was there too. Was that a coincidence, or did they know each other? Here was another possible suspect, and she wanted to talk to him. "Does he live around here?" she asked.

"Top of the hill somewhere," George said. "Bill always had to go back and wake him up when we stopped."

"Thanks, George, you've been a big help," she said, reaching for her card. "If you think of anything else—I guess my card wouldn't do you much good, though, would it?"

"Just tell me the number. I'll remember it," he said, his sightless eyes fixed on her. So she did.

Then she made her way to the passenger door and climbed down, sucking in her breath when the icy wind hit her. Poteet came around the front of the bus, cloth in hand, and began wiping the headlamp.

Danutia considered how to proceed. She'd offended Poteet. How could she get him to open up? She recalled the article on eye movements Alyne had sent, with its suggestions about "matching" the client's language and behavior to establish rapport. Maybe she should give the method another try, see if she could tap into Poteet's memories of Labor Day.

"Mud's splashed all over this door," she said. "You got another cloth?"

He looked surprised but pulled an extra out of his back pocket and handed it over. She went to work. "Not much traffic out here," she said. "Is it always like this?"

He'd finished the headlamp and moved onto the passenger mirror. "Pretty much."

"So you would have noticed if there'd been any other vehicles around on Labor Day," she said, still scrubbing.

He paused and glanced up and to the right: visual memory clicking in. "That's right," he said. "Just me and the white Honda."

She too paused, copying his body language. "So it seemed natural to suggest they might give her a ride."

"Yeah, I thought the car belonged to the gal who was drawing the poplars. Then the Paki got out."

Danutia let the comment go. Revealing bias was a lawyer's job. Her job was to see the right person brought to trial. "Did he talk to the girl?"

Poteet frowned and shook his head. "Not that I saw." The hand holding the cloth dropped towards his back pocket. "I'd better be heading out."

"Just one more thing," Danutia said, resuming her cleaning. "When you stopped at the top of the road to let off your passenger, was the car still there?"

"I didn't really notice," he said, changing his mind and taking another swipe at the mirror. "I was running late by then, so I just pulled in long enough for Trav to hop off."

There it was, the name she was waiting for. She tried to keep the excitement out of her voice. "You didn't have to wake him up?" she asked.

"Naah, for once. The commotion the girl made must have waked him up."

She'd heard enough. She handed back her cleaning cloth. "Do you know where Trav lives?" she asked.

"Sure, there are only two places up there. He and his mom live in that fire hazard on the right. Want me to drop you off? I gotta split. I'm two minutes overdue."

"I'll take my car. Thanks anyway," she said, but by then he'd already climbed aboard. She stepped back as the idling engine engaged and the bus began to move.

A few minutes later she stood on a porch stinking of kitty litter and the garbage spilling out of black plastic bags. While she waited for an answer to her knock, she poked among the broken furniture and cardboard boxes of empty bottles. Vodka bottles, presumably for Mom's Harvey Wallbangers, and beer bottles. The beer bottles were the same brand as the bottle caps Sharma had recovered from the bridge site; they were also the same brand Sunil bought at the Crossroads the afternoon of Crystal's death.

She'd knocked a third time and was turning away when she heard a chain rattle and the door open behind her. Trav's mom peered out through half-shut eyes, clutching a stained terry cloth robe around her. Seeing her in the daylight, Danutia wondered why the woman had reminded her of Cher. Without makeup her eyes seemed small and set too close together, her cheeks sunken. She was tall and big-boned, as though she'd been built to carry more weight than she'd ever allowed herself. She obviously preferred a liquid diet.

"I recognize you, you're RCMP," she said, yawning widely. "You here about my jewelry?"

"I have some questions to ask," Danutia said, glancing past the woman. Pop music played softly from somewhere, but there were no sounds of movement from the other rooms.

"You'll have to excuse the mess," the woman said, holding her bent left arm away from her body like a chicken's wing. "My arm's still swole up from my operation and I haven't been able to do much. Keeps me awake at night something terrible if I don't take my pain pills, and then I can't wake up." She retreated to her nest, a recliner chair covered with a tiger-striped fleece blanket and surrounded by overflowing ash trays, dirty dishes, and discarded clothing. A scrawny calico cat jumped up into her lap and began clawing the robe.

Danutia cleared a space on the sofa. "Tell me about the missing jewelry," she said.

"First I thought both my rings was gone," the woman said, "but then coupla days ago this one turned up in my lingerie drawer, right where I told Trav to put them." She stretched out her right hand to show a turquoise set in silver. "See, when I went into hospital for my surgery I forgot to leave them at home, so I told Trav to bring them back. Then when I got home and asked about them, he said he must have forgot and they must still be at the hospital. That boy can't remember to come in out of the rain, so I gave him shit and called the hospital. Well, of course they said they had no record of them and anyway it wasn't their responsibility. That's when I called the police. Not that it did any good."

Trav had access to his mother's rings. A ring was found in Crystal's purse. Pieces of the puzzle. Did they fit? "Can you describe the missing ring?"

"Course I can," said the woman. "It was my mother's dinner ring, wasn't it?"

She pushed herself out of the recliner with her good arm, the other cradling the cat. "I gotta feed this thing though before she scratches me to death."

Just get on with it, Danutia thought, following the woman into the kitchen, where she began half-heartedly poking in drawers and moving dirty plates and glasses around the counter.

"Is this what you're looking for?" Danutia asked, producing a can opener she'd spied beside an empty soup tin.

"Thanks," the woman said, opening a cupboard. "Now I hope Trav remembered the cat food."

"Here, I'll do it," Danutia said, reaching past her for a flat tin that she quickly opened and dumped into an aluminum dish beside the garbage. "Now tell me about your other ring."

"It's a diamond set in a circle of rubies," the woman said. "I think the stones are real, anyways. It's more the sentimental value, you know, being my mom's and all."

"Platinum band? Size eight and a half?" Danutia asked, unable to restrain herself any longer.

"How'd you know?" the woman asked, her eyes narrowing.

"A ring of that description turned up in the course of another investigation," Danutia said. "When exactly did your rings go missing?"

"My surgery was the Friday before Labor Day," she said. "I should have gone home the next day, but I got an infection and then of course there wasn't a doctor around to release me till after the holiday. It must have been the end of the week before I asked Trav about them. He swore up and down it wasn't his fault, but if he'd done what I told him to start with, I wouldn't of had all this trouble."

Lady, you don't know the half of it, Danutia thought. The time fit. Did Trav give Crystal the ring, or did she steal it, as she'd stolen her mother's jewelry and her boyfriend's cash? Did they spend some time together here, in this house for once empty of his mother's carping presence, before he showed her Sitting Lady Falls? If so, Forensics would have no trouble finding evidence. It was clear that nothing had been cleaned or tossed out in months. "Your son may be able to help us figure out what happened," she said. "Is he around?"

"Was the car out front? White Tercel?"

"No. Any idea where he might be?"

"No telling. He asked to borrow the car today to show around some friend of a friend who's visiting from Toronto."

"Tell him to give West Shore a call when he gets in," Danutia said, though she had no intention of waiting. She'd call in an APB as soon as she reached her car. "I'll need your full names for my report," she said. "Yours and your son's."

Nineteen

The kid pulled into a parking lot, still yakking away about his mother and her cancer. Kelly said, "That's too bad," though Ritchie could tell she wasn't really listening. How could she, knowing what they were about to see.

Ritchie climbed out of the back seat. So this was Witty's Lagoon. He'd passed the park sign on his way to and from William Head. The name reminded him of that old horror movie on late night TV, *Creature from the Black Lagoon.* He'd never known what a lagoon was. Now maybe he'd find out. In the film some scientists find a fossilized skeleton of a hand with webbed fingers and sail up the Amazon to try to find out more about the creature it belonged to. A monster comes out of the water and mauls one of the heroes to death. It felt creepy to think about that now. Somewhere near this lagoon, a monster had killed his daughter.

A bunch of little kids and their parents were hanging around the Information Centre. Ritchie hoped they'd be going in a different direction. It was bad enough having Zitface blabbing all the time, he didn't want to hear little kids screeching around while he was trying to say goodbye. What were they doing here, anyway? It was too cold for the beach to be much fun. Maybe there were fossils. He tried to imagine Crystal among this bunch at eight or nine, with her long straight hair in a pony tail and her impudent blue eyes. He couldn't, though, and it made him sad.

The creek was running alongside them and then the kid took them down a broad trail to the left. Ritchie could hear the falls, roaring but invisible.

"I used to come down here all the time," the kid said, stopping beside a low wooden fence with a Trail Closed sign. "You can see where the trail ran down the cliff. There was a bridge at the bottom. A tree fell on it during the Labor Day storm and smashed it to bits. So they closed this off and moved the trail over."

"Which way would Crystal have gone?" Kelly asked. She was bundled up in a puffy coat with a hat pulled over her ears, and still she was shivering. You'd think it was twenty below instead of several degrees above freezing. "It's the damp," she kept complaining on their nightly walks to the Imperial Garden. "It goes right through my bones." She wasn't complaining now, though, he had to give her that.

"The old way," the kid said. "The new trail wasn't opened till around Thanksgiving."

"Then what are we waiting for," Kelly said. She threw a leg over the fence and scrambled over. Ritchie looked around. No one else was in sight so he followed the kid. He didn't think they'd throw him back in the pen for ignoring a trail sign, but you never knew.

"A lot of the guys in high school bring girls down here at night to drink beer and go skinny dipping," the kid said as they scrambled down the trail, wet from the recent rain and the blowing spray from the falls. "I'll bet that's what happened with that Sharma guy. It was really hot that day."

The dark face floated into Ritchie's mind, along with what he'd learned about the Sharma family. After avoiding the newspapers and television all week, he'd let Frenchy drag him in to see the local news last night. The toothy announcer had smilingly promised the latest developments in the investigation. A shot of the falls, then the sketch of Crystal, then a glimpse of the killer with his lawyer flashed across the screen, though of course the announcer referred only to "the last person known to have seen the girl alive." Hearing that, Ritchie felt like he'd been kicked in the nuts. All he'd seen was that glimpse of her decaying body.

The anger churning inside had kept him awake and he'd risen early this morning, heading for the kitchen. As he took a pan of brownies out of the oven, Nancy came in, bringing two cups of coffee. He told her about the trip today, and she said, "No wonder you're baking brownies. Chocolate is so soothing."

He'd cut them each a big square, no icing—"Who needs it?" Nancy had whooped—and he'd wolfed his down, hardly noticing the taste.

"Looks like the police have a suspect," Nancy had said. "There's a photo in this morning's paper. You never know about people, do you? My daughter went to school with Sunil Sharma and I met him a few times. He seemed like a nice enough kid. His parents too. There was a photo of the family in the local paper a few days ago—did you see it?"

He hadn't, and didn't want to, but she'd gone off anyway.

"It's about the Diwali festival last weekend," she said when she returned, newspaper in hand. "'Festival organizer Yasmin Sharma, owner of Spiceland, her husband, RCMP Corporal Surinder Sharma, and members of their family,' the caption says. That's Sunil with them. There's another son, I think, but I haven't met him."

Ritchie had reluctantly taken the paper from her. Sunil Sharma was a big guy—it would have been easy for him to overpower Crystal. But it wasn't the killer he'd focused on, it was the girl in the sari, the one who looked like Sita even more when she was laughing, as she was here, as Sita had been when she climbed on his motorbike. The newspaper identified her as a niece from Toronto. A long-buried memory struggled towards the surface.

"I think Sita's name was Sharma," he said.

"Probably a coincidence," Nancy said. "Sharma's as common among East Indians as Smith or Jones among Anglos."

At the time he'd agreed with her. Now, as he followed Kelly and the kid down the steep trail near the cliff's edge, he wondered whether it was coincidence or fate that had brought Sunil Sharma into his life. He remembered a Greek play they'd read at the Head, looking for something for their next production. The story was about a king who'd unknowingly murdered his father and married his mother while attempting to escape a prophecy that he would do exactly those things. They'd rejected the play, finally; they were too uncomfortable with the idea that you bring your troubles on yourself and the people around you suffer for it. Maybe that was a truth he'd have to face: that his daughter had died because of the life he'd accidentally taken so many years ago. If that was the case, what was the point of taking revenge on her killer?

He stumbled over an exposed root and grabbed for something to hold on to. The others had stopped at a wide spot in the trail, waiting for him to catch up.

"You slipping in those runners?" Kelly called. "Me too, and I'm wearing boots. How'd Crystal make it in those high-heeled sandals they say she was wearing?"

"Oh, it wasn't—isn't—so bad," the kid said, breathing hard. He turned his head to look back at Ritchie, a flicker of something like fear in his eyes. "In the summertime, I mean. The trail would be dry then. Not like now."

The kid's runners were as worn as his droopy jeans, though his light gray hoodie was clean. Trying to impress Kelly? Fat chance. The kid was getting on his nerves. "You bring your girlfriends down here?" Ritchie asked, a little jab.

A pink flush crept up the kid's neck, making his zits look angry and red, though he tried to smile. "Who me? I don't have time for girls, what with work and school and all." He licked his lips, looked at Kelly with big pleading eyes. "You bring any water?"

"What's the matter, you don't like girls?" Ritchie said. "Or they don't like you? They wouldn't, would they? Ugly, overweight, just like that East Indian guy, only you're white."

"Don't," the kid said, throwing his hands up like Ritchie was about to punch him, which he might, just for the hell of it. He hated guys who groveled. Ritchie could feel the hot tongues of anger flare up, spread from his belly to his hands.

"Don't what?" he said, his right hand flicking out, a little tap on the head, that's all. "Don't call you ugly? But you are, aren't you? I bet even your mother thinks so."

The kid's fat face crumpled and then he lunged at Ritchie, grabbing his jacket.

"My mother's a fuckin' bitch and you're just like her, you and your fuckin' daughter," the kid yelled. "You bastard, you cunt, I thought you'd be different, the way she talked that night, Dad this, Dad that, but you're just the same, always picking on me—"

His hands were around Ritchie's throat and squeezing hard, but he wasn't a street fighter. Ritchie kneed him in the groin and when he was down, choking, kicked him in the ribs. The kid grabbed his ankle and before he could catch himself Ritchie stumbled backwards, towards the cliff edge. He heard Kelly screaming but all he was thinking about was if he was going over, he'd take the bastard with him. He grabbed the hoodie and pulled. Then the earth slid out from under him and they were in the air, falling, as Kelly's screams mingled with the thunder of the Sitting Lady.

"Still no response from Farrell," the dispatcher reported.

"Keep trying," Danutia said. "I'm in the parking lot at Witty's Lagoon. I'll check back in a few minutes." She signed off and strode towards the Information Centre, wondering why Farrell wasn't answering her pager. Maybe she was occupied with Mike the dog handler again this weekend. Too bad for her if she missed out on the excitement.

Inside the trailer she found a pleasant middle-aged woman in a brown Parks Department uniform talking to a group of school-age children about how the First Nations people used moss. She waited in the doorway until the children were turned loose to study the various exhibits, and then motioned the woman outside.

She introduced herself and showed her ID. Then she explained about the chain.

"Oh dear," said the woman. "I'm Joan Goodman. I found the girl's body. A couple of weeks later, right after the big storm, I rescued a locket from some crows, but I didn't dream it was hers. It's the kind of thing much younger girls wear. I put it in the Lost and Found box, so it should still be there. Come inside while I look."

The noise level inside had risen as children overcame their shyness to share microscopes and discoveries. "We'll be going into the forest in about ten minutes," Joan Goodman said, handing out sheets of paper and crayons laid ready on the desk. "First you can color these pictures of the plants we'll see."

As soon as the children settled to their task, she turned to Danutia. "Now for the Lost and Found," she said. She hefted a square wooden box from the floor onto the desk. A small padlock secured the hinged lid. She located the key on her ring and unlocked it. "Some people are inclined to help themselves," she said, opening the lid and rummaging among the contents.

"Hold these," she said, handing Danutia assorted bits of clothing. "It must be in here somewhere."

"I'd better take over," Danutia said, handing back her armload of stuff. She lowered her voice. "If the locket was the girl's, the killer's fingerprints may be on it."

Goodman moved aside. "Mine will be too," she whispered, "though God knows I didn't kill her. I didn't open it, though. That really would have messed things up."

Danutia spotted a thin gold chain twisted around a pair of sunglasses. "I need a pencil and a small plastic bag."

A redheaded boy with a runny nose had sidled up to the desk and stood on tiptoe, trying to peer in. "Can I see?" he said.

"You can help me find a plastic bag," Goodman said, handing Danutia a pencil and inching the boy away.

By the time Danutia had worked the chain free, Goodman was back with the plastic bag. Danutia dropped in the locket and chain and dug out her pocket knife.

"The kids are getting restless," Goodman said. "I'm going to have to get them out of here."

"Just a second," Danutia said. She held the locket inside the bag while she took the knife to the clasp with her other hand. "Let me see if it's the right one."

The locket fell open, revealing two tiny photos: a younger Ritchie on the left, facing a girl of six or seven, unmistakably his daughter.

Goodman peered over her shoulder. "Why, that man walked past here not twenty minutes ago!" she exclaimed. "Except he was older. That's the girl I found, isn't it, and he's her father, coming to see where she died. I should have a word with him."

"You're sure it was this man?" Danutia asked, startled. "Was he by himself?"

"No, he was with a young guy lives up the road, name of Trav, and an older woman—not Trav's mother, I know her."

"This Trav. Is he heavy, bad case of acne?"

"That's him. Poor kid. When he was younger he used to come to the programs here, but his mom would dump him and never pick him up on time, and we had to stop accepting him. I still see him walking here sometimes."

"Thanks for your help," said Danutia. She stuffed the plastic bag into her jacket pocket and hurried out the door. Time to radio dispatch for backup. Before she reached her car, she heard someone yelling for help. She ran towards the woman panting up the Lagoon Trail.

"Call 911," she gasped out, hugging her puffy coat around her. "Two guys went over the side of the cliff."

Joan Goodman had appeared beside Danutia. "That's the woman with Trav," she said.

"I'm RCMP," Danutia told the woman. "I'll put in a call." Turning her over to a shocked bystander, she asked Joan Goodman to unlock the gate to the service road—the children would have to wait—and radioed in for two ambulances and backup at Sitting Lady Falls. If Farrell missed out, it was her own fault.

Danutia sprinted down the trail, wondering if she was already too late. Goodman had told her the new trail had no view of the water before the platform, so Danutia slid through the fence blocking the old trail and hurried downward as fast as the treacherous footing allowed.

Ahead she could see trampled leaves and broken ferns where the men had fought. She slowed. It was impossible to tell exactly where they'd gone over the edge, or where they might have landed. She could hear the roar of falling water and feel the cool spray blowing on her cheeks but a rocky outcrop hid the falls from view. She recognized the slope: That's where Penny Pinscher had signaled, where she'd climbed down the rope to retrieve the pink purse. If they'd fallen on those rocks, the men could be dead or badly injured. The adrenaline rush that had masked her fear of heights had begun to recede, and she felt her mouth go dry. What if she had to attempt a rescue?

Nothing stood out against the green of ferns and gray of rock. She should have asked what the men had been wearing, but she hadn't taken the time. No binoculars, although Joan Goodman would surely have had some, if she'd thought to ask.

Danutia's vision began to blur and she shifted her focus to the water, where a pool widened out below the falls. Chunks of wood and other debris swirled on the surface and disappeared and popped up again, before being picked up by the current and carried away. To the left, a long finger of water rippled out towards the gully where the Douglas fir had come crashing down on Labor Day. Less than two weeks ago, the water had seemed quite shallow. Then the big storm hit, and after that, sporadic rain. Would it be deep enough now for a human to survive the plunge?

Anyone alive after hitting the water would have had plenty of time to get to shore, she realized. She wasn't doing any good here. She set off towards the gully. Trailing blackberry vines snaked across the path, prickling her ankles and threatening to trip her up.

Young firs and alders blocked her view of the shoreline. Then there was a break and she glimpsed where several logs had washed up. Something didn't seem to fit, but her legs had carried her past the break before her brain registered what she'd seen: patches of gray and navy alongside the brown logs, and movement. One of the men, at least, was alive.

She broke into a jog. Had backup arrived yet? She'd advised covering all the park exits, but now she remembered the crisscrossing trails she'd encountered with Barb and Penny, many more than showed on Farrell's map. If she lost Trav, he could easily elude his pursuers.

And what if it wasn't Trav who'd survived? Her mind geared up to consider all the possibilities that lay ahead and she tried to switch it off again. Too late. Distracted by her thoughts, she tripped on a rock and went sprawling, barely registering skinned knees and hands before she was off again. Another minute and she broke into the clearing where the bridge had been.

A slender man in a navy jacket was dragging a limp body farther away from the water. He looked around at her.

"You, is it? Don't matter. I ain't goin' back to prison," Taylor said.

No gun, no backup. Keep him talking. "What happened, Mr. Taylor?"

"It was self-defense. He came at me and we went over the edge."

"You think a jury's going to believe that, Mr. Taylor?"

"It's the truth," Taylor said, laying the body down. "This fucker's heavy."

Danutia took a step closer, alert for any sudden movement now that Taylor had freed himself of his burden. "When did you figure out he'd killed your daughter?"

Taylor hawked and spat on the sodden gray hoodie. "I shoulda seen it comin', him hangin' around all the time, always bringing up the fact he lived out here, but you know, it didn't actually click till we were in the water and his fingers were around my throat and I looked into his eyes—"

"Then you panicked," Danutia said. After all, what did it matter now if she gave him a story?

"No," Taylor said. "My mind was real clear. I held onto him tight."

"You drowned him," Danutia said dully.

"You got me all wrong," Taylor said, nudging the body with his shoe. "I held onto him real tight, like Frenchy said. I looked into his eyes and saw this scared kid just like I used to be, and then I knew. But I didn't kill him. Come see for yourself."

Cautiously she crossed the ground between them and knelt beside the prone figure, her fingers searching for a pulse. Faint, but there.

Danutia looked up at Taylor. He was shivering in his wet jeans and jacket, but his face was full of wonder.

"Camossung gave me a blessing," he said.

PART 4

You must stand under
god's burning tears as under
rain, blessing.

and then you must lend her
your tongue.
—Anne le Dressay, "Speaking in Tongues"

Epilogue

Joan Goodman unlocked the gate to the Witty's Lagoon service road and stood aside to let the white Honda pass. Good thing she'd decided to come early. It was only ten thirty and the gathering wasn't supposed to start until eleven o'clock. That's what Corporal Sharma, the East Indian RCMP officer, had told her when he'd come into the office last week.

The car stopped as it drew even with her. Corporal Sharma rolled down the passenger window and leaned out.

"Good morning, and thank you," he said. He gestured towards the driver. "My apologies for being so early. My son Sunil and I have some preparations to make. Are you sure you won't join us?"

"That's very kind of you, but no," Joan said. "I'll lock up after the last car and then stand guard at the trail junction so you won't be disturbed." She'd stay on the periphery, where she'd been throughout this tragedy, where she belonged.

"Namaste," he said, hands folded together, and the car moved on.

Sunil parked where his father indicated and they began unloading. Leanne's easel. Ajji's small three-cornered shelf to make a shrine. A box of candles and icons and the carefully wrapped photo of his Aunt Sita. Pots of winter pansies and a basket of shiny green leaves from his mother's garden. The small clay bowls they'd spent the weekend making. The food would stay in the car, away from the crows, until it was time to assemble the offerings.

They worked in silence, the easy silence of those who know what has to be done and do it. It reminded Sunil of the times they'd gone camping, just he and his dad, when Rajit decided he was too old for such things. Pitching the tent, chopping wood, building a fire. Then, after a day on the beach, falling asleep to the sound of the surf and his father's steady snores. They hadn't talked much, hadn't needed to.

And that had been true this time, as well. He'd been furious when his dad had doubted his story, even though the story hadn't been true.

He'd gradually come to see that if he hadn't trusted his dad with the truth, he could hardly blame his dad for not trusting him. So when Corporal Farrell had told him he'd been cleared, he'd called to ask if he could come home.

"Son, you will always have a place in our hearts and in our home," his dad had said, and that had been enough.

When he set the last box down on the viewing platform, he asked, "What next?"

His dad looked up from where he was placing candles on the shrine. "The bank is too steep here for Ajji to get to the water. See if you can find another spot not too far along the trail."

As Sunil clattered down the steps, Sharma heard car doors slam in the clearing and went to investigate. It was his colleague, bringing the girl's parents. They had been reluctant to come, at first, but then he had expressed his gratitude for Taylor's part in clearing his son and had explained about Leanne's painting. "She too has played a part in your daughter's story," he'd said. "She would like a chance to tell you what it's meant to her."

Sharma introduced himself.

"Ritchie Taylor," the man said, drawing the woman's arm through his. "And this is my soon-to-be-wife Kelly. I brought some cinnamon buns, and my friend Frenchy sent some sweet grass. He showed me how to use it. Are you folks okay with a little smudge? If not, that's okay. Kelly and me can do it here."

"We would be honored," Sharma said.

"Do you think I could sing a song?" the woman asked. "There's one that Crystal really loved when she was a kid. It's turned out so beautiful today; it just seems the right thing to do."

"The weather couldn't be better," Danutia agreed, joining them. The sun had burned off the morning fog and now the forest was bathed in golden light.

"Of course," Sharma said, "whatever you want. You decide when it's the right moment. The viewing platform is straight ahead. I'll join you when the rest of my family arrives. They should be along soon."

Taylor took his bundle of sweet grass from the backseat and Danutia locked her car. When she and Sharma were alone, she said, "I'll be in a bit of a rush when the ceremony's over. Can you give the Taylors a ride back?"

"Yes, I understand, you must pick your sister up from the airport," Sharma said.

"It isn't just that. I have to take care of something at the office," Danutia said. She didn't elaborate. Why spoil this moment?

A horn tooted and tires crunched to a stop beside Danutia's car. Yasmin slid out of the driver's seat. "Sorry sorry," she said, "we were all ready to go and then that Rajit phoned to say they weren't coming, some nonsense about Kumala being sick but I know she isn't, she was over last night and perfectly fine, but what can you do?"

Yasmin shrugged her shoulders and turned towards Leanne, who was helping Ajji from the car. "We'll see to her, you get your painting, it's almost eleven," she said, taking Ajj's elbow. "Come, everyone."

Soon they arrived at the viewing platform, where Taylor was waiting with the smoldering sweet grass. As she wafted the smoke over her head and arms, Danutia tried to still her mind, to put aside thoughts of the task awaiting her at the detachment. This morning as she was preparing to leave, a fax had arrived from Serious Crimes in Sidney, Nova Scotia. A Micmac woman had been strangled and both feet severed. They were asking for information from other jurisdictions with similar cases.

Despite all her efforts, it seemed as though Handy Dan had slipped through her fingers. She hadn't been able to convince a judge to issue a search warrant for the house Richard Hawkins had rented on Lampson, and when she talked to the owner again, she found that he'd moved out, the place had been thoroughly cleaned, and new tenants were in residence. The dates of his official visits to the Naval Museum didn't coincide with the dates of the murders. Interviewed by an RCMP colleague in Kingston, Hawkins had indignantly denied everything except the mix-up over the credit card with which he'd paid for the car rental. Even though Nathan's Plymouth showed traces of white paint, there was no way of proving it came from the Achieva Hawkins had rented, now beyond recovery.

The Detroit Tigers ball cap she'd confiscated from Phoenix was the only tenuous link between Richard Hawkins and Handy Dan. In the absence of other compelling evidence, its priority rating had slipped. The Vancouver lab would get to it eventually. It might yield a smear of blood or bodily fluids that matched Marie Wilson's, a DNA profile of its wearer or wearers. A match might be found as a result of the Nova Scotia investigation, or not until years later. Or never.

She put that possibility from her mind and took her place in the circle.

Everyone was in place. The seconds clicked past on Sharma's watch. At eleven o'clock, he rang a small brass bell and closed his eyes. Two minutes of silence for those others who had died violent deaths, victims of wars. He thought of his father, who had served as a medic with the British Army during the Second World War, a terrible time, though not so terrible as the Partition that followed, independence bought at the cost of how many million lives. It was his father's army contacts that had allowed them to immigrate, first to England, then to Canada. The war that might have killed his father when he was still a child had instead brought them to a land of peacekeepers. Here, as everywhere, there were violent deaths, but no slaughters in the name of religion. How thankful he was to have his son restored to him, to have peace at last between Ajji and his long-banished sister. So much had happened since his niece entered their lives.

So much, Sharma thought, some good, some bad. Rajit's last-minute phone call troubled him. He had been acting strangely ever since Sunil was cleared of suspicion. Had he believed his brother to be guilty, *wanted* his brother to be guilty? Did he envy his brother's life so much? Rajit had always seemed so independent, so determined to make his own decisions. How many times had he rejected his father's offers of help? Yet there must be some lack in his life. I must spend more time with my elder son, Sharma thought.

And that brought him to the decision that had been quietly

forming about his own life. He must quit his job. Not because he was being pressured to, far from it. Forensics was so backed up that Sergeant Lewis had phoned him the minute that other boy was arrested, asking him to return to work. And so he had. He and Carl had gone over the house on Lombard, as well as the mother's car, looking for trace evidence of the girl's presence. It hadn't been hard to find, and corroborated the boy's story about leaving the girl at the house while he went to visit his mother in the hospital. None of it proved he killed her, but it didn't need to—that was a fact he readily admitted. He'd gone to look for her when she'd left the bridge to take a leak and hadn't returned, found her squatting in a clearing, pants around her ankles, passed out. When he shook her awake, she'd lashed out at him, accused him of being a pervert, a dirty slob, a pimply freak. Something had broken inside him.

Still, Sharma's work had been good, and necessary. For him that was not enough. He no longer had faith in his ability to be dispassionate about the evidence he and others so meticulously gathered. Ever since he'd seen that fingerprint and known it to be Sunil's . . .

Leanne stood beside the easel that held her painting, waiting for Sharma Uncle to signal the end of the silence. When the bell rang again, she felt her palms go sweaty. Why was she doing this? It was crazy. They'd never understand. She fumbled with the string and loosened the brown paper wrapping, though she wasn't ready to remove it. Not until she'd tried to explain.

"As some of you know," she said, turning to face the circle, "I've been working on an art project about Emily Carr. Before I'd ever been to the coast I'd fallen in love with Carr's twisted trees, with the light that transformed her landscapes and made them magic. I thought if I immersed myself in Carr's life and in those landscapes, I could learn to see the world as she did, and create wonderful paintings like hers.

"But I was wrong," she said. "And Sunil knew that. One day he said to me, 'What about the world as *you* see it?' I wasn't too happy about that at the time," she admitted, smiling at Sunil, "but then I realized I couldn't paint the world as I see it because I didn't know who I was. There'd only ever been half of me, because I was ignorant of half my heritage. Then Yasmin Auntie gave me the *Ramayana* and I started studying Hindu art and the stories and beliefs behind it, and one day I suddenly understood about the beings with many heads and arms and legs. They express the many-sidedness of our identity, all of us. The gods are multiple. I am multiple. We are all multiple."

She looked around at her Indian family to see if she was making sense. Ajji was studying the boards at her feet, but Sunil flashed a thumbs-up and Sharma Uncle nodded encouragingly. So she continued, speaking now to the girl's parents, whom she'd just met. "But I am also a young Canadian woman of this time and place. And we are here today because of two young Canadian women who were not as fortunate as I have been, young women whom most of us didn't even know . . ."

Ritchie wasn't sure what the girl was going on about, but he wished she'd hurry up. He needed a smoke. He'd only agreed to come because Kelly had insisted. The scolding call of a bird came like a reproach, stopping his thoughts dead in their tracks. He watched the kingfisher skim over the water, searching for fish, and land empty-beaked on a low-lying branch. In a moment the kingfisher tried again, this time scooping up a wriggling silvery fish. A week and a day ago he'd plunged into that water not knowing whether he'd live or die. Whether the kid would live or die. There they'd struggled with each other and he'd struggled with himself. A blessing had come from that struggle. You'll lose it if you start lying to yourself again, he told himself. You're not here because Kelly made you. You are doing this for Crystal. And for yourself. And for Sharma's family, who need to hear the story you need to tell. You're lucky that the cop is leaving early and Sharma and his son are giving you a ride back, you and Kelly. That will be your chance.

There was a rustling around him as people shifted. The girl had taken the wrapper off the painting and stepped aside. A groan escaped him as he took in the three-headed figure: a veiled Sita on the left, Crystal in her bandana on the right, and in between a goddess whose flowing locks and flowing tears became the waters of Sitting Lady Falls. Tears of sorrow or tears of joy? He couldn't tell. And then he felt the wetness on his own cheeks and knew it didn't matter.

Beside him, Kelly sang the opening lines of "May There Always Be Sunshine," the rest of the words lost in sobs that came from himself or others, he couldn't tell.

When they'd sung the chorus with as many variations as fit the occasion, they brought the food from the cars and began filling the small clay bowls.

"Your friend Arthur," Yasmin said as she added bright pansy faces to a bowl and passed it to Danutia, "what do you hear from him? How is his mother? He will be home from England soon, yes?"

"Next week," Danutia said. "His mother seems to have recovered from her stroke." She didn't mention that she might be going to England herself. Arthur had sent her a news article about a pilot project that was planned for the Peak District where his mother lived. One of its aims was to reduce crime by providing positive alternatives for at-risk youth. She couldn't help wondering whether such a program would have made a difference in Trav's life. Sergeant Lewis had encouraged her to apply for an exchange, and for the first time she didn't wonder whether he was criticizing her. "Things like that look good on your record at promotion time," he'd said.

She did wonder whether she was attracted not only to the potential of the British program but also to the idea of spending time on Arthur's home ground. One of the many things she'd discuss with Alyne in the hours ahead. It seemed clear to her after the events of the last few days, after this morning's ceremony, that she couldn't let her life be dominated by what had happened in the past. The past was gone; she had to let it go. The future lay ahead, unknowable. This was the present, putting bits of cinnamon bun into clay bowls and passing them on to Ajji for rice, Yasmin for flowers.

Across from the viewing platform where they filled bowls, the waters of Bilston Creek thundered over the Sitting Lady and crashed into the pool below in a headlong rush. When the bowls were ready, they carried them to the spot Sunil had found and set them afloat. The current picked up the tiny clay boats and whirled them around and carried them outwards, bobbing and tipping. Relieved of its heavy glass, a wooden photo frame bearing the likeness of a young girl skimmed after them. A larger canvas caught on a trailing arbutus branch and then, freeing itself, hurried after, to the open sea.

Acknowledgments

If it takes a village to raise a child, it takes a community to produce a book. I'd like to express my warmest thanks to the many people who have helped me bring *Sitting Lady Sutra* to fruition.

Those who helped me with my research: Staff Sgt. Bruce M. Brown, West Shore RCMP; Constable Melissa Brown, West Shore RCMP; Grant Keddie, Curator of Archeology, Royal British Columbia Museum; Joseph M. Lenarcik, Assistant Curator, CFB Esquimalt Naval & Military Museum; Community Coroner Barb McClintock and former coroner Robert Stevenson; Jay Rastogi, Wildwood; Director Kathy Roy and Judy Chouinard, Manchester House; Jerry Simpson; archaeologist Joe Stewart; and Deb Thiessen, Capital Regional District Parks Department. Your assistance was invaluable in providing the factual underpinning for this fictional work.

Friends who explored various settings with me, gave me a place to write, discussed the project with me, and/or read parts or all of the manuscript: Tina Bonkowski, Kathy Crandall, Caterina Edwards, Nancy Henwood, Sandra-Lynne Janzen, Bonnie Moro, Ann Pearson, Sue Rickles, and Fred and Kathleen Schloessinger. Your interest and enthusiasm kept me writing.

Readers who critiqued the manuscript: Caitlin Beck; David Bergen, Humber School of Writing; RCMP Corporal Nedge Drgastin; and my writing group, Chris Bullock, Bruce Patridge, May Partridge, and Carolyn Redl. Your sharp eyes, insights, and probing questions helped me shape this narrative.

I'd also like to thank readers of early sections of the manuscript: Alvin Abrams, Mary Liz Bright, Sharon Crawford, Irene Gargantini, Ron Kenyon, Betsy Ryder, Keri Wehlander, and Beth Yim.

At TouchWood: special thanks to publisher Ruth Linka, who believed in Danutia, and to editor Frances Thorsen, who prodded me into developing her more fully. Thanks to designer Pete Kohut for the fantastic cover, to proofreader Lenore Hietcamp for her attention to detail, and to Promotions Coordinator Tara Saracuse for ensuring I submitted all the bits. Many thanks as well to photographer friend Gary Ford for his skill and patience.

At Crime Writers of Canada, board members who gave me courage and a silver dagger: Lou Allin, Catherine Astolfo, Anthony Bidulka, Alison Bruce, Melodie Campbell, Nancy Grant, Sue Pike, and Garry Ryan.

I am also indebted to the following books and articles:

Beavan, Colin. *Fingerprints: The Origins of Crime Detection and the Murder Case that Launched Forensic Science.* New York: Hyperion, 2001.

Carr, Emily. *Hundreds and Thousands: The Journals of an Artist.* Toronto: Irwin, 1966.

Cornwell, Patricia. *Portrait of a Killer.* New York: Putnam's, 2002.

Crean, Susan, ed. *Opposite Contraries: The Unknown Journals of Emily Carr and Other Writings.* Vancouver: Douglas & McIntyre, 2003.

Jackson, Steve. *No Stone Unturned: The True Story of NecroSearch International, the World's Premier Forensic Investigators.* New York: Kensington, 2002.

Keddie, Grant. "The Legend of Camosun." *Discovery: Friends of the Royal British Columbia Museum Quarterly Review,* (Autumn 1991) 19 (n. 4): 4–5.

Knott, Kim. *Hinduism: A Very Short Introduction.* Oxford: OUP, 1998.

Minaker, Dennis. *The Gorge of Summers Gone: A History of Victoria's Inland Waterway.* Victoria: Desktop Publishing, 1998.

Murphy, P. J., Loyd Johnsen, and Jennifer Murphy, eds. *Paroled for Life: Interviews with Parolees Serving Life Sentences.* Vancouver: New Star, 2002.

Ramayana: A Tale of Gods and Demons. Illus. B. G. Sharma. Text by Ranchor Prime. San Rafael, CA: Mandala, 2001.

Singh, Chitralekha, and Prem Nath. *Hindu Festivals, Fairs and Fasts.* New Delhi: Crest, 1999.

For all you've given, I am truly grateful. This is a work of fiction, and though I've tried to be faithful to the spirit of these and other sources, I've also taken liberties when necessary. Any errors or blemishes are my responsibility.

Writing this book has been a long process. I thank my husband, Chris Bullock, for understanding my need to write and encouraging me to keep at it even under difficult circumstances. You deserve more dancing. I'm pleased that we're again collaborating on the third novel in the series.

Kay Stewart is the co-author of the mystery novel *A Deadly Little List* (2006). She taught English at the University of Alberta for twenty years, and has co-authored two textbooks on writing, *Essay Writing for Canadian Students* and *Forms of Writing*. Her creative work has appeared in the periodicals *Other Voices* and *NeWest Review*, and in the anthologies *Eating Apples* and *Wrestling with the Angel*. She lives in Victoria, British Columbia.